Deeper Than Skin

A novel from the recent past

Jack LeMenager

Anna —
I hope you
enjoy my
book. I'd
love to hear
your thoughts.
Jack

Fells Publishing

Fells Publishing, First Printing April 2019
Copyright © 2019

Address all inquiries to:
Fells Publishing
10 Johnson Road
Winchester, MA 01890

Independently published
Printed in the United States of America

ISBN: 978-1-090-235589

Title: Deeper Than Skin
by Jack LeMenager

1. Man-woman relationships – Fiction
2. New Canaan, Fairfield County, Conn. – Fiction
3. 1980 – Fiction

Cover Design by John Granville Leonard
The Granville Group
Nevada City, CA

Cover photograph: Pexels.com

"*A portrait is a picture in which there is just a tiny little something not quite right about the mouth.*"

John Singer Sargent

1: Happenstance

Friday, May 30, 1980

When he first saw the woman he would marry, Rick felt a surge in his chest. She radiated a classic yet understated beauty, capturing his mind and holding his eyes.

From thirty feet across the noisy room, he studied her. Something washed over him as he looked at her. Like a rising wave spreading over a flat sandy beach. The face. Familiar, somehow. A sense of *déjà vu*. That he'd once been similarly transfixed. A misty memory. Then it receded, and, like the wave, was gone.

As he continued to stare at her across the room, he realized she was in trouble.

A large man hovered. Physically intimidating. Speaking sharply. Jabbing an accusing finger at her repeatedly. The argument intensified.

Rick could hear the man's muffled loudness rising over the party's din. His instincts urged him to intervene. He began in their direction. Simultaneously, the woman took a half-step back and threw her glass of wine in the brute's face. Then, she turned and hurried outside through the adjacent doors.

Rick stopped. Watching, he held his breath. The man stood a moment. Blinking, he put his hands to his face, wiped at the wine. Unbelieving. Lifting his eyes to the door, the man took one step, stopped, and then turned to walk briskly in the opposite direction through the crowd toward the men's room. Rick exhaled.

Rick's presence at the gathering awakened in him a discomfort he'd acquired in college with some of his classmates—the preppies, that is. Those with whom he had had so little in common, from whom he'd felt detached. It came as no surprise, then, that he felt awkward and out of place here at this alumni get-together of prep school graduates.

The product of a frugal, hard-working middle-class family, and a scholarship-funded Ivy League education, his four years' exposure to numerous preppies in college had established and repeatedly confirmed his impression of them: their teen years, spent cosseted within expensive private schools without regular parental talks, advice, squabbles and love, instilled in many an ersatz sophistication, a cliquish superiority that smirked, *you can't join our club.*

Happenstance had brought Rick to this alien crowd of Hotchkiss School grads and their dates. His pathetically open Friday night offered little resistance to the urgings of his roommate to come along to Salisbury for a night of, he promised, drinking and women and partying.

Bill Crenshaw had been Rick's college roommate—and was once again, some four years after graduation. Bill was Hotchkiss but proved one of a few exceptions to Rick's rule: a good guy and a solid friend, who also happened to be a preppie.

He didn't begrudge him his expensive secondary education. However, he did sometimes needle him about his privileged upbringing and latent preppie tendencies. Bill rolled with the ribbing and gave it back in equal quantities.

The two drove the ninety minutes from their Stamford apartment in Rick's 1972 VW Beetle, turning into the inn's parking lot as the sun drew near the treetops, the party underway.

Bill introduced him to a couple of his classmates and their dates. But Rick forgot their names as soon as Bill had spoken them. The quarrel across the room had already seized his attention.

2: Saint Kitts

Maggie had grown accustomed to conversations with Pete that would blow up into nasty, no-win arguments. This one was shaping up as yet another.

"So, what do you say? Sounds like fun. Huh?" he asked her, with a hopeful smile, as they turned onto Route 44 North toward Salisbury.

How to say *no* without ticking him off. She had dodged the question before, postponing the inevitable. Fact was, she simply did not want to spend a week with him in Saint Kitts. Or anywhere else, for that matter. She'd grown weary of him.

"I can't, Pete. I'm buried at work. Besides, I've already used up all my vacation time this year."

A lie, but credible. Greeted with a frown and sullen silence.

Five minutes later, he pulled his car into the White Hart Inn parking lot. Switching off the engine, he turned to her slowly—one of Pete's tells, she'd learned. It meant his anger was simmering, ready to burst into a full boil.

"It's not even June and you've already used up your vacation time? Really? What's the real reason, Maggie?" he quietly asked, with a sneer in his voice. The cynical tone was another tip-off to what was coming.

"Why don't you want to go with me to Saint Kitts? You didn't want to go last year when we had the chance. My friend is being really generous letting us use his place for free. If I say no a second time, he may not offer it again."

"Pete, I'm serious. I have *no* vacation time left. I used it last February when I went with my family to Vale. And even if I did, we just landed a new client and Ken wants me all over it, *like white on rice*, he said." Another lie. There was no new account. "No way could I go away for a week. Not even a long weekend."

"But we're not going until September. You should have that new client under control by then. Besides, we *love* each other. You could find the time if you wanted to."

She grimaced, pausing before her own quiet words. "Pete," she sighed, "I don't think *love* is the right word for our relationship. I like you, and I've enjoyed the times we've spent together." Not really. Best to humor him. "But I've never said that I loved you."

That did it.

"You can tell me. I can handle it," his voice rising. "You're seeing someone else, right?"

"Oh, for God's sake, Pete, let's not go there again. Of course, I'm not seeing anyone else. Let's just go to the damn party," clipping her words as she opened the door and climbed out of his ridiculous muscle car. "Can you please be civil?" and slammed the door.

As he got out, she continued. "These people are your classmates, not mine. Let's try to have a good time. Walk me in like you're a gentleman. Buy me a glass of Chardonnay. Introduce me to your friends."

Pete silently escorted Maggie into the colonial-era inn. The noise down the hall guided them to the party. It was about seven-fifteen and already the ballroom was full of talking, laughing young men and women. The men were mostly Hotchkiss School, class of 1972, a private high school about four miles down the road in Lakeville. Most of the women, their dates, had attended private all-girls schools at the same time—as had Maggie.

After stopping by the bar to get himself a bottle of Heineken and a glass of wine for her, Pete spotted two hockey teammates. Neither had dates, and he hadn't seen them since graduation, he told her.

"C'mon," he said, pulling her by the arm across the floor with him. Billy Sampson and Sam Kellogg each shook her hand in turn and mumbled a *nice to meet you* while staring at her chest.

She stood by silently throughout the detailed hockey reminiscences, the mind-numbing recitation of statistics and recollections of game-winning goals. Pete's friends clumsily snuck repeated glances at her body, as though she wasn't noticing.

After a few minutes of jock talk and gawking, Maggie spotted a friend across the room. "Oh, there's Jane Dothan, over there," and pointed. "She's an old friend of mine from Farmington," and she walked away.

Jane was an acquaintance, not really a *friend*. But she offered a convenient excuse to escape Pete and his leering pals. Joining Jane and her date, another Hotchkiss alumnus, their banal conversation reminded Maggie of why she had avoided Jane at school. She still had the personality of a dial tone—as did her date, apparently. At least Maggie was away from Pete, she thought.

She could see him scowling at her from across the room. Five minutes later, Pete walked to the bar for a second beer. But, instead of returning for further hockey remembrances with his friends, he walked straight to Maggie, grabbed her by the elbow and pulled her away.

"Pete, *what are you doing?* I'm talking with my friends." They watched in silent indifference as he marched her away.

"We need to talk." His height and heft walled her off from the party.

"About what? That I can't go with you to Saint Kitts?"

"The real reason you don't *want* to. Why not? It makes so much sense. All we'd have to pay for is air fare, a rental car, and food."

She snorted. "Yeah. That and a massive bar tab, because you'd be drinking like a fish the whole time."

"Bullshit! I promised you I'd cut down on the booze. Because I love you. And I *thought* you loved me. But apparently I was deluding myself." He took a swig of beer.

Here we go again.

"Just like I told you in the car, Pete. I don't love you. I never have. I think you're using the term too loosely. I don't think it applies to our relationship. We've had fun the past year, done a lot of things together. You've been generous. But, unlike you, I don't confuse my pleasures with my happiness. And I'm not happy anymore when I'm with you."

"I *was* right. I should have *realized* it before. You *are* cheating on me," thrusting his index finger repeatedly at her chest in rhythm with his accented verbs.

"Oh, for Christ's sake, Pete. Don't be *absurd.*"

"So. You're denying it? How do you explain that you've been quote unquote *busy* the last three weekends in a row? Obviously, you're *two-timing* me."

"Oh, for God's sake, Pete, I told you. We had a family gathering last weekend because my aunt and uncle were in town from Philadelphia—"

"—You *could* have invited me."

Her explanation of the other two weekends didn't mollify him, either, and he continued berating her, belittling her comments, and wagging his finger at her repeatedly to emphasize his fantasy accusations.

Finally, in exasperation, he cursed her. She threw her wine in his face and stormed from the room.

3: Beauty Through Tears

When the woman retreated outside, Rick followed. Stopping at the double French doors, he could see her petite figure on the deck, silhouetted through the window panes against the wispy orange-red clouds and setting sun.

He opened the door, stepped outside, and then quietly closed the door behind him. She was leaning forward on her elbows on the railing, chin on both fists, her back to the party, looking into the distant hills.

Rick feigned indifference as he walked past her and stopped at the far end of the terrace. Leaning on the railing himself and gazing at the same backlit ridges, he stood still, listening to the tranquil dusk. Too early for summer insects, it was quiet, save the muted sounds of the party, leaking through two partly-open windows at the other end of the deck.

After a few minutes, Rick turned and walked back casually, as though to return to the party, while actually hoping he might catch her eye and perhaps engage her in conversation. She was still studying the distant landscape. And, as he'd hoped, she glanced at him. She'd been crying.

Nodding slightly, he said a quiet "Hi." She returned a blank look. He stopped. "Are you okay?" She continued staring at him. Her face again transfixed him.

"I. Um." His tongue clicked softly. "I'm sorry. I don't mean to pry. It's just that, uh I couldn't help but notice you were arguing with that guy inside a few minutes ago. And I, uh." He cleared his throat. "And I could see he was verbally abusing you, and I didn't like what I was seeing. I just wanted to make sure that you were okay."

She continued looking at him. "Yeah. I'm okay," she said, without conviction.

Closer now, he could see that his assessment from across the room fell short. Though upset, she was gorgeous. Hers was a natural beauty. She didn't need the artificial enhancement of lipstick, mascara and all that other stuff—which she didn't appear to be using anyway. Even her fingernails were plain, neatly trimmed and without fingernail polish. Despite the tears, her eyes sparkled. He was mesmerized, nearly rendered mute.

Again, that feeling he'd seen the face before washed over him, lapping at his consciousness.

"Well, it's uh, it's none of my business. Sorry." The pause became unbearable. Desperate to start a conversation, he asked, "Uh, can I, uh Can I getcha anything? A glass of water? A Kleenex? Another glass of wine, maybe?" nodding at her empty glass as she simultaneously shook her head slightly. She looked at him curiously through the awkward silence before returning her gaze to the horizon.

Rick felt as though he had his pants on backwards. After a moment, he said, "Well, okay then. I'll leave you alone," turning to walk toward the door.

"You don't have to go," she said quietly.

He stopped and turned around. "Are you sure?" She gave a shallow, sad nod, wiping at a stray tear on her cheek with the back of one hand.

He inhaled audibly. "Actually. Well. To be honest, I did follow you outside. Like I said, it really bothered me the way that guy was treating you."

She eyed him. "I'm fine. But thanks for asking." She paused and looked away again, and then turned back to consider his face briefly.

He looked at her, couldn't think of what to say next, and looked down, embarrassed as though caught staring. Both turned and studied the hills through another uncomfortably long silence.

"I love this view," she murmured, scanning the hills.

"Yes, it is nice," he replied quietly. He paused, took a deep breath, and spoke softly, slowly, deliberately. "The sun's backlighting and the bright clouds give it a real sense of depth and expanse," he said, as he straightened himself, extending his arm and gesturing toward the sunset.

"The hills and trees are layered into the distance, shades of grays and greens," as he pointed with the edge of his hand, as though touching each successive ridge line while staring to the west. "It's like a watercolor painting. It's… It's like something Winslow Homer would have captured perfectly—you know who Winslow Homer was?"

She had turned toward him at the mention of Homer. She smiled and nodded at his question. "Oh, yes."

"I'll bet it's quite pretty when the leaves turn in the fall," he added.

She returned her gaze to the hills. "Yes, you're right. It does get beautiful here around mid-October."

Another few moments of silence.

She turned back and offered her right hand. "My name is Maggie."

He took her hand and shook it gently, smiling as he spoke his own. "Rick."

He felt a little wave of elation and, at the same time, a sense of relief and calm.

"Glad to meet you."

Another pause.

"Are you a Hotchkiss alum?"

"Nope. I just tagged along with my friend, Bill Crenshaw. He's the alum. Not me."

"Oh, I think I've heard that name before. He probably played hockey with Pete."

Rick nodded. "Um, yeah, that sounds about right. I know that Bill did play hockey in high school. Class of '72?" She nodded. "Uh, is Pete the guy you were arguing with?"

She scrunched her nose, nodded again, and sighed. "I didn't want to come tonight, but Pete insisted. I'm not a big fan of these parties. The conversations are always so predictably boring. People get too drunk and make fools of themselves." She brightened as she looked at him, "But you're a fresh face. Where did you go to school?"

"Dartmouth," before realizing she had meant high school. "Oh, I'm sorry. Wilton High School."

"Oh. So, you're not a preppie? I should've realized that," and she laughed quietly, eying his clothes. "You're not wearing the standard issue preppie uniform. That's refreshing. Care to stay a bit longer? I'd like to talk to someone from the real world." She paused, continuing to appraise him with a smile.

"Sure, happy to." He laughed, and then grinned—probably too broadly. "You know, I almost didn't come either. I don't really care much for parties like this. There's too much smoke. It's too loud. You stand next to someone trying to talk and only hear about every third word. You find yourself yelling to be heard. By the end of the night, your ears ring and you're hoarse. But, hey, it's a great way to meet people. And, uh, sometimes they're pretty cute," smiling at her as he said it.

She smiled, too, and their eyes locked for a few long moments before he turned away self-consciously.

4: Hat Trick

Pete had to wait nearly five minutes to get close enough to the bar to ask for another round. He treated himself to two more Heinekens. Then, it was back to rehashing hockey memories with his former teammates.

"What happened to your date? What's her name? Maggie?" Sam asked, when Pete got back.

"Yeah. Maggie. Oh, she's on the rag tonight."

"That's one good-looking woman," Billy added, with a wink. "Where'd you meet *her*?"

"Uh, we met last summer on Cape Cod. But we're having another one of our arguments tonight. She's playing her *Little Miss Perfect* role. And as usual, I'm wrong."

"Exactly. You have to learn how to argue with women," Billy said, snickering. "Doesn't matter what the argument is about. They're right. You're wrong. It's that simple. End of story. End of argument."

"Yeah, right." Time to change the subject. "But anyway, as I was saying before you two girls went to the ladies' room—who got the hat trick against Westminster his senior year, one of which was short-handed?"

"That would be you," Billy said.

"And who scored four goals against Taft the very next game?"

"Again, that was you."

"And how well did Osborne do in those games?"

"As I recall, he was held scoreless."

"Which proves my point," he added, taking a big gulp from one of his beers for emphasis.

"Okay, okay, I give up. You were the big producer, not Reggie Osborne," Billy replied. "But who got the assists on most if not all of your goals?" Billy had been Pete's line mate for most of their three years together on the Hotchkiss varsity team.

"You're my set-up man," jabbing his arm lightly with his elbow. "Couldn't have done it without you."

"But who spent the most time in the penalty box?" Sam laughed.

"Uh, that would probably be me," Pete said. "But hey, I was working the ice for you guys, keeping the amateurs under control so you had some room to maneuver." Turning to Sam, he added, "and so you could get some rest."

Sam had been their starting goalie.

"True enough," Sam chortled. "So much so that you were willing to knock yourself out with a flying header into the boards when you missed that third period check against Exeter. They took you off the ice on a stretcher."

"You had to remind me. Not my favorite Hotchkiss hockey memory. And it was *so* much fun to stay overnight in Sharon Hospital for observation. I missed the next three games because of that little incident." And he took another pull on the beer bottle.

"Yeah. That, and it made you goofy for life," Sam said, still chuckling.

"Fuck you very much," boxing his shoulder softly and belching loudly simultaneously.

On and on they bantered with their beer-infused memories. Glancing around the room at one point, Pete didn't see Maggie. Was she still outside on the deck? He told Billy and Sam he needed to take a leak.

When he exited the men's room, he placed his empty beer bottle on a passing waiter's tray, took a swig from his other bottle, his third beer of the evening, and then stepped through the door to the porch. Maggie was still outside, but she was talking to some guy Pete didn't recognize. Her back was to the door, so she didn't see him. He reversed course and returned to his buddies.

5: Send Me No Flowers

"I try to avoid big parties like this because I treasure my hearing," Rick said. "I love good music and I'd like to be able to enjoy it for the rest of my life." They both laughed quietly.

As he was talking, a door at the far end of the deck opened and some guy stepped outside. It was the oaf Maggie had been arguing with earlier. With her back to the door, she didn't notice him. He scowled at Rick, turned, and went back inside.

Rick talked through the intrusion. "I'm glad you went outside when you did. It gave me an excuse to get away from the noise." He paused. "I'm sorry. I don't mean to be such a blabbermouth." He'd grown tired of hearing his own voice and told himself to shut up.

She spoke into his silence and looked straight at him. "Listen, Rick, I appreciate your concern, I really do." She hesitated and looked away briefly. "I guess that was an ugly scene in there. Did everyone notice?"

"Uh. Not sure. I don't think so. But, uh, I sure did." He waited a moment before asking, "Where did you go to school?"

She smirked. "Boston College," adding, with a little laugh, "actually, Boston College after Farmington."

Farmington? Rick had never heard of a school named Farmington but didn't want to seem like he was out of it, so he just nodded with a half-grin, hoping she'd explain.

"Actually, I mean Miss Porter's School. We got into the habit of calling it Farmington. Miss Porter's is a private all-girls' school. It's in Farmington. Uh, Connecticut?"

"So, that makes you a preppie, I guess. Well, I won't hold it against you," he said smiling. "Are you wearing the preppie uniform for women?"

"Absolutely not," she said, laughing. She paused again. "So, how do you know Bill?"

"We were assigned as roommates our freshman year at Dartmouth and got along so well that we continued rooming together all four years. Neither of us joined a fraternity, which at Dartmouth is weird. And now we're roommates

11

again. In Stamford… Bill's a preppie, too, but not the typical sort. He's a good guy." And he laughed again.

"Do you work in Fairfield County or do you commute into the city?"

"I have an easy ten- or fifteen-minute commute to my job at Hamilton Forest Products, to their new headquarters in beautiful downtown Stamford. If the weather is pleasant, I walk."

Her eyebrows arched. "Hamilton? *Really?*"

"Yeah. Why? Do you know the company?"

"Well, yes, I know a little bit about it. My father works for World Paper Company and he knows a lot of your executives. Plays golf with some of them occasionally."

"Oh, really? World's our biggest competitor. What's he do for them?"

"He runs their Haines Paper subsidiary."

"Oh, wow. I know the Haines brand."

"How'd you wind up at Hamilton?"

Rick explained briefly that, through Dartmouth's careers office, he had learned that his fellow alums included Hamilton's CEO, as well as several of its executives. After a series of interviews, they offered him a job. Settling in quickly, they invited him to join the leadership track program.

"Sorry. I shouldn't have gone into such detail. I'm sure that was boring."

"No, no. Not at all."

The awkward pauses tailed off and they fell into easy conversation as the darkening sky blossomed stars. A few early summer moths had begun swarming the porch lights.

It was nearly ten-thirty when Pete stumbled out onto the deck, a half-empty beer bottle in one hand. After glaring at Rick, he gruffly slurred at Maggie, "Let's go." She stood still and scowled at him. "*Are you comin'?*" he growled, a little louder.

She narrowed her eyes. "No. Go on without me," she said through a taut jaw. "I'll find my own way home." He gawked at her for a moment, incredulous, before she added sharply, "And by the way. Don't bother calling me in a couple of weeks to apologize for your *vile* behavior tonight. I'm tired of your crap. We're breaking up." Pause. "And *don't* send me flowers. Save your money."

"*Fine*. Be that way."

Pete turned his frown and dagger eyes on Rick momentarily before pivoting and leaving. Maggie glowered at his backside as he lurched through the door and returned to the party.

"Drunk… Again," she muttered, looking at the now-closed door. "I'd walk home before accepting a ride from *him*."

Reacting to the tension, they both turned and resumed silently looking into the distance, now dark, leaning forward on the railing on their elbows again. Their arms nearly touched. Rick could feel the soft hairs on Maggie's arm against his own. After several minutes, he quietly asked, "Maybe it's none of my business, but—but, how long have you been dating him?"

She sighed, continuing to look into the distance. "Oh God, too long. Almost a year… a year of on again off again dating. Mostly off. We met last June. Late June. Dated for several weeks last summer… Then we had a big argument. I forget what it was about. But it established the pattern. We'd fight, split up, not see each other for a while, and then get back together again. We must've done that four or five times."

"If you don't mind my asking, what was tonight's fight about?"

"Oh, it's *so* boring"

Turning to him, "A buddy of his owns a small house on Saint Kitts. Pete talked him into letting us use it for a week in September—in the middle of the hurricane season, of course. I mean who else would want to use it then? The guy probably can't rent it out then anyway. So, what's he got to lose if he lets Pete use it for free? I waffled the last time he asked, so he brought it up again on the way here. I finally told him *no*. But I lied and said I'd used up my vacation time for the year. That set him off. He claimed that if I loved him, I'd find the time. The argument dragged on here—which is what you witnessed."

"I saw you throw your wine in his face. What provoked that?"

"Oh God. He claims I don't want to go with him because I'm cheating on him. Me? Cheating on *him*? That's absurd. When I denied it, he called me a lying… uh, a lying bitch. That's why."

Her eyes darted about as she talked. She was getting upset all over again. Rick resisted the urge to hold her, to comfort her.

"So, after tonight's argument, I can expect to get a groveling, apologetic phone call from him in two or three weeks. And, he'll probably send *flowers*, too, which is why I told him not to. You *did* hear me say that, didn't you? Because I'd bet my last dollar that he'll do it anyway," anger in her stare.

Rick nodded. "I hope I'm not being too forward, and you don't have to answer this, but, uh, it doesn't sound like you like him very much. Why do you keep dating him?"

Maggie frowned and looked down into the darkness in front of her before coming back to him. "That's an excellent question and I wish I knew the answer. In fact, I keep asking myself that. Truth is, I don't know." She shrugged and paused a beat. "I guess I'm a glutton for punishment," and she snickered. "Maybe it's an inertia thing. I honestly don't know... It's one of life's eternal mysteries," and laughed again.

Time to steer the conversation in another direction. "You said you live in South Norwalk?" She nodded. "I grew up in Wilton and can't say I've spent a lot of time there. Except I do go to Lajoie's junk yard on Meadow Street occasionally to hunt for cheap spare parts for my car. If you don't mind me saying so, the place is kinda rundown, isn't it? —you know, abandoned old warehouses? Stuff like that? Your rent must be pretty cheap. But what's it like to live there?"

She brightened. "Well, you're right on both counts. Actually, my apartment is really nice. It's a third-floor walk-up, the top floor of a renovated brick warehouse building with high ceilings and exposed red brick walls and big old wooden beams. The neighborhood is a bit dumpy—though Lajoie's is several blocks north of my neighborhood, closer to the turnpike. But, anyway, yeah, they're cleaning it up. It's in the early stages of a renaissance of sorts. At least, a lot of the people there think so. They call it SoNo. Kind of a play on SoHo, I guess. But the name is sticking. Not a lot of places to buy groceries, though. So, I usually stop in at Stew Leonard's or Hay Day on my way home from work."

He watched her as she continued describing her neighborhood. The change of subject had calmed her. Her allure glowed again as her anger dissolved. Rick felt comfortable in her presence. Her contralto voice, with a hint of a smoky rasp, warmed and welcomed him. She smiled as she spoke about SoNo and used her arms and hands a lot for emphasis. He found himself absorbed in examining her face, watching her gestures, and listening to the sound of her voice more than paying attention to what she was saying. So, when she interrupted herself with an unexpected question, it caught him off guard.

"Rick, can I catch a ride home with you? I *really* don't want to go home with Pete."

14

"Uh, uh, yeah, sure. Of course. I was going to offer. Besides, Bill's girlfriend met him here and they're staying overnight. So, I'd be driving home alone. It'd be nice to have your company."

He paused and looked down a moment to steel his courage before looking back at her. "You know Maggie, um, I've *really* enjoyed talking with you, and I like the idea of continuing our conversation on the ride home." Pause. "And, um uh, I'd like to see you again." She smiled broadly. My God, Maggie has such a magnetic smile. "This has turned into a *very* special evening for me, considering it's a party I didn't even want to come to. But I'm sure glad I did... And I'm glad you came, too... Sorry about that argument."

"I've really enjoyed talking with you, too. And, yeah, I'd like to see you again, too," and she smiled again. "Maybe we could get together for dinner sometime soon."

Rick stifled the urge to jump up and down and shout for joy.

"I appreciate you listening to me whine and complain. I don't normally do that. Only when provoked."

"Oh, I didn't hear that as whining and complaining. I heard it as letting off steam. Glad to oblige," as they continued smiling at one another.

"Rick, would you mind if we left soon?"

"Now?"

"Sure. But I'd like to visit the ladies' room first."

"Okay. I'll meet you outside at the front door near the parking lot." She nodded and turned to go back inside. He took his own detour to the men's room and got to the front door at ten-forty-five, pleased that he'd be alone with Maggie for another ninety minutes.

When she stepped outside, she walked to him, moved her face near his, put her hand lightly on his wrist, gave it a gentle squeeze, and smiled.

He thrilled at her touch.

"Let's go," she whispered.

They crossed the parking lot, got in his car, pulled out, and turned right onto State Route 44, heading south.

6: Intriguing Intruder

Why did that strange man follow me outside? Maggie wondered. She'd noticed him when he first opened and then quietly closed the door. She watched warily out of the corner of her eye as he walked further down the deck, leaned on the railing just as she was, also staring into the lush, green hills to the west.

Initially, she was annoyed that someone was intruding on her much-desired solitude. But he kept to himself at the far end of the porch and didn't distract her from her dilemma. And fortunately, he wasn't smoking, as she'd first feared he might.

How to be rid of Pete? He was driving her crazy. She suddenly realized, oh my God, she'd have to endure a ninety-minute drive back home with him. With more of his harangues, shouting and tantrums. Made worse by his drunkenness. No way! Could she go back with Jane and her date? It was so damned frustrating. She could feel her tear ducts filling, her throat tightening.

After about ten minutes of sharing the deck with the stranger, as she considered whether to go back inside to ask tedious Jane for a ride, the young man began walking toward her, looking at her all the while. Would he notice that she'd been crying? *Oh, so what.*

He said *hi* and quietly asked if she was okay.

Maggie looked at him, trying to discern his intention. She gave him a terse assurance. "Yeah, I'm okay," though she knew it didn't sound convincing.

He stammered, trying to start a conversation. She looked at him, unsure of what, if any, response would be right. She was touched by his effort to reach out in her moment of distress. She could see that he was good looking. His warm, soft voice was kind and reassuring. She appreciated his hesitancy. But she stayed silent, unsure of what to do or say. When he gave up and said he'd leave her alone, Maggie panicked, and quietly urged him to stay.

They were both silent for an uncomfortably long minute, staring into the distance together, before she broke the ice with an innocuous comment about the scenery. That opened his flood gates. She was both surprised and pleased by his mention of Winslow Homer, one of her favorite painters—to say nothing of the perceptiveness of his allusion. He was right. In truth, the landscape did have a certain Winslow Homer quality to it. She introduced herself.

His name was Rick. She sensed that he was unaffected and sensitive—aware and considerate of her bruised feelings. He said he knew she'd gone outside to escape Pete and admitted he'd followed her but had done so out of his concern for her. That was nice.

Unlike most men in such circumstances—and though she was wary at first—she didn't get the feeling he was creepy or just there to hit on her. Of course, he was interested, of that she was certain, just as she was interested in him. He was pleasant, polite and handsome. And she was charmed.

The more they talked, the more her initial fears melted away. She found herself drawn to him, unthreatened, calm and emboldened in his presence. She liked his thoughtfulness and quick mind. He spoke knowledgeably on a range of topics, listened well, and responded genuinely and appropriately to what she had to say.

Rick dressed smartly, not in the cynically formal-sloppy manner of most preppies, with the wrinkled button-down Brooks Brothers shirt, sock-free penny loafers, and all that. So, her guess was right: he was not a preppie. He'd gone to Wilton High School and won a full scholarship to Dartmouth.

Pete made Maggie's decision easy when he drunkenly stumbled out to the porch and commanded her to leave with him. "No. Go on without me," she told him firmly. She'd walk home first—which is what she said to Rick when she later asked him for a ride. It was a gamble, but a safe one since they clearly were hitting it off and he was obviously a gentleman. Maggie was enjoying the conversation. When he said he'd like to see her again, she got a little tingle, and responded in kind.

Rick called her Wednesday night as they'd arranged. They chatted for more than an hour, readily picking up where they'd left off Friday. It pleased her how naturally the conversation flowed. They laughed together, trading jokes, and had much more to talk about. They would meet for dinner Saturday night.

Still, she hesitated, wondering whether it was a good idea to jump into a new relationship so soon. She worried that she was only seeing Rick in a positive light because he wasn't Pete, that she was not seeing his flaws yet, just as she had been blind to Pete's when they'd first started dating.

Playing it safe, she told Rick she'd meet him at a place walking distance from her apartment, in case the evening turned into a disaster. Though she was pretty sure it wouldn't go that way, she wanted a ready means of escape. Just in case. A stormy year of dating Pete had taught her that much.

7: Happy Daydream

Saturday, May 31st

The morning after he'd met Maggie, Rick awoke with a grin and the same sense of euphoria. She truly was a remarkable woman. Intelligent, well-read, kind, ironic, funny, and knowledgeable on so many subjects.

On the ride back to Maggie's place, he was also pleased to learn that they had more common interests. For one, they both enjoyed everything John le Carré wrote. She'd just finished *Smiley's People*, she said, as he had the previous month. They'd spent several minutes discussing the book, comparing their interpretations of the final scene where Soviet spy Karla defects at the Berlin Wall, and British MI6 agent George Smiley's subtle reaction to the gold cigarette lighter that Karla dropped at his feet—the same lighter Smiley's wife had given to him many years before.

A joy to talk with, she put him at ease. He felt confident in her presence, completely natural, like he'd known her his entire life. Her beauty completed her perfection.

As he fixed his breakfast, he couldn't stop smiling, recalling the details of what they'd talked about, and how good it felt to be with her, absorbed in studying her gorgeous face as she spoke, rapt at her gleaming smile, listening to her warm voice, taking in her scent in his car on the ride home. Not perfume. Something subtler than that, but—

The ringing phone interrupted his happy daydream. It's Saturday morning. A little after nine. Probably Julie.

"Good morning," his sister chirped.

"Hi Julie. Just back from your morning run? You're out pretty early today. How many miles?"

"Yeah. I was up at sunrise, ahead of today's heat. Supposed to get up to a hundred. I hit the Mount Sanitas trail at five-thirty and had it all to myself. Ran a little over five miles out and back. I would have gone further but I'm still a bit sore, recovering from the race."

"Bolder Boulder? That was Memorial Day, right? How'd you do?"

"Yeah. And, actually, I did pretty good. I took sixth among the women—only three minutes off the winning time. And, I ran a new personal best for the 10K. Forty-one, fifty-two."

"*Pretty good?* Bullshit! That's incredible! That's under a seven-minute pace." Julie had been a track star at Wilton High School, and her the record-setting finishes in the 10K at University of Colorado put her among the top collegiate distance women runners in the country.

"Yeah. To be precise, it was a six-forty-five pace," and she laughed quietly. "The conditions were ideal. I actually had fun. So, what's new with you?"

"Well, a lot, actually. I met the most amazing woman last night. Her name is Maggie Haines. She's from New Canaan. Not only is she the most beautiful woman on the planet, she is the sweetest, smartest, kindest, most charming woman I've ever met."

"Whoa, down boy. Beautiful how so? I need some details."

"Oh my God, I can't think of the words. Let me see. Well, she has sparkling brown eyes. A beautiful smile. Long, wavy brunette hair. I can still see her face vividly. She has a natural beauty, like she doesn't need make-up. How do you describe perfection?"

Julie laughed. "I get it. I get it. So, how'd you meet her?"

He told her about the events of the previous evening, including Maggie's argument with Pete and what he'd learned about their relationship.

"Uh oh. You sure you want to get into the middle of that? You know, catching her on the rebound with all the usual bad baggage? I mean, you just said they'd broken up and gotten back together again a few times before. Why not again?"

"Oh, I think it's definitely over this time. She was pretty adamant about it. We'd been talking outside for nearly two hours. Totally into each other. And this drunk meathead comes out and says *Let's go!* I mean, he practically commanded her to leave with him. I wouldn't talk to a *dog* like that. She told him off. Said the relationship was over. Not to call her later to apologize. She even told him not to send her flowers. Sounded pretty final to me. After all, I did see her throw a glass of wine into his face."

"Yeah, yeah, I guess it does sound over. So, what's your next move, Romeo?"

"Well, I gave her a ride home—which was also great. We swapped phone numbers and agreed to get together for dinner sometime soon. I'm supposed to call her Wednesday night to arrange that."

"Way to go. Keep me posted."

"How 'bout you? How's the job hunt going?"

"I've given up on Boulder. I'm looking around Denver... Oh, and before I forget, I gotta tell you, I spoke to Uncle Frank last week and asked about the estate, whether there's enough money for me for a down payment on a house."

"You're gonna buy a house?"

"Yeah. Well, if I get a job in Denver, that is. Boulder's too expensive, but Denver has a lot of affordable neighborhoods. I'm tired of paying rent. So, I called Frank last weekend to find out what I could afford."

"What'd he say?"

"No problem. He said I could cover the full cost of a modest house. It sure would be great not having to pay a mortgage—or monthly rent."

"How much are we talking about?"

"As much as three hundred thou, he said."

Rick blew a low whistle. "Wow. Maybe I should talk to Frank. I'm tired of paying rent, too. I'm also tired of having a roommate. At least you don't have a roommate."

"You should, Rick. You know, with the airline payouts, the life insurance policies and everything else, there's a pretty hefty balance there. Somewhere north of three million in all, Frank said."

"*Three million?* Whoa. I had no idea! But, you know, it kind of bothers me, knowing what that money represents. I really don't like to think about it."

She paused a moment. "Yeah. Yeah, I know what you mean. Me, too. But, hey, look at it this way. It's their legacy for us. It's tough, but what else can we do?"

"I suppose you're right," he said, sighing.

"Listen, I should get off. I need a shower. Badly. But I wanted to check in with you before my weekend got too crazy. I'm working lunch and dinner both today and tomorrow at McKinney's Pub. Weekends are crazy this time of year. Lots of tourists in town. Too bad they're such lousy tippers. But listen. I'm so happy for you. I hope it all works out."

"Thanks for calling. Take care buddy. I love you."

"And I love you, too. Keep me posted on this Maggie business. Sounds promising. Oh. And send me a photo of Maggie when you get one. I want to see what your definition of beauty is all about."

"Will do. And good luck with the job hunt."

8: Rippowam Girls

Friday, June 6th

Since moving into his rented house on High Ridge Road the previous fall, Pete had come to appreciate the fringe benefit of watching the parade of high school girls every morning on their way to classes at Rippowam High School next door.

He stood at his second-floor bedroom window putting on his tie, his eyes focused on the sidewalk fifteen feet in front of his house. The summer break would begin later that month, which depressed him, knowing he'd miss his daily opportunity to consider the nubile talent.

And they were walking by right now, in groups of two, three and four; some with and some without boys. Several were plain and skinny. Others were chubby. But Pete zeroed in on those worth checking out closely. It had been especially warm lately and the good-looking ones weren't terribly modest about their choice of clothes. Skimpy was their preferred style—and his. His favorite girl usually came along by herself, around seven-thirty.

Anticipating her arrival, as he often did, he grabbed the Grateful Dead's first album and put the needle on the third cut, "Good Morning Little School Girl." It was one of his most-played albums from his high school days— the Dead was a dorm favorite at Hotchkiss—and he knew the lyrics by heart. Right on cue, there she was, and he sang along with the tune to the closed window.

After the first couple lines, he stopped singing, just to admire her. "Oh, that's very sweet. I like that snug shirt you've got on today. I've never seen you wear that before. It really shows off your tits. And the cleavage is a nice touch, too." He'd seen the buxom brunette several times before and she'd become his top choice for fantasy sex. He took a mental picture of her for later reference.

"I'll bet you'd be even more beautiful naked in my bed. *I think I love you,*" he said loudly, admiring her tight short blue-jean skirt and shapely rear end as she walked by. "I sure hope you're not a senior. I'd like to see more of you in the fall. Maybe we could go out for a date, my *little school girl.*"

After she'd passed, Pete resumed singing the song as he returned to the bathroom mirror to straighten his tie. Fiddling with it in frustration, retying it a fourth time, he couldn't get the two ends to match up. He stopped singing, yanked the tie off and threw it on the floor among a pile of dirty clothes. Reaching into the closet for another tie, his irritation took him back to the Hotchkiss party.

What he'd witnessed Friday night still gnawed at him. He hadn't left the party right away after telling Maggie that he was heading home. He wanted to see what, if anything, came of the conversation she was having with that stranger. The guy was not Hotchkiss. Never seen him before. With his sixth bottle of Heineken between his legs—or was it his seventh? —he sat in his idling car at the far corner of the dark parking lot, waiting. He wasn't too drunk to see what was going on and soon realized his worst fears: Maggie was climbing into the stranger's VW—the same guy she'd been talking to for so long outside. He even opened and closed the door for her. Pete admitted to himself that he'd never done that.

He also owned up to having blown it with Maggie. Shouldn't have been so pushy. Probably got kind of obnoxious. Shouldn't have sworn at her. Yeah, he'd love it to go to Saint Kitts with her. She does look great in a bikini. Very sexy. It was that bikini she wore on Cape Cod a year ago that caught his eye when they'd first met.

But maybe he was too aggressive. He decided to call her later that day and apologize. Before it's too late.

Putting on his sports coat, he walked out the door.

9: It's Over

Molly Shepherd, the Williams Advertising receptionist, buzzed Maggie on the intercom. "Maggie, it's Pete Conley on line two for you."

It's only Friday, a week since the fight. He's earlier than usual. She sighed aloud, which Molly probably heard. "Okay. Thanks, Molly."

"What do *you* want?" Maggie asked, omitting the conventional *hello*.

"I'm really sorry, Maggie. Really, I am. I was totally out of line Friday night when I insisted we go St. Kitts together, and then losing it when you said you couldn't and—"

"—Pete, stop—"

"—and I said some things I regret, and I'm really sorry. I really am. I know what you always say about that, but it's just that I love you so much and my feelings for you overwhelm me sometimes and I—"

"—*Stop!*" she yelled.

He stopped. "We've been through this too many times, Pete, and I am *sick and tired of it*," she said in a quietly loud voice, so as not to be heard by others in the office. "You blow up and hurt me. Later, you always apologize and promise to change your ways, and then, a few weeks later, you're doing the same damn thing all over again. Like I told you Friday night, our relationship is over. You cannot sweet-talk your way back into my life anymore. I don't want to hear from you again. Do you understand? Our relationship is *over*. Do not call me again."

"But Maggie, *if you'd just listen to me. Please!* I know I was wrong. I know I hurt you—"

"—I've heard it all before. I'm done with your excuses. I'm done with your groveling. I'm done with you. And I'm done with this call!" She hung up and went back to work.

10: Dinner Date

Saturday, June 7th

It had been eight days since they met at the White Hart Inn. As agreed, Rick met Maggie at seven-fifteen at Al Fresco, a small Italian restaurant near her apartment. They settled in a corner banquette. He asked about her job.

The autumn after Boston College, she explained, she'd taken an entry level position as receptionist and go-fer at Williams Advertising in Westport. Ken Williams, the owner and creative director, appreciated her drive, strong work ethic and creativity—his words—and promoted her to account executive a few months later.

Over the course of the nearly four years since, she had advanced in the company and now managed four accounts and a team of four account executives. Over the same period, Ken had continued to build the agency, adding ten new people since Maggie had come aboard. The agency now numbered thirty-five professionals, and she was one of the more senior people.

As she scanned the menu, she asked, "So, how do you like working at Hamilton? Dad has always been high on that company. He knows a lot of people there, so he gets a lot of insights into it. I know he's tried to recruit some of their top people—without success, so far."

"Doesn't surprise me," and Rick laughed quietly. "It's a great organization and I can't imagine that someone worth poaching would want to leave. Hamilton is pretty progressive, which I really like. They give us a lot of freedom and encourage innovative thinking and new ideas."

"When you told me about it last week, I got the sense that you kind of fell into the job, that the Dartmouth alumni office steered you that way. Is that true?"

"Well, yeah, I guess so. I went there more out of curiosity than in any expectation of landing a job. They said they expected me to interview them as much as they were interviewing me, which I found intriguing. I really liked the people I met and felt they treated me with respect I'd never seen in any other interviews I'd done up to that point. So, I was pleased to be offered a job there. I think that, traditionally, people are just happy to get a paycheck. I feel like that's changing and that Hamilton is at the forefront. They want to cultivate independent thinking and a loyal team."

"I know what you mean. My agency is the same way. I love the place and my job. I can't imagine going to work every day just for the paycheck."

"You're lucky, then. Like I say, I think it's a new trend in business today. It's like… Uh… Well, take my father, for instance. He was married when he graduated from college. My mother was already pregnant with me. So, he scrambled to find a job. He landed one selling insurance in Stamford. Later, he went out on his own, and did pretty well. But was selling insurance what he really wanted to do? I mean, when he was studying business is college, was he thinking he'd go out and sell insurance? Why not some other business? I never got the impression that he liked it—at least, not the way I like my job. Did he really intend to spend his life selling insurance? I'll never know."

"He sells insurance? What sorts?" Maggie asked.

Oh shit. Bad move. Rick regretted that he'd brought up his father. Looking past her into the middle distance, he thought how he might give her a brief but satisfactory answer. Too late. He'd already put his foot in his mouth.

"Uh, yeah. He sold insurance—fire, auto, life. That sort of stuff. He had his own agency in Wilton. Did it since I was a baby."

"You say he *sold* insurance? Has he retired?"

Rick sighed, looked down at the table, and then looked back into her eyes. "No. No. Actually, my father is no longer alive. And neither is my mother."

"Oh, I'm sorry, Rick. Both your parents?"

"Yeah."

"Recently?"

He paused, continuing to look at her. "Actually, four years ago. Do you remember that plane crash in Aruba in April 1976?"

Maggie inhaled sharply, pursed her lips, and shook her head slightly.

"Well, the pilot overshot the landing and crashed into the ocean. The plane split in half. Forty-eight people survived, but thirty-six were killed, including my parents."

"Oh, my God. That's horrible."

Looking down, he paused a beat and then looked back at her. "Yeah. It was pretty awful." He paused for another moment. "I was near the end of my senior year at Dartmouth and I had to drop out to deal with it—and to be with my sisters."

"Sisters? How old are they?"

He took a deep breath. "Julie's now twenty-three, and Sarah turned twenty-one last Saturday."

Maggie had reached across the table as he was talking and put her hand on his.

"Sarah was a junior in high school at the time. Julie was a sophomore at University of Colorado and, as I said, I was finishing up at Dartmouth. Even though I hadn't taken my finals, they gave me my degree anyway. I think the dean felt pretty badly about the whole thing."

He took a sip of ice water. Maggie absent-mindedly massaged his hand, which he found comforting.

"Oh, Rick, that's very sad. I'm so sorry."

This was difficult to talk about, especially in light of his growing attraction to Maggie. He looked at her forlornly and sighed again.

"The plan had been for Sarah to stay with our aunt and uncle in Weston while Mom and Dad were away those two weeks in Aruba." He felt a catch in his throat, coughed involuntarily, and resumed. "After we found out about the crash, Julie and I came home to be with Sarah and to sort things out. Fortunately, my aunt and uncle took over. They handled everything. All the arrangements, the funeral—we had a double-funeral. Sarah moved in with them and finished high school, commuting from Weston."

The waiter came to take their orders. "Could you please give us a few more minutes?" Maggie asked.

Rick paused again for a few seconds. He could tell she'd been getting upset as he told her about the tragedy. He'd noticed that she had dabbed at the corners of her eyes with her napkin a couple times. Looking down again, he said, "I'm sorry this came up tonight. I guess it's spoiled the evening."

"No, Rick. It's okay. I can't imagine being in your place. You must have been completely devastated. I'm sure you miss your mom and dad terribly. That's just awful."

"Well… I guess I've gotten past it and accepted it, as much as anyone can. My aunt and uncle have been very supportive… You just have to move on."

"It's good that your aunt and uncle were there for you. Even better that they lived close enough that your sister could finish high school."

"Yeah." He exhaled. "Well, anyway, would you mind if we ordered dinner and changed the subject?"

In truth, his memories of those nightmare days and weeks after his parents' deaths still tormented him. Though he felt he'd shown a brave face, he sensed he'd been on the verge of breaking down all over again, as he often was whenever anyone asked him about the tragedy.

"Sure. Uh, sure. Of course." She released his hand and picked up her menu. Getting the waiter's attention, they placed their orders. He left and soon returned with the bottle of wine they'd selected.

"We haven't talked about your family. All I know is what you told me last week… that your dad is a senior executive at World Paper. As I recall, you said he was in charge of their Haines Paper Group. Is it just a coincidence that your last name is also Haines?" he asked with a grin.

Maggie opened her mouth as though to answer, but then closed it and stayed silent, averting her eyes.

11: Louise Pomeroy Inches

Learning of Rick's family tragedy had stunned Maggie. What's the right thing to say? How do you put yourself in the shoes of someone who had lost both parents so suddenly, so cruelly? It was incomprehensible. His story touched her deeply. She'd choked up. She didn't know what to say, how to empathize, and couldn't imagine how that must feel or how anyone could live with that.

Understandably, Rick wanted to change the subject. But did he have to steer the conversation to her family?

"What's the matter?" he asked, concern on his face.

Maggie looked—and felt—uncomfortable, grimacing slightly, averting her gaze and staying silent. Too many times, she'd seen the effect that knowledge of her family's vast wealth had had on new acquaintances, particularly new boyfriends—like Pete. Her attraction to Rick and her growing feelings for him amplified her discomfort. How would he react when she told him that she had so much money that she really didn't need to work? How would it change his feelings toward her? She still hadn't answered him.

He looked perplexed. "Uh, can you tell me something about your mother. Do you have any brothers or sisters?" he asked.

She'd give him the bare minimum. "Well, Mom is a couple years younger than Dad, born and raised outside Philadelphia. She was always a stay-at-home mother. Once I went off to school, she got back into her ceramics and started a little business, making and selling her pieces and, later, offering classes. My brother Charley is a year-and-a-half older than me. He went to Yale and now works at World Paper, in marketing. But Rick, if you don't mind, I'd like to leave it at that. I have a hard time talking about my family with new friends. Can we postpone the details, please? I'm afraid a discussion about my family would just spoil the evening."

She reached across the table again to put her hand on his for emphasis. He turned his palm over so that they were holding hands. She squeezed it. They locked eyes. Both smiled. She held his hand firmly.

"I'm sorry Rick, but all that just seems so trivial right now. And I'm having a hard time dealing with what you just told me about your parents. I still have my parents and I love them very much. I cannot even begin to imagine how you must feel. Believe me, I'm just happy to be here with you, all by ourselves, in this quiet restaurant. If we start talking about my family, there'll be no end to it. I'd much rather talk about anything else."

"Um, okay. Some other time. Whenever you feel like it… Enough talk about families. Let's eat," he smiled, seeing the waiter approaching with their salads.

As they ate, they continued their meandering conversation. It came easily, and they discovered several more shared interests. They began reminiscing about their college years and their studies.

Rick talked about his senior thesis on Teddy Roosevelt.

Maggie had majored in Art History, with a minor in Music. She'd focused on John Singer Sargent, an artist that Rick had especially appreciated in the art history class he'd taken at Dartmouth, he said. His questions impressed her, demonstrating a genuine familiarity with Sargent and affection for his work. He showed a depth of understanding that pleased Maggie. Many of his questions about Sargent gave her pause, forced her to think about aspects of Sargent's works she hadn't thought about since college.

They'd been so absorbed in one another, neither had been paying attention to the clock. Both were surprised when they realized it was past ten. Having finished dinner and their bottle of wine, they drank ice water and continued talking, smiling often, laughing occasionally. Only one other couple remained in the restaurant.

"Rick? Let's pay the tab and let our poor waiter go home," lifting her purse to the table to take out her wallet. Rick put his hand atop hers.

"This is my treat. I invited you—"

"—Actually, I invited you," she interrupted with a teasing smile.

"Never mind. I insist. But I don't want the evening to end. I don't mind hanging out here a little longer. Would you like dessert? Or an after-dinner drink? Do they serve Grappa? Or would you like some espresso? We can make it worth our waiter's time."

She grinned and tilted her head slightly.

"Instead of an after-dinner drink here, how about you let me treat you to one in my apartment? And I have some Pepperidge Farm cookies, too, if you feel like dessert. It's only a couple blocks away."

"Are you sure? I remember what you said on our drive home, that you were feeling like you needed space after what's-his-name—Pete." She grimaced.

"Sorry. Really, I do understand. It's okay."

He amazed her, giving her an out like that.

"Rick, you're sweet. But, yes. Really. It's okay. Just come up for a little something."

After getting the waiter's attention, Rick paid the check and they left. Walking the three blocks slowly from the restaurant to her apartment, they continued their quiet conversation.

It was a pleasant evening with clear skies, but it was early June and the night had taken on an unseasonable chill, with a light but steady breeze off nearby Long Island Sound. Both were under-dressed. She hugged herself and shivered. Rick noticed, put his arm around her shoulders and pulled her close. She welcomed his embrace, leaned into him and thought how nice the evening had turned out.

Maggie felt completely at ease with Rick. Though she worried that she'd been too forward inviting him to her apartment, his hesitant response reassured her that it would be okay. Many other men would have started drooling at such an offer. She laughed out loud at the image of Rick drooling, angling to pounce on her.

"What's so funny?"

"Nothing," and smiled at him.

He gave her a long curious look, smiled, and then pulled her tighter to himself. She put her arm around his waist. Her smile broadened.

Climbing the two sets of stairs, she locked the door behind them as they entered her apartment. Rick checked out its high ceilings, ample living room, open kitchen, dining room table and chairs, and half-bathroom off the living room. She showed him the separate bedroom with its own bathroom.

"You weren't kidding. This is really a nice apartment."

"Thanks. What would you like to drink?"

"Maybe a bit more wine, if you have something open," as he settled into the couch.

She poured two glasses of Chianti. Handing him one, she set hers on the coffee table and sat down next to him, tucking her bare feet under herself and leaning toward him with one arm on the back of the couch.

As he continued to look around, he said, "I love the high ceilings with the exposed beams. It's so roomy. How many square feet?"

"I think it's about a thousand."

"It has a nice open feeling. What do you pay for rent… if you don't mind me asking?"

"Two-fifty a month."

"Wow! Two-fifty? No wonder you live in SoNo. Bill and I pay more than double that for our Stamford apartment, and it's not even this big, and only has one bathroom. Maybe I should move to SoNo, too."

After further small talk, Rick resumed their earlier dinner conversation about John Singer Sargent. He pursued a point she'd made on their way to the apartment about the mystery of Sargent's portraits.

His portrait of "Mrs. Charles Inches" had always been his favorite Sargent work. It had been included in a Sargent retrospective at the Museum of Fine Arts while Rick was at Dartmouth, he told her, and he'd made a special trip to Boston to see the show. Maggie had seen the same show, too, with her class. The portrait had riveted him at the time—so much so that he'd bought and framed a three-quarter-sized copy that still hung on his apartment wall, he told her.

"In my opinion, few painters of that era captured personalities as skillfully as Sargent. Mrs. Inches' expression really intrigues and mystifies me. It's a shame it's still in a private collection. It deserves a wider audience. I've always thought of Mrs. Inches as America's own *Mona Lisa*. She's beautiful and enigmatic at the same time."

"Hmm. That's an interesting observation. I never thought of that."

"I can't decide what her mood is. Who is she looking at, and why is she looking that way? In one sense, she looks kind of worried. About what? But look at her another time, you think she looks happy. Or maybe bored. Distracted? Reflective? I think it's all about her mouth. It has a slight twist that is both a smile and a pout at the same time. It's hard to decide what she's thinking—as though Sargent wasn't sure himself and left it vague… Despite the mystery, or maybe because of it, I've always found her to be a fascinating woman, and remarkably beautiful. Did you know that her husband was a wealthy Boston doctor twenty years older than she? It makes you wonder all the more about her mysterious expression and who exactly she was."

Maggie remembered Rick's casual reference to Winslow Homer the night they met. And now, this mini-lecture on Sargent. Of course, she already knew all this about the painting's provenance—and more. But it pleased her immensely that he had thought so much about this particular painting and could talk so comfortably about art, especially about two of her favorite artists—and so many other topics, as well—unlike Pete, with whom most conversations seemed to focus on his daily routines, complaints about work, the last party he'd been to, and the next party on his calendar. How wonderful it was to be with Rick. She felt far more comfortable than she'd ever been with any man. She leaned closer to him and smiled.

"What? Why are you looking at me like that?"

Her smile grew. "Rick. I don't know what's going on. I'm not sure if I should trust it, but I have to tell you, it just feels so good to be with you right now. I feel like myself and so comfortable. It's like I've known you for all my life."

Rick smiled and looked at her for a moment before speaking.

"I feel that way about you, too." He put his glass down next to hers. "Would you mind if I told you how beautiful you are? I just love looking at your face." She giggled self-consciously and looked down.

"In the days since we met, I was able to recall your face so clearly in my mind," and he reached out with a bent index finger, put it under her chin, and gently lifted her face so that they were looking into each other's eyes again. Maggie got a bad case of goosebumps, which she could feel on her bare arms.

"My sister, Julie, called the day after we met, and I told her all about you—at least all that I knew. I had trouble finding the right words, but I tried to describe your beauty to her. I did forget to tell her about the light sprinkling of freckles across your upper cheeks and over the bridge of your nose that I find so charming," and he lightly traced the tip of his index finger over the freckles on one cheek. She giggled again, embarrassed by his attention and touch.

"Something else I forgot to tell her about is your smile. It's wonderful. It makes my heart skip." She smiled broadly. "You see? You did it again," as he clutched at his chest. She laughed out loud.

Continuing to scan her face, "You know, come to think of it, there are aspects of your face that remind me of the portrait of Mrs. Inches."

"Stop it."

"No, really. That portrait is imprinted on my brain. The copy I bought at the MFA show has hung on my wall ever since and I often find myself admiring it. Do you know that when I first saw you at the party last week, I had an eerie feeling that I'd seen your face before? Like from a dream. And I think that's why. I think you reminded me of her. Still do."

"Don't be silly."

"I am *not* being silly. I'm quite serious. That's what I saw. If you put your hair up like hers, I think you could do a stand-in. Are you sure she's not an ancestor of yours?"

Maggie laughed. "Oh, come on."

He scanned her face. "The very shape of your face is like hers. The soft arch of your eyebrows." He touched her right eyebrow, and then lightly placed the palm of his hand gently against that side of her face, moving closer, continuing to look into her eyes and speaking quietly. "Your warm, dark eyes. Your face, a perfect oval like hers. The mouth is a mystery, though—both yours and hers... Except for the freckles, I'd say it's a perfect match." And he grinned. "Or maybe Mrs. Inches had freckles and Sargent didn't include them in the portrait," and he laughed softly.

The touch of Rick's hand, his gentle voice, and his gaze were sensual and exciting. She felt a deep, tingling sensation, leaned her head into his hand, kissed his wrist, moved toward him. She closed her eyes and sought his lips. He pulled her to himself and they locked in a long, deep kiss. She found herself utterly lost in it.

After a few minutes, they released, and she looked at him, and whispered, "Rick, I told myself I wasn't going to hurry this, no matter how I felt. But I'm having a hard time ignoring what I'm feeling right now. Would you stay tonight?"

Rick smiled, scanned her face again for a long moment, and lightly stroked her cheek with the back of his fingers, until she grew uncomfortable, worried that she'd drunk too much wine and been too forward.

"Maggie, I can't think of anything I'd rather do, but..."

But? But what? She'd always assumed that any man would leap head-first at such an invitation. Rick didn't. Why was he hesitating?

Rick interrupted her thoughts. "Don't get me wrong. In the past, I'd have jumped at an invitation like that from a beautiful woman like you. But this is different. *You're* different. I wonder if it's a good idea to rush into this."

Rick looked at her closely. His directness froze her.

"Maggie, you are special. You're thoughtful, smart, funny, and utterly gorgeous. It feels so good, so right just to be with you." He paused a moment, continuing to look into her eyes before resuming.

"I'm overwhelmed by my luck, that we'd both be at a party that neither of us wanted to go to. That I'd witness your passion, the range of your emotions. That I'd experience so soon the depth of your intelligence and compassion in two short evenings. And now, here we are. And I'm *so* happy right now. I've *never* felt this way about a woman before."

Maggie melted inside. It was as though he'd been reading her mind, caressing her insecurities, making them evaporate. There was no appropriate response but to smile back at him.

She kissed his cheek, stood, took his hand, guided him to his feet, and led him to the bedroom, leaving behind two glasses of wine.

12: Two Family Dynasties

Sunday, June 8th

When the morning's sunlight touched Rick's face through a gap in the curtains, he opened his eyes and looked around, remembering he wasn't in his own bed but in Maggie's. The thought gave him a smile. He reached out gingerly to the other side of the bed. Empty. Rolling his face into her pillow, her scent gave him a tickle of recollection of the previous evening.

Lying still a moment, taking in the aromas of the room and the bed, tracking the sun beams across the ceiling, he smiled again.

What an amazing woman Maggie is. He couldn't believe what had happened the night before. She is such a sensuous and sensitive woman, so sexy, and so beautiful.

Hearing sounds from the kitchen, he sat up and looked for his clothes on the floor, but saw only his boxer shorts, pants, shoes and socks. He remembered having carefully hung his shirt on the back of her desk chair the night before. But it wasn't there now.

Getting out of bed, he put on the boxers and made a detour to the adjacent bathroom to rinse his mouth and brush his teeth with the tip of an index finger and a dab of stolen toothpaste. Rick found Maggie in the kitchen washing the wineglasses from the night before, wearing nothing but his shirt.

"Good morning, beautiful," he said, smiling and walking to her.

She wrapped her arms around the back of his neck and pulled him to her for a deep kiss.

"What a nice evening that was last night," she cooed. "I had fun. And I believe you did, too. That felt *really* good."

"Oh yeah. It certainly was, and it certainly did. You are really amazing," as he put his hands on her hips. "I like that shirt on you. Just about the right size, too. Plenty of room for maneuvering," as he lifted the shirt bottom. She snickered at the touch of his hands wandering up her bare back.

"You know, in addition to your beautiful face, you have a beautiful body, too," continuing to rub her backside before dropping his hands to massage her bare butt.

"You're pretty hot yourself." He resumed the hug, kissed her neck and gripped her butt firmly with both hands, pulling her hips snug to his. They shared another long, deep kiss. His erection grew against her belly. He broke off from the kiss and smiled again, whispering, "Care for an encore?"

She laughed, backed away, took his hand, and led him back to the bedroom where they resumed making love.

Afterwards, lying naked next to each other, Maggie looked at him and smiled. "Where did you come from, Mr. Hewson?"

"Hah. I already told you. What else do you want to know? But what about you? I still know next to nothing about you."

Maggie sighed and frowned a faux grimace.

"You told me about your job, and a little bit about your mother and father, and you mentioned your brother, Charley. But that's about it. Tell me how wonderful your family is—or maybe they're not?"

"Do I have to?" and she pouted. He mirrored her pout and she laughed. "Okay. Let's take a quick shower and go around the corner to Ernie's for breakfast. You'll love the place. It's a classic diner. We'll sit in a booth with a little tabletop jukebox, and I'll spill the beans about my family."

The quick shower lasted almost twenty minutes, and included a lot of nuzzling, groping, kissing, tickling and giggling.

After being seated in a booth at Ernie's, Maggie began to talk about her family. "We have a lot of family money that goes back a few generations… old money."

The waitress arrived at their table with a pot of coffee. After filling their mugs, she took their orders and left.

"You were paying attention the other day. Yes, you're right. It's not a coincidence that my dad runs the Haines Paper Group. The company was founded in Maine nearly a hundred years ago by my great-great-grandfather, who emigrated from Wales just after the Civil War."

She explained how the company grew and evolved over the subsequent decades in Maine, expanding later into New Brunswick and Quebec. The business had been passed down through the sons. Her uncle and father took it over in 1965.

The waitress brought their breakfasts and freshened their coffee.

Maggie continued, about how her father and uncle had decided to accept an acquisition offer from World Paper in 1968. Maggie's father became

CEO of the subsidiary. "His brother, my Uncle Henry, who's older than Dad, took early retirement. He and my Aunt Maureen wanted to travel, which they've been doing the past several years."

In fact, asking a few questions around the office and perusing industry reference books, Rick had learned as much. So, she was confirming what he already knew.

"We all got World Paper stock and cash from the sale. After Grandpa Tom and Grandma Abigail passed away, the rest of the family wealth was shared among us all."

"Sounds like you're probably wealthy enough that you don't have to work for a living. Right? Why do you?"

"We all do. Dad, Charley, and my cousins Hank and Olivia all work at World. Dad wants me to join the company, too, but I'm happy at Williams. And Mom has her ceramics business." She paused and sipped her coffee. "None of us *need* to work. We do because we've been raised that way. Dad commutes into the city every day and continues to operate with the same philosophy and dedication as always. It's the challenges. It's meeting and working with people from different backgrounds every day. How boring it would be to live a life of leisure. I wouldn't know what to do with myself. What? Become a jet-setter? I think jet-setters must be the most boring people—they have no connection to the real world."

Rick nodded. "Tell me more about your mother."

She smiled. "Mom is the greatest. She's my buddy. She's a great listener and friend. Mom comes from old money, too. A similar multi-generational thing."

She explained that her mother's grandfather had founded a few small local electric utilities in the Mid-Atlantic region in the early days of electricity around the turn of the century, a business inherited by her mother's father who continued to build the business, Maggie explained.

"Mom grew up outside Philadelphia. She's the second of two daughters. Graduated from Bryn Mawr College. So did her sister, my Aunt Alice. Mom and Alice inherited the family wealth when Grandpa Chuck and Grandma Margaret passed away a few years ago."

Incredible, Rick thought. Maggie is the product of a merging of two family fortunes. And she's totally normal and charming, unlike his past two girlfriends: Not self-centered and unfocused like Karen, nor an elitist back stabber like Linda. And she's sitting here with him. Right now. And he thinks he's falling in love.

But he also struggled internally with this new information. Here he was once again, falling for another wealthy woman, like Linda and Karen, someone who had more money than he could ever dream of, a woman who didn't need to work. Why? Was it pure luck, or was there something—an aura—about rich women that he was attracted to?

"I don't believe you," he said, with a grin. "You made it all up." She shook her head. "But look at you. Your lifestyle does not betray wealth and privilege. You're down to earth, nothing like the rich women I've known. You even drive a used VW."

"I live on my salary alone. My trust fund did pay for my college education. But otherwise, I've never touched a nickel of it. I'm not even sure how much money there is—I mean, yeah, I know what it is as a ballpark number, but not exactly. We have financial advisors manage it, and Dad has fiduciary control. Charley and I won't have control until we turn thirty-five. It's how Grandpa Tom set them up."

As comfortable as he was with Maggie and as happy as he was just being with her, the gulf between their respective bank accounts troubled him. Trust fund? How he would have loved to have a trust fund, especially his junior year when he had to take the waiter job in the dorm dining room just so he could eat.

And, on top of that, the open question of the former boyfriend nagged at him, too, as she was talking. Rick felt the matter was still unresolved, but didn't say anything, not wanting to spoil the moment. And then he scolded himself for even thinking about it.

13: Unwanted Roses

Wednesday, June 11th

Maggie got to her office early Wednesday to prepare for a meeting with a new client, who was expected at eleven. She'd been at her desk for nearly an hour when Molly Shepherd called to say that a dozen red roses in a glass vase had just been delivered for her at the front desk.

Oh shit. Pete, again. That means he'll be calling. "Okay, Molly, thanks. Can you leave them in the reception area for everyone to enjoy, please?"

"Do you want the card that came with them?"

"Nah. Just toss it. I know who they're from."

About an hour later, Molly buzzed her again. "Maggie, it's Pete Conley for you on line three."

"Thanks."

She paused and took a deep breath before picking up the phone.

"What is it Pete? I'm very busy. I'm about to go into a meeting." Which was true. It was ten minutes before eleven.

"Maggie, I hope you got the flowers," he said in a cheerful tone.

"I told you not to send me flowers." She was getting sick of the sight of roses.

"Did you read the note that came with the flowers? I'm trying to apologize. But last week you hung up on me. Please let me finish—"

"—Pete, I already know what you're going to say. I've heard your spiel too many times. I have it memorized. I reminded you last week that our relationship is over. I told you to stop calling me. *Please Stop Calling Me. Leave Me Alone.* And stop sending me flowers. Send the flowers to your other girlfriends."

"But Maggie, I don't have any other girlfriends. Only you. Please, Maggie. Please listen to me. I know I said some hurtful things and—"

"—I've heard it all before. This call is over." She hung up, stood and walked to the reception desk.

"Molly, would you please do me favor?"

"Sure."

41

"From now on, whenever Pete calls, I don't care what I'm doing, I am, quote unquote, busy and I cannot take his call. Okay?"

"Got it."

"You know Pete's voice, don't you?"

"Yes."

"He may try to get around you with a fake name. Don't let him."

"Okay."

Maggie knelt so that she was looking directly into Molly's eyes. Putting her hand on Molly's forearm, she lowered her voice. "Look, Molly, I'm really sorry to bring you into this mess, but I broke up with Pete two weeks ago and he doesn't seem to believe me. He's being a total jerk and won't leave me alone. It's interfering with my work. He leaves me no other choice."

Molly was a few years younger than Maggie, a 1979 Wesleyan College graduate who'd been hired earlier that year. She'd been working hard, learning a lot in the fast-growing agency, eagerly tackling the same kinds of tasks Maggie had when she'd started there. They'd become good friends.

"Okay. But do you want to know if he calls again? Because you know he will. I remember the last time you broke up with him in January. He must have called a dozen times."

"You're right. Good idea. Yes, I do. If it's not too much trouble. Just let me know? Oh, you know what? Better yet, can you just keep a log? Or whatever's easier." Molly nodded again. "Thanks, Molly. I really appreciate it. You're a pal."

Maggie stood and returned to her office. Though she had some last-minute details to review and about five minutes before the client arrived, she couldn't get her mind to focus. She was still obsessing about Pete. *Dammit!* Pete really was interfering with her work. She wasn't even talking to him and she couldn't get him out of her mind. Why wouldn't he just leave her alone? She wished he would just get out of her life and move on—

"—Maggie, the client team is here," Molly said over the intercom. "They know they're a little early and said they're happy to wait."

"Okay. Thanks. Tell them I'll be right out."

14: The Art Happened

Saturday, June 14th

Maggie stood with Rick in the first gallery on the third floor of the Museum of Modern Art in New York City, taking in the largest, most amazing oil painting either had ever seen: Pablo Picasso's *Guernica,* an epic portrayal of the April twenty-sixth, 1937, joint German-Italian *blitzkrieg* destruction of a Basque village by the same name in northern Spain.

The MoMA was under increasing pressure to repatriate the painting to Spain since the constitutional government that Picasso had long sought had been established upon Francisco Franco's death some five years earlier—a condition of Picasso's will. It looked as though it would be leaving New York soon, so this might be their last chance to view it.

They'd learned all this and more watching a story on the MacNeil/Lehrer Report the previous week.

"It was first shown in Paris the summer after the attack. Picasso completed it in thirty-five days," she aloud read from a pamphlet she'd picked up in the museum.

"Obviously, if he did it that quickly, it was a work of profound passion and grief," Maggie whispered. "I think he's really captured the anguish, horror and violence of war." Rick nodded.

For about fifteen minutes, they studied the massive twelve by twenty-five-foot surrealistic work. Stepping closer, they examined its many painful details—the ghoulish, ghost-like, dismembered and distorted humans and farm animals, and their terrified faces—and then stepped back to take in its full import.

Eventually, they moved on to see the many other treasures in the museum. They left around three, tired from being on their feet on hard floors for nearly four hours.

The weather was warm and humid, but tolerable, so they strolled the half-dozen blocks north up Fifth Avenue to Central Park to enjoy the vast green scape. A shaded bench just inside the park near the Grand Army Plaza provided them their desired respite.

Rick bought a couple of Italian ices from a nearby street cart vendor. After sitting quietly for a few minutes, enjoying their ices, Maggie suggested a walk in the park. Hand in hand, ambling aimlessly, they took in the greenery, and breathed the fresh air, heard dogs' barks and children's squeals of delight. Walking past the carousel, full of happy youngsters and loud calliope music, Rick remarked on the ironic contrast between the horrific painting they'd just seen and the joy of being together in Central Park on a warm summer Saturday.

Their wanderings brought them to Tavern on the Green at a quarter-to-six where they had an early dinner. Afterwards, they grabbed a cab back to Grand Central and caught the next train back to South Norwalk.

After they'd settled into their seats, Rick said, "I don't think I've ever seen a piece of art that's quite so powerful as *Guernica*."

"Paintings *can* be powerful. The greatest ones are. You know, an art history professor of mine once said that the painting we see on the wall is not really the art but merely a representation of the art, which in fact is the act of creation."

"What do you mean?"

"Well, the art happened all at once—or over a period of time as the artist's ideas and passions evolved and found expression. Viewing the painting afterwards—years or decades, even centuries later—can only give us a foggy window into what the artist may have been feeling and thinking during the act of creation. So, when we look at *Guernica*, what we are doing as best we can is belatedly bearing witness to Picasso's own sense of loss and personal grief, the emotional intensity he felt at the time of creation. And we know it was intense by the speed with which he completed the painting."

"Hmm. I've never heard it explained that way."

"Until my professor explained it, neither had I. But I think *Guernica* is an excellent example. The intensity of Picasso's emotions and grief drove the artistic act that we now know by its name and reputation, by the static art we see hanging on the wall. It's a powerful painting because you can really sense the passion that created it. We weren't there during its creation. But we can revisit it repeatedly by viewing the painting."

"Oh. I see. So, when we look at a painting, we can infer the act, but we can't really share the experience of its creation—unless we go to the artist's studio and watch him in the act," and he chuckled.

"Um, yeah, that's right. Well, I suppose we could create our own art and appreciate it first-hand." And she laughed quietly. "Heck, we could go watch my mother make one of her beautiful vases and talk to her about her feelings as she's creating the piece."

"Good idea! I'd like that. In fact, I'd like to meet her. And your father. And your brother, too."

"And I'd like them to meet you, too. What are you doing Fourth of July weekend?"

"Um, I was going to suggest we go away for the weekend—maybe stay a couple nights in a Vermont bed and breakfast. Why do you ask?"

"Oh, I like that idea. A lot. But let's postpone that because I have a better one. I want you to meet my parents. They always have a family party at their house on the Fourth of July. They have a great view of New Canaan's town fireworks from their patio. It's all very informal and relaxed. It would be a perfect setting for you to meet them. And you could meet Charley, too. And everyone else. Why don't you come with me? Be my date. Okay?"

"Well, if you think so, then, sure. But we've only known each other for two weeks."

"I wouldn't have asked otherwise," and she leaned into him and put her hand on his thigh. "Besides, that's not for another three weeks and that gives us a lot more time to get to know each other better. Heck, I might learn some deep dark secret about you and disinvite you."

"Not likely. What you see is what you get."

"And I like what I see." She leaned closer and kissed him.

15: A Mother's Skepticism

Thursday, June 19th

Maggie's mother answered the phone on the first ring.

"Hi, Mom. What're you up to?"

"Hi Maggie. I'm in the studio, getting ready for my class this afternoon. Haven't talked to you lately. You're at work?"

"Yeah. Just got some free time and thought I'd call."

"So, what's new?"

"Well, a lot, actually. I met the neatest guy."

"Oh? Do tell."

"Well, his name is Rick Hewson. He's originally from Wilton and he's amazing. So intelligent, and so knowledgeable on so many topics."

"What's he do?"

She filled her in on Rick's background, job, education, and their many common interests. "We've been spending a lot of time together. We went into the city on Saturday to the MoMA to see *Guernica* after we saw a story about it on McNeil/Lehrer Report a couple weeks ago."

"Oh, we saw that story, too. We saw the painting a number of years ago. But, uh, what about Pete? Didn't you just get back together with him?"

"Oh, Mom, I am so fed up with Pete. We had another fight, and I told him it's over. I don't want to ever see him again. And I told him not to call me to apologize like he always does."

"Okay," elongating the two syllables. "Let me guess. He called you."

"Of course—twice. He tried to give me his standard BS apology, but I cut him off and told him for the second and third time that it's over, not to call me again, and I hung up on him—both times."

"Hmm. I see. So, now what? Do you think you've heard the last of him? As I recall, you've gotten together with him again after these fights in the past. How many times?"

"Not this time, Mom."

"Maybe he doesn't believe you based on what's happened in the past."

"Well, he'd better. It's over. I mean it. I've had it. He's history. But, anyway Mom, I feel so right being with Rick. I've never felt like this before."

"You said the same thing about that other fellow a couple summers ago. Uh, Ron? Ron something? And look what happened then."

"Yeah. Thanks for reminding me. His name was Ron Marion and I'd rather not think about that lying bastard. No, Mom. Rick is a real gentleman. Completely honest and up-front. I feel like I can totally be myself when we're together. He's very smart and has lots of interests. He loves art. Rick really listens. He has a good heart. He's comfortable in his own skin and makes me feel that way, too. He's well-read, interested in a lot of different things, always excited about new ideas. He's just so positive. It just feels good to be with him. Oh, and he's very handsome."

"Okay, then. I like what I'm hearing. When do we get to meet him?"

"Well, actually, that's why I called. I hope you don't mind, but I invited him to our Fourth of July party. I do want you guys to meet him, and I want him to meet you and everyone else."

"If you feel comfortable enough to bring him over, then he's welcome. I think we all learned a lesson with Pete when you brought him over."

"Yes, Mother. I know. Believe me, I know. But Rick is totally different than Pete. You'll see. I don't want to prejudice the jury, but I think you'll really like him, and I think you would have even if I hadn't just said that."

"I trust you, dear. I just think that Pete somehow pulled the wool over your eyes."

"Yeah. Thanks for pointing that out, Mom. Believe me, I've learned a lot and I'm not going down that road again."

"Well, that's good to hear. Why don't you guys plan on coming over before cocktail hour."

"Okay. Oh, you guys are really going to like Rick. He's so wonderful."

"I'm sure we will, dear... Look, I've got to get back to work and get the studio ready for my class. My students will be here in less than twenty minutes."

"Okay Mom. I'll check in with you again a few days before the party to see what we can bring."

"Okay. Thanks. Bye, Maggie. I love you."

"I love you, too, Mom."

16: Thurman Munson

Tuesday, June 24th

The second quarter would end in less than a week. Pete and his team still had to close nearly a dozen open orders. Otherwise, they wouldn't be recorded, and they would miss their numbers, which would adversely impact everyone's commission checks.

He had come in early that morning to whittle away at the backlog and didn't get out of the office until after seven. One customer had asked for a revised quote. It had to be on his desk first thing the next day or he couldn't give Pete a purchase order in time for the close of the quarter. No purchase order, no commission. And it would be a substantial order, so Pete was totally focused on it.

The sales rep was on the road so Pete had to deal with it himself. To get the quote to the customer on time, he had to fax it before he left for the day. But, with no secretary around to do it, he had to figure out the fax machine by himself—a frustrating ordeal. It took him nearly twenty minutes and involved strapping the sheet of paper on a rotating drum. When he finally got the beep confirming it had gone through, he put on his navy sports coat and left.

To hell with going home and heating up some shitty TV dinner, he thought to himself. He'd go to Victoria Station and treat himself to dinner, "that and a beer or three. Maybe a couple of shots of Jack, too," he told himself out loud as he walked out the door.

Striding past his car, Pete walked the block-and-a-half to the restaurant. Once inside, he turned right toward the bar and took his usual stool on the corner at the far end, greeting the bartender.

"Hey, Stan my man. How ya' doin'?"

"Terrific, Pete. What'll it be? The usual?"

"Yup. And a menu, too? I'm starved." Stan nodded, handing him a menu.

When Stan returned with a frosty mug of Michelob, Pete ordered a bacon-cheese burger with all the fixings and a side order of steak fries. He then turned his attention to the TV over the bar, pleased to see the Yankee game had just gotten underway. Fans had packed Yankee Stadium to see them play the hated Boston Red Sox.

By the time he'd finished dinner and had asked for his third beer, the Yankees were in the middle of a third-inning rally. A guy a little older than Pete had taken a seat two stools away a few minutes earlier as the bottom of the inning got underway. The game riveted him, as well—clearly a Yankee fan, judging by his enthusiastic reactions. Pete struck up a conversation during the commercial break.

"Yankees are looking real good this year. That was a helluva little rally they just had there," Pete said.

"Absolutely! Put 'em back on top, six to five. That three-run homer by Rick Cerone was a thing of beauty. Almost gave me a hard-on."

Pete laughed heartily and slapped his thigh. "I'll say!" and continued laughing, choking momentarily, trying to catch his breath. The other guy beamed.

"You know, Cerone has really stepped up and filled some big shoes behind the plate," he said. "It was a real tragedy to lose Thurman Munson last year. Sad ending for our captain."

Pete nodded solemnly. "Yeah. No kidding. Thurm was the heart and soul of the Yankees. But, hey, Cerone is the man."

"Amen. I was listening to the game on my car radio on the way over here from work. The Sox were on top when I turned it on. Then, right after I sit down here—BOOM! Cerone parks one in the bleachers. Well, I sure hope they can hang onto that one-run lead."

"Of course they will. Have faith, my friend." Pete smiled, and reached out to offer his hand. "Pete. Pete Conley."

"Andy Greene. Pleased to meet you. You a regular here?"

"Yeah, I guess you could say that. Me and Stan are on a first-name basis," as he nodded toward Stan. "He knows all my secrets," and Stan smiled as he wiped down the counter several seats to Pete's left.

"My office is just down the street and I'd rather come here when I have to work late than go home to an empty house and a shitty frozen pizza. This is my back-up office, isn't it, Stan?" Stan nodded and grinned again.

"Yep. I know the drill. I work a mile or so up Post Road in Norwalk." They traded business cards. Andy was a manufacturer's rep. They chatted about business and baseball during commercial breaks and lulls in the game. After finishing his dinner, Pete ordered his fourth beer and asked Stan to bring him a shot of Jack Daniels as well. Andy perked up.

"Want one, too?"

Andy grinned and nodded. "Make that two, Stan."

"Thanks. That's very generous of you."

At a quarter to eleven, with the Yankees up seven-to-five after seven innings, Pete stood to leave. "Well, I should get going. It's a school night tonight. Gotta be back to the grind first thing tomorrow."

"Yeah. Me, too."

The two left the bar together. By then, Pete had had a total of six beers and three shots of whiskey. They left the bar together, shaking hands again in the parking lot and slurring good-nights. Pete slapped Andy on the back and turned away. Rediscovering the sidewalk, he followed it back to his car. Before getting in, he glanced around the area and then took a leak in the dark parking lot in front of his car. He chuckled to himself at the thought that, had this been broad daylight, everyone in his second-floor office would have been able to see him pissing there.

Sitting in his car, thinking about his futile efforts to connect with Maggie, Pete grabbed a nip bottle of Jim Beam bourbon out of the glove compartment and sucked it down in a couple of quick swallows, chucking the empty out the open window.

She wouldn't talk to him on the phone, even when he sent her flowers. Dammit, to hell with the phone. He decided to go over to her apartment. She'd have to talk to him.

17: Drunken Wake-up Call

The intercom's persistent buzzing awoke Maggie. She'd fallen asleep on the couch while reading *The New York Times*. Glancing at her watch as she crossed the room, Maggie wondered who it might be at five-after-eleven. With Rick out of town overnight on business, it couldn't be him. Had to be a mistake. Someone's buzzing the wrong apartment.

"Hello? Who's there?"

"Hi Maggie. It's me, Pete," he slurred, with a jovial lilt.

"Great. That's all I need," she said aloud before pushing the talk button again. She replied with an intentional note of irritation in her voice.

"What do you *want?* It's after eleven. It's a work night. You woke me up."

"Oh. Sorry. I just wanna apologize. You keep hanging up on me and won't let me finish. Can I just come upstairs for a couple minutes so we can talk?"

"Pete, as I said at the party, and as I told you twice when you called my office, our relationship is over. There is nothing left to talk about, and there is nothing to apologize for—except for waking me up. Go away and leave me alone," and released the talk button.

The buzzing resumed. She didn't answer. It was warm and her windows were open, so she could clearly hear him when he started yelling at her from the sidewalk three floors below, persisting and getting louder until a downstairs window opened and a man started shouting at Pete.

It was Paul Jenkins, Maggie's downstairs neighbor. A kind, elderly gentleman, she had befriended him and his bedridden wife, Lilly, and often ran errands for them.

"Get out of here, you drunk. You're waking up the whole neighborhood."

"*Fuck off, old man.* Maybe you want to come out here and make me."

"If you don't get lost by the count of three, I'm going to call the cops."

"Go fuck yourself."

"Okay. That's the way you want it." The window slammed shut.

Maggie turned off her lights before peering out the window. Pete stormed around the sidewalk for another minute, continuing to yell and swear at both her and Paul.

She spotted a patrol car rounding the corner. Pete did, too. He started walking away casually, as though out for a late-night stroll. The police car stopped at the building. An officer got out, and buzzed Paul's apartment.

The next afternoon when she came home from work, she bumped into Paul as he picked up his copy of *The Hour*, the local evening newspaper, from the front stoop.

"I'm really sorry about last night, Paul. It's all my fault. That was an old boyfriend who can't accept the fact that we've broken up. The next time he shows up—if there is a next time—I promise to call the police before he starts making such a racket."

"That's okay Maggie. It's not your fault. Obviously, the guy's a jerk."

18: Unheeded Advice

Thursday, June 26th

Thursday evening, Maggie was home alone again. Rick's boss had scheduled a business dinner for his team after work in Stamford. She hadn't talked to Amanda Olsen, her best friend from BC, for a few weeks and had the urge to chat.

After their graduation, Amanda had stayed in Boston, landing a plum job as an analyst with a mutual fund company there, and had advanced at the company in the years since.

After they caught up on Amanda's latest doings, Amanda asked, "Are you still dating that creep, Pete what's-his-name? Last time we talked, you'd just gotten back together with him for the umpteenth time—against my advice, I might add."

"No. I am not. I broke up with him three weeks ago. For the last time, by the way."

"Thank God you finally saw the light. Please, please, please get away from him! Burn that bridge. Do not—I repeat—*do not* go back to him again. *Please!*"

"You don't need to convince me, Amanda." And she filled her in on the events of May thirtieth—including all the messy details, Pete's subsequent calls to her office and his drunken visit two nights earlier. She also told her about meeting Rick and raved at length about him and their blossoming relationship.

"Amanda, am I doing this right? I'm feeling so conflicted."

"Doing what right? Conflicted about what? You dumped an abusive boyfriend—as I said you should have a long time ago. And now you're dating a guy who sounds to me like Mr. Right. On the one hand is a complete asshole. While on the other, you now have your dream-come-true. What's there to be conflicted about? Sounds like a no-brainer to me—unless, God forbid, this guy turns out to be another Ron Marion."

"*Amanda!* Ron Marion was a lying turd. You can't compare the two. They have nothing in common. Except Rick is handsome, and so was Ron. And they're both very smart and well-read. But that's where the similarity ends."

"Okay, okay. Sorry for bringing it up."

"But, anyhow, I don't know. I mean, am I getting ahead of myself here, moving too quickly into a new relationship after just getting out of one?"

"Honestly, I wouldn't say you just now got out of one. Based on all that you've told me over the past year about Pete—all the arguments, the time he hit you, the breaking up and the getting back together again—I think that for all intents and purposes that relationship was over a long time ago. At least, it should have been. You just ignored everyone's advice and didn't follow through until now. And now, you've met and apparently fallen for a great guy. So, the true nature of your lousy relationship with Pete has become even more apparent—in sharp contrast to Rick."

"But I can't help but think that I'm only seeing Rick as a port in a storm. Am I simply willing myself into this relationship with Rick? Will his flaws become apparent soon, too? How do I know I'm not jumping from the frying pan into the fire?"

"Maggie, based on all that you just told me about him, all the adoring details you just shared, his love of art and music, it sounds to me like you're in love. It also sounds like Rick is not just a port in the storm. I'd say he's what you've been looking for."

Maggie smiled and nodded to herself.

"At the same time, maybe you haven't been able to see how awful Pete truly was until you had someone so vastly superior to compare him to."

"Hmm, yeah. I guess so. Yeah. That makes sense."

"Maggie, I remember you telling me about Pete last fall, about how he'd hit you and that you'd broken up with him. At that time, you swore to me that you'd never see him again. But then you did. *Why?* I was worried about you, getting back together with a guy who had shown that he could and would physically hurt you. Why did you go back to him? And what's to stop you from going back to him yet again?"

"I don't know. I really don't know. Rick actually asked me the same question the night we met—and he doesn't even know that Pete had hit me. I told him that I'm a glutton for punishment. I probably shouldn't have been so flip about it with him." She thought for a few moments. "It's a fair question. I should have a better answer for Rick. I just don't know what that answer is."

"Okay, that's all past history and you don't have a good answer for that, but you also haven't answered my main question, which is, what's to stop you from getting back together with Pete yet again?"

"There is no way that is going to happen" She hesitated. "Look, Amanda, I haven't been completely honest with you. I didn't tell you, but he actually hit me a second time, when we got together briefly in January."

"Wait a sec. *What?* You got back together in January? You never told me that. What happened?"

"Yeah. I know. I guess I didn't tell you because I was too embarrassed to admit it. But, yeah, after two months of being apart, he talked me into dating again. He took me out to dinner at an expensive place and gave me a cultured pearl necklace over dessert. Said it was his way of apologizing—"

"—*Oh my God*, Maggie. That's standard operating procedure for men like him. I thought you knew that. They give their girlfriends expensive gifts to ease their feelings of guilt. I mean, that kind of behavior is right out of a psychology textbook."

"I know, I know." She sighed. "Well, anyway, it was literally on our second date the following weekend that he got drunk and picked a fight. When I got angry and argued back, he hit me again. It was like an instant replay of the incident in November. So, when we got back together yet again in April, he gave me another gift—a pair of diamond earrings. But I warned him that if he ever laid a hand on me again, I'd go straight to the police and file assault and battery charges."

Maggie sighed again. "But, yeah, I know, that still doesn't answer your question or explain why I went back to him for the umpteenth time. I just don't have any answers."

Amanda was silent for a few moments before she spoke, quietly. "I thought you guys were apart from November until April. Now I'm even more astounded that you went back to him in April. It's worse than I thought."

"Well, like I said, I guess I was just too embarrassed to admit it. Actually, no one besides Pete knows that we'd gotten back together again in January. It only lasted for two dates."

"So, my advice last spring was given not knowing he'd hit you a second time? Wow. Just wow. Maggie, you're smarter than that. You're too good for a beast like him."

"I know. I feel like an idiot."

"Well, based on what you're telling me, Rick should serve as a pretty good deterrent to help you resist the temptation permanently."

"Yeah, you're right. Rick is really very much different than Pete, in so many ways. I mean, he's like the complete opposite. He's *such* a wonderful man. Gentle, thoughtful and so handsome. And, he genuinely appreciates art Amanda, do you know that on our first date, he compared my face to Sargent's portrait of Mrs. Charles Inches? He said I had her eyes and eyebrows—that our faces have the same shape."

Amanda chuckled. "My, my. He's smart, handsome *and* he's quite the romancer. Did he seduce you with that line?" she asked, laughing.

"*Stop that. Be nice!* And Amanda, get this. He also adores Winslow Homer. Can you believe it? When he was at Dartmouth, he actually came to the MFA to see that special Sargent show as well as their collection of Homer's works. I mean, Amanda, my two favorite painters! How incredible is that?"

"Wow. A match made in heaven. Pretty amazing."

"You're right. In comparison, Pete's faults really do stand out as never before. I'd never thought of it that way. But, you know, I'm worried about rushing into a new relationship."

"Sometimes, rushing into a new relationship is okay because it was meant to be. You know, like I just said, a match made in heaven."

"Yeah," and Maggie smiled to herself again. "It does kind of have that feel to it. You know, the same thing happened to my parents. Their wedding was less than two months after they met."

"I know. Your mom told me that story a long time ago. But what you are implying? Are you thinking of marrying Rick? You only met him three weeks ago."

Maggie wondered to herself why she had brought that up if she wasn't thinking that way.

"Oh dear. Is that what that sounded like?" and she laughed. "I don't know. Interesting idea, though," and she grinned to herself.

"Hey. When do I get to meet Mr. Wonderful so I can help settle this for you, and make sure you're making the right decision? I have an idea. How about you guys come up to Boston for a weekend?"

"Not a bad idea. Rick is adventurous and, like I said, he's an MFA fan. We could check out the Homer and Sargent collections."

"You guys can stay at our place. You know, the new place I told you about? Jeff and I moved into this huge two-bedroom apartment on Comm Ave two months ago. It's embarrassing how much space we have. Do come up for a weekend. It'd be great. You and Rick, and me and Jeff. We could have a blast. We could go to the Eliot Lounge on Friday night and see Heidi and The Secret Admirers. We saw them last Sunday. They've become the house band every Friday and Sunday night. It's less than two blocks from our apartment. We could stay out late and stumble back to bed."

"I remember seeing that band at the Eliot. They were incredible. I didn't know they were still together. I'll talk to Rick about it. Sounds like a wonderful idea. We could see them Friday night and go to the MFA on Saturday."

"Think about it Listen, I gotta go. Speaking of Jeff, we're going out for dinner tonight. He should be home any minute and I'm not ready yet. Still wearing my work clothes. Anyway, I hope that I helped put things in perspective for you."

"Yeah. Yes, you did. Thanks."

19: Village Gate

Saturday, June 28th

Rick and Maggie drove into the city to the Village Gate Saturday night to see Johnny Hartman, one of Rick's favorite living jazz singers. Hartman was past his prime, but Rick hoped and assumed he retained the best qualities of his rich, expressive baritone.

After a successful career with many collaborative LPs and live performances with a range of jazz greats, Hartman was now playing mostly festivals and doing occasional guest appearances on TV variety shows, Rick explained to Maggie on the way into the city. Dates at name clubs like tonight's in Greenwich Village were rare.

This would be their second straight Saturday together in New York, but for an entirely different cultural experience.

Hartman's opening number was an upbeat tune unfamiliar to Rick. Maggie grinned widely, her foot tapping time. Rick took her hand across the tiny cocktail table, pleased to see her enjoying herself so much.

Four songs into his set, Hartman chose one of Rick's favorite standards, "Lush Life." Hartman had recorded the song with John Coltrane and McCoy Tyner for a 1963 LP that had long been Rick's favorite.

As the crowd applauded with the song's final notes, Maggie leaned into Rick's ear. "That was so beautiful. But so depressing."

"Billy Strayhorn wrote that for Duke Ellington. I think it was personal for Strayhorn, about mourning a break-up, as his life goes on without purpose, sitting alone in a dingy bar getting drunk."

"Will he sing any songs that are cheerier?"

Rick laughed. "Of course. And I'm hoping he sings another one of my favorites," as the pianist began playing the opening bars of the next song.

Hartman sang a few more numbers before Rick got his wish, recognizing it with the first half-dozen notes of the piano. "You Are Too Beautiful," written by Richard Rodgers in 1933. He was thrilled to hear that Hartman's phrasing was still perfect.

"That was lovely. The sentiment is so sweet," she said, as it ended.

"I think that song perfectly sums up how I feel about you."

Maggie smiled, leaned over and kissed his cheek. Hartman's set, including two encore numbers, wrapped up at nine-thirty because he was scheduled for a second show at ten.

They drove the long trip back to Maggie's apartment. Though the traffic was light, they didn't arrive home until eleven-thirty. Maggie had fallen asleep on the way with her head on his shoulder. He woke her with a kiss on the forehead when they parked in front of her apartment.

20: One-Woman Judge and Jury

Wednesday, July 2nd

Pete was depressed at the realization that he'd be spending the long July Fourth holiday weekend alone. Needless to say, there would be no date with Maggie. In his mind, that was still an unresolved issue.

Wednesday had been another tough workday, mostly due to a client who was irate because a shipment had gotten screwed up, which in turn had messed up their production schedule. Pete didn't leave the office until he'd gotten the situation straightened out—which included a fawning apology and a deep discount on the customer's next order. Since the problem originated in an erroneous order and not in Shipping, that discount would have to come out of his team's commissions.

It was well past seven when he walked down the street for dinner and a few beers at Victoria Station.

"Stan, my man. How ya' doin'?" he said, as he walked into the bar.

"Hi Pete. Doing great. What'll you have? The usual?"

"Yup. And I'm hungry. Tough day at the office today. I need a beer or three and some serious protein. I've had French dip on my mind all afternoon. You got it on the menu tonight?"

"Yes, sir. As usual."

"Great. And can I substitute onion rings for the fries?" Stan nodded as he handed him a mug of Michelob.

Pete was just taking his first sip when a familiar voice called out from behind him. "Hey Pete. What's up?"

"Hey Andy," he said as they shook hands. "Good to see you again. How you doin'? Another lonely night like me?"

"Yeah, I suppose Well, shit, the truth is, my wife threw me out."

"Oh no. What happened?"

"I thought we were having a trial separation. But the trial is over, and I got convicted by the one-woman judge and jury."

"Ouch. Sorry to hear that. Let me buy you a drink. What'll it be?"

"That's generous of you, Pete, but I'll empty your bank account tonight. I feel like drinking myself into oblivion."

"How long you been married?"

As he ordered a bottle of Rolling Rock for himself, Andy began his tale of woe, of working late nights and coming home drunk to an angry wife. He had chugged the beer and ordered a second one before he'd finished his story. Then he asked Pete why he was there alone again.

"Well, I got my own girl problems."

"Got a bum marriage, too?"

"Nah. Haven't gotten that far yet with her. Been dating this girl on and off for the past year. She's real easy on the eyes, if you know what I mean. Got a beautiful body. She's from New Canaan, and her family is loaded."

"If you don't mind me asking, what's the problem?"

"She's a perfectionist. Whenever I step out of line, she's on my case. We had an argument a month ago and she broke up with me. But we've broken up like that before and I've always been able to patch things up with her after a few apologies. She usually makes me grovel, eventually accepts my apology, and then we get back together. I usually give her a make-up gift—something expensive like a necklace. I also send her flowers—which is what I did again this time, a couple weeks ago."

"Oh boy, I know that routine."

"The flowers usually do the trick. But not this time. I went over to her apartment last week, but she wouldn't even open the door for me. Something's up. All I can figure is that she must have a new boyfriend."

"What do you know about him?"

"Nothin'. The night of our argument, we were at this big party. After the fight, she went outside and wound up talking to this guy most of the night. And then I saw her leave with him in his car. I don't know his name. Don't know anything about him. But she's totally different now than she was in the past when I've tried to make up with her. She won't listen to me. Keeps hangin' up mid-sentence."

"Uh oh. Sounds like she's turned the corner on you, man, especially if she's got a new boyfriend. Not good."

"If there's another guy in the picture, how do I get rid of him? Threaten him?"

"Ooh. I don't think that's a good idea, Pete. Not if you're hoping to get your girlfriend back. She'd take that the wrong way, for sure. You just gotta be patient. If she loves you, she'll see the light, get tired of him and come back to you. If she doesn't, then it wasn't meant to be."

"Hmm. Well, maybe. But I'm not giving up that easily."

"Listen, Pete. There're always other fish in the sea. Got any prospects?"

"Uh, yeah. Good point." And then a grin slowly creased his face as he stroked his chin. "Yeah. There's this hot new secretary in my office. Started last week. She seems really nice. Stacey something. And she's stacked. Plus, there's no wedding ring. And, she's a real flirt. Shows a lot of cleavage. Flaunts her tits at me all the time. Perfect ass, too."

"Well, there you go. That sounds like the ticket."

"Think I will."

Later, as Pete drove home, the thought of Maggie still nagged at him. Yeah, he'd make a play for Stacey. But, at the same time, he would get to the bottom of whether Maggie had a new boyfriend. Since he had no plans that weekend, he decided to hang around outside her apartment to learn whether that guy came and went with her.

21: Two Newbies

Friday, July 4th

Over the past five weeks, Maggie had spent a lot of time with Rick. In addition to seeing *Guernica* and Johnny Hartman, they'd been to a couple of foreign films at the SoNo Cinema and gone out for dinner twice.

Maggie's fondness for Rick had grown so quickly that it surprised her. And clearly the feelings were mutual. It felt so good being together, Maggie thought, so easy to talk on such a range of subjects, so nice to just sit quietly and cuddle, too, and not talk at all.

She especially enjoyed making love with him. Rick had spent every Friday and Saturday night at her apartment, as well as a few weeknights. They'd made love two, sometimes three times in a night. Often, the next morning, they'd make love again before getting ready for work. They couldn't get enough of each other. She grinned to herself thinking about their love-making as she sat in his car on the way to her parents' house.

He'd stayed over Thursday night ahead of the Independence Day party. They left at four for the short drive to New Canaan.

Rick interrupted her blissful thoughts. "Maggie, I know you said your parents are going to like me and all that. What about your brother? And are there going to be other people there, too? Anything about what not to do or not to talk about?"

She laughed. "Relax. Be yourself. I probably don't need to tell you but it's best to avoid politics. My parents don't see eye-to-eye. Dad's all gung-ho for Reagan, but Mom's for Carter. They started disagreeing about politics back in the Nixon years, with the Watergate mess and all that. Just to keep the peace, they stopped discussing politics."

"So, who else will be there?"

"My Uncle Henry and Aunt Maureen, plus my cousin Hank. He's coming solo because he and his girlfriend broke up last month. Mom said Olivia, my other cousin, isn't coming because she's out on Shelter Island with friends for the long weekend. My brother Charley is bringing his new girlfriend. They've been dating for two or three months now, but none of us has met her yet. She's an interpreter at the UN and travels a lot for her work. So, you and she will be the newbies."

"Anyone else? Any non-family?"

"Yeah, our neighbors will be there, too. Stan and Helen Jackson. You'll love Helen. She's a real trip. She's always quick to tell you what's on her mind. I'm sure she'll say something to embarrass me in front of you."

Rick slowed as Route 123 approached New Canaan town center.

"Take a left onto East Avenue at Mill Pond, at the light," she said. "Okay. Go right at the next signal, onto Main Street." As their progress was slowed by cars backing out of diagonal parking spaces, she pointed out the sites.

"That's Gristede's on the right where Mom buys her groceries. It's a small, old-style grocery store." Maggie went on to explain how her mother phoned in orders for delivery right to the house, "through the back door, which they leave unlocked so that their delivery guy can even put the food away. And they send her a monthly invoice. Kinda friendly and old-fashioned."

As they wound through town, Maggie pointed out the town common, known as God's Acre, a sloped triangular parcel of neatly trimmed lawn, flower beds, shrubbery and trees, tended by the New Canaan Garden Club, said a decorative little sign at the corner.

Above the common sat the whitewashed Congregational Church with its modest steeple. Her family used to attend the church there when she was younger, she said. "We still go on the major holidays, like Christmas and Easter."

They continued through town and headed north. There were more churches. The spacious, manicured yards and houses grew the further they drove away from town center.

"There's the Roger Sherman Inn on the right. It's a nice place for dinner. We used to go there fairly regularly when I was growing up. Slow down. You're going to want to turn right at that red mailbox up ahead."

22: Louise and Tom

Rick found New Canaan homey and appealing, with its quaint little shops in single-story red brick buildings downtown, and classic New England churches. He'd grown up a few miles to the east, but this was an unfamiliar place. His time in the town had been limited to track meets at New Canaan High School and cross-country meets at the adjacent Waveny Park—both of which were at the southern end of town near the Merritt Parkway. If he'd ever been in the middle of town, he didn't remember.

The waist-high stone walls that lined both sides of Oenoke Ridge north of town center gave way occasionally for entrances to long driveways leading to landscaped yards and large, elegant homes.

They were pulling in at the red mailbox, and onto a crushed gravel driveway, shaded by the tall maple and elm trees that lined it. Looking ahead, Rick saw an enormous white colonial house about fifty yards down the drive to the right, facing left, toward an open grassy field. He spotted a swimming pool between the house and Oenoke Ridge, shielded from the road by dense rhododendrons.

The landscaping was immaculate. The shrubbery and lawn were neatly trimmed and free of debris. Clearly, it was professionally maintained, he thought. Looking further down the driveway beyond the house, Rick saw a bright white carriage house, with a cupola and a brass rooster weathervane.

The house rose gracefully above the lot's flatness, with four broad, tapered granite steps leading to a large screened, covered porch. Like the carriage house, the house itself was highlighted by black enamel trim.

The front door was opening.

"Come meet my parents," and Maggie took his hand to lead him toward the house. Louise Haines stood in the open doorway. She looked like she could pass for Maggie's older sister, Rick thought. Her hair was cut shorter than Maggie's, just above her shoulders. She had the same trim figure, about five-foot-six, and most of the same facial characteristics that had so entranced Rick when he first laid eyes on Maggie five weeks earlier.

"You must be Rick," and she extended her right hand.

Rick smiled and shook her hand. "And you must be Mrs. Haines."

"Please, call me Louise. Maggie has told me so much about you. Come in." Louise led them into the entry hall.

Rick was struck by her voice, which had a timbre similar to Maggie's—that hint of a smoky rasp.

A broad staircase swept up in a curve to a large open landing on the second level, with a crystal chandelier hanging in the middle of the two-story open room, sun-lit through second-floor windows, splashing dozens of tiny shimmering rainbows on the foyer's ivory-colored walls.

"It's a bit early for cocktail hour, you guys, but would you like something to drink? Whatever you like—alcoholic, non-alcoholic."

"No, thank you."

"Maggie?"

"No thanks, Mom."

The three stood and talked for several minutes before Maggie turned toward the back of the house. "Rick. I want you to meet Dad. Is he out on the patio, Mom?"

"Yes. He's dusting the patio furniture. Helen just called. She and Stan are on their way over. They want to see our new Frank Stella lithograph. I'll just wait for them here. You guys go ahead."

As they walked through the house, Rick whispered, "Your parents have a *Stella*?"

"Yeah. I'll show you later."

As they walked through the house, Rick took in its immensity, rooms and hallways going this way and that. Helen and Stan Jackson were long-time neighbors, Maggie explained. They had moved into the neighborhood about the same time as the Haines, in the early 1950s.

"I should warn you. Dad's a real talker. And he's gonna give you the third degree, I guarantee it," as they stepped outside. "Hi Dad," and she gave her father a hug. His eyes were on Rick.

"Call me Tom," as Maggie's father gave him a firm handshake and a broad smile.

Tom Haines stood a little over six feet tall, handsome, trim, with a full head of salt-and-pepper hair. Rick guessed he was about fifty, fifty-two tops.

"So, even though Maggie told me not to grill you—her words—tell me a little about yourself. I understand you work for Hamilton."

"*Dad!*"

Rick smiled at Maggie and turned back to her father. "Yes, I'm in Hamilton's leadership training program."

"Maggie mentioned that. Great company. I know Brent Bigelow, your CEO. Known him for years. He's a good guy. We play golf occasionally. You know he lives in New Canaan?" Rick shook his head. "Actually, not far from here, over on Ponus Ridge, just down the street from Philip Johnson's Glass House. In fact, Philip designed his house for him about twenty years ago. You probably know that Brent's a Dartmouth alum like you. And Brent Junior is there now. I think he'll be a senior in the fall."

Rick was astonished at how much Maggie's parents already seemed to know about him: where he worked, what he did at Hamilton, and his alma mater. Clearly, they'd learned it all from her. He wondered what else she had told them.

He nodded and laughed. "Yes. In fact, a lot of our top executives are Dartmouth. I keep bumping into my fellow grads at all levels of the company. It feels like a daily reunion in the lunch room. There're a couple of guys in the leader program with me who were in the class ahead of mine."

"We have something like your leadership program at World Paper—I assume Maggie told you that I work there."

"Yes, she did. Terrific company, though a competitor. Uh, yeah, they're exposing me to all eight of the main operations—three months in each. After which, they and I decide which department I will settle into. I started in Sales, which I finished at the end of May. And I'm now in Purchasing until the end of August."

"Purchasing? Brad Freeman is another golfing buddy of mine."

"Small world. Brad's been very kind to me. Anyway, I still have six more departments to go, with Marketing next, starting in September."

Tom did a quick mental calculation. "So, let's see. By my estimation, sometime in early 1982, you'll be settling into one of those areas. That about right?"

"Exactly. If I cut the mustard, that is, and they decide to keep me."

"My dad owned the company when I was starting out and he made sure that my brother and I got a taste of every operation. You're going to find that knowing something about the different aspects of the paper business is invaluable. So, when you become the CEO and ask someone to do something, you'll know what's doable and what's unrealistic," winking as he said it.

"Dad, can we talk about something else, please? Besides, as much as I think Rick is going places, I don't think we should be promoting him to Hamilton CEO just yet." They all laughed. "Rick is really into a lot of other things, too. Like skiing, jazz, art, baseball—"

"—Yankees?"

"Of course. Is there any other team to root for?"

Tom hooted. "That's my boy. Go Yankees."

"Twenty-three World Series championships and counting. Next up: 1980. Good squad this year, too. Reggie's healthy. And then there's Randolph, Nettles, Cerone and Guidry. Plus Goose in the bullpen."

Maggie wagged her finger and clucked. "*Tsk, tsk.* The Red Sox are looking pretty good this year." Rick raised his eyebrows. "Yaz, Fisk, Rice and Lynn. They're all back and they're hitting."

"We have a traitor in our midst," Tom said, grinning at Maggie. "Well, she did spend four years in Boston. I think they brainwashed her."

Maggie punched her father lightly in the shoulder. "They went to the World Series my junior year, in 1975—"

"—where they lost to the Reds in seven games," her father quickly added. She frowned at him.

"Well, seeing as how the Yankees swept a three-game series from the Red Sox this week and are solidly in first, up seven-and-a-half games over the Tigers, I'm not too worried," Rick added.

She punched him, too. "You guys are so mean."

"The truth hurts," Rick said, and laughed. She snarled.

"Let me buy you a beer," Tom said. "Or would you prefer a glass of wine? White? Red?"

"No, thank you." Tom left to go into the house.

Maggie turned to Rick. "You'll have to excuse Dad. He can get pretty hyper. But I think he likes you."

He tilted his head and looked at her with a fake frown. "Red Sox? Really?"

They heard voices and laughter from the kitchen. Rick looked over to see Louise walking out with two others who Maggie quietly identified as Helen and Stan Jackson, the neighbors that her she and her mother had mentioned.

"Where's this Rick I've heard so much about?" Helen said loudly, looking at him across the patio. "That must be you," as she strode briskly to Rick. He smiled and extended his right hand. She softly batted it away. "Never mind the hand shake. Give me a hug." And she wrapped her arms around his shoulders. Rick limply put his hands on hers.

Releasing him, she stepped back to take his measure. "My my. You're every bit as handsome as Louise said." Rick blushed. "I hope you know that you've cleared a mighty big hurdle, young man. Any boy that Maggie feels is good enough to bring home to is all right by me."

"*Helen.* Is that really necessary?"

In the midst of the back-and-forth, a young man and woman came around the side of the house and onto the patio. When Rick noted the young man's resemblance to Tom, he assumed it was Charley and his girlfriend.

Approaching the group with his arm around his date's waist, Charley said, "Everyone, this is Beth Meeks. Beth, this is my mother, Louise, our long-time neighbors and surrogate parents, Stan and Helen Jackson and my sister, Maggie. And, I assume you're Rick, the man of the month, it would seem—or maybe man of the year."

Charley smiled and shook Rick's hand firmly. "It's good to meet you finally. We've talked about little else in this family the past few weeks."

"Good God almighty, my family is such a bunch of blabbermouths," Maggie exclaimed. Everyone but her laughed. Rick grinned at Charley and then looked sideways at Maggie who once again took his hand in hers.

Tom returned to the patio with wine glasses and a couple bottles of wine. "What'd I miss? Hi Charley. Say, who's this pretty young lady?" looking at Beth as he put the tray down. Charley made the introduction.

"Beth, please take center stage away from Rick," Maggie pleaded, after shaking her hand. Everyone laughed again. Beth smiled nervously.

Maggie whispered to Rick, "Let me show you the house," and led him inside.

23: That Stella

Maggie's parents had both smiled a lot as they talked with Rick. Her father was his usual chatterbox self. But it was getting a little intense and though she felt he was getting on well with them, she thought that Rick needed a break, so she pulled him away for a quick house tour.

They returned to the entry hall. "Let me show you that Stella in the front room," she said, leading him through the tall double doors on the left. Hanging over the fireplace mantle was a large horizontal Frank Stella lithograph, a vibrant mix of sharp-edged polygons overlaying one another.

"Mom and Dad are friends with Philip Johnson. You know, the architect Dad mentioned?" Rick nodded as he studied the lithograph. "They met him a few years ago at his Glass House for a charity gala he held there to raise money for the Committee to Save Grand Central Station. Several celebrity types also attended, like Jackie Kennedy Onassis, Gore Vidal, and Tom Wolfe. They've been back a couple times since then to other parties. I went to one party with them.

Mr. Johnson owns several Stella lithographs and hangs them along with a lot of other amazing paintings in the underground gallery at his compound. A few months ago, Dad jokingly told Mr. Johnson he has too many Stellas and that it wasn't fair." She laughed.

"Mr. Johnson wouldn't dispute the point, so when Dad asked if he could buy one, he sold him this one. I don't know how much he paid for it, but I'm sure it was a lot. Dad had an alarm installed on it, which is set to go off if anyone tried to take it off the wall."

They stood a few moments, studying it. "I like it—a lot," Rick said. "I remember seeing a couple of Stella's pieces at the MoMA when we were there. I also remember that we both admired them. But you didn't mention that your family owned one."

She shrugged. "Come on. Let me show you the library."

Across the entry hall, another double-door led into the wood-paneled library. "These are mostly Dad's books," she said, gesturing toward the shelves that lined most of two walls.

Rick scanned the spines. "Nice collection." He surveyed the room: the long leather couch and two leather wing chairs facing a Sony Trinitron TV. It was the largest television he'd ever seen outside an electronics store. There were a couple shelves of family photos, where he spotted a wedding shot of Maggie's parents.

"Wow. Your mother was beautiful—correction. Your mother *is* beautiful. It's remarkable how much you look like her in this photo. The only difference is your hair styles."

She stood next to him with her cheek pressed against his shoulder, her arm on his waist and thumb hooked in his belt loop, looking at the photo with him. She reached out and picked up another one off the shelf. "This is my Grandma Margaret, Mom's mother, here with Mom before the wedding."

"Your mom looks like her mother, too."

"Uh huh."

They studied both photos a few moments in silence before they replaced them. Then she picked up a photo of her father with his parents at the wedding reception and smiled. "I have to tell you a very funny story about Dad. It was before he met Mom. Shortly after graduation from Yale, he went into the city, intending to visit Haines' new offices as he got ready to go to work there. But he thought he'd stop by the Yale Club first to check it out. So, when he arrived at Grand Central Station from New Haven, he jumped into a cab on Forty-Second Street and told the cabbie to take him to the Yale Club. Do you know where that club is?"

Rick shrugged.

"On Vanderbilt Avenue, between Forty-Fourth and Forty-Fifth streets, across the street and about a block from Grand Central's west entrance." She started laughing and continued laughing as she finished the story. "So the cabbie gave Dad a ride around Midtown before dropping him at the club, just to run up the meter. Dad had no idea he'd been had until he came out of the club later and saw Grand Central across the street."

Rick laughed, too.

"So, you only know that story because he admitted to it?"

"Oh yeah. I've heard him tell the story on himself several times."

"Hmm. Seems to me your father has a pretty good sense of humor if he can poke fun at himself like that."

"Yeah. You're right. Dad can be pretty funny. I'd never thought of it

71

that way."

They turned from the shelf of photos. In the corner near the window facing the front yard was a baby grand piano. As he looked at it, Rick said, "You told me you'd minored in music at BC and that you studied classical piano. But I've never heard you play anything. Would you play something for me now?"

"Oh, I'm a little rusty."

"Ah, please? Just one. When was the last time you played?"

"The weekend before we met."

She walked to the piano to see what was on the music stand. "This is still open to the last thing I played. My Aunt Alice was here that weekend and she asked me to play this."

"What is it? Play that."

"It's Chopin's Twelfth Nocturne. I played a selection of his Nocturnes for my final recital at BC. This is my favorite. It's also Alice's favorite." Maggie sat, lifted the keyboard cover, looked over the sheet music and settled her fingers on the keys before starting. Rick stood behind her as she played the quiet, lilting melody, rocking her torso in time with the music. When she finished the piece, Rick was silent for a long moment, until she turned to him.

"I'm... Uh. I don't know what to say," he stammered. "That was exquisite." He squeezed her shoulder gently.

She closed the keyboard cover. "That's enough for now," she said quietly, before standing. He hugged her.

"I've never heard that before. But, wow! What an amazing piece. And so beautifully performed."

"Thanks. I've always felt that the Twelfth is the sweetest of Chopin's Nocturnes, as well as the most emotional. It's also very peaceful. To me, it sounds like a quiet stream flowing over rocks."

"Yes. I can hear that" His voice broke. He cleared his throat and spoke quietly. "You know, listening to you play that reminds me of what you were telling me a couple weeks ago about the artistic act—the passion of the artistic act. I think the same applies to live music versus recorded music. I really see the difference here. Being here when you play a mesmerizing piece of music like that—it's a totally different experience than listening to a recording. The fact that you are playing it *for me* adds a very special meaning. I don't mean to sound corny, but it really touched me." He squeezed her shoulder again. She smiled.

"I'm glad you liked it."

"I'd like to hear you play the other Nocturnes."

"Sure, but some other time. Come on. I wanna show you the rest of the house," leading him through the rear library door, through the mudroom, and up the rear stairwell.

Her bedroom and adjoining bathroom still had a few trappings of her teen years: assorted posters of rock stars like David Bowie, Rod Stewart and Billy Joel; a nearly-empty bottle of L'Air du Temps perfume; assorted dusty souvenirs from family travels; and a framed photo of her younger self with a half-dozen college dormmates. She pointed to a grinning young woman.

"That's Amanda Olsen mugging there on the left. She's my best friend. I've mentioned her to you before. She still lives in Boston. I told her all about you when I talked to her last week. She wants us to come visit some weekend soon. We really should. It'll be a blast. We could go to the MFA. Or maybe Fenway if the Sox are in town." She grinned and winked.

"Yeah. Good idea. Let's do that—if the Yankees are playing," and he smiled back at her. She smirked back.

She led him down the hall, showing him Charley's room, the guest bedroom and the master suite.

"Let's go see the carriage house now," and led him back down the rear stairwell.

Inside were three cars that Rick carefully checked out: a new red Mercedes-Benz 230 sedan, a bright blue BMW 633CSi and a dark green GMC Suburban.

"That's Mom's new Mercedes that Dad gave her for her birthday earlier this year. Dad drives the BMW, and we use the Suburban for family trips, like for ski weekends to our place at Stratton." As he eyed the cars, she continued up the stairs in the rear. "C'mon. Mom's studio is up here."

She opened the door to the airy, sun-lit room. "After Charley and I went off to prep school, Mom resumed her ceramics work that she'd given up after college, and she had this studio built here where it used to just be a cob-webbed storage space. She's quite talented and sells a lot of her stuff now in arts-and-crafts shops in in the area. Plus, she teaches ceramics classes to groups of three or four people at a time—right here. I think she's making a pretty good little living at it."

Rick took in the roomy space and all it held: potter's wheels, an electric kiln, work tables, storage bins, a utility sink, supply cabinet, glaze buckets, a small bathroom, and a bank of tall windows on the north wall, affording lots of natural light, plus several shelves full of both finished items and covered works in progress.

"These are beautiful. Your mother does lovely work," Rick said, as he carefully handled an earth-toned, textured vase.

"I think we should get back to the party. They'll be wondering what happened to us," Maggie said. The tour had taken more than a half-hour. "I hope Beth has distracted them enough so that you can just relax and have a good time."

They walked around the back of the house to the patio. Henry, Maureen and Hank had arrived in their absence. Maggie introduced them to Rick. They also spent time talking with Beth who, they learned, had a PhD in international relations from Columbia, was fluent in five languages and worked as a translator for the American mission to the United Nations.

Dinner was served outside at seven. Nine were seated at the large table. At the conclusion of the town's fireworks, Maggie nudged Rick and suggested they leave. She stepped aside to speak to her mother as Rick said good-bye to Tom.

"Mom, we're leaving now," pausing before she whispered, "so, what do you think?"

"Well, I saw a lot of touching, hand-holding and kissing. I think the only time you two weren't was when you were eating, and even then, you snuck in a couple of kisses," she said, smiling. "That's sweet. Rick is a fine young man. So smart, yet modest at the same time. And so handsome, too. You've found yourself a real winner," and she hugged Maggie.

"I think so too. He's really a great guy. But I'm kinda worried. This is going so fast."

"Oh, that's fine, dear. Just remember, your father and I—"

"—Yes, yes. I know. You guys had known each other for less than a month when you decided to get married. And that's less time than I've known Rick. Anyway, we're leaving now."

Louise crossed the patio to speak to Rick as Maggie moved over to say goodnight to her father. They then walked to Rick's car and left.

24: Interrupted Kiss

Rick hadn't gotten his car down the driveway before Maggie started apologizing. "I'm sorry they were so nosy and chatty."

"It's okay, Maggie. You don't have to apologize. I really like your parents. They're lovely people, and so friendly. And everyone else, too. You have a wonderful family. I felt so welcomed and at ease. And your mother there as we were leaving. Wow."

"Why? What'd she do?"

"Well, when I went to say goodnight to her, she gave me a big hug. And, she kissed me on the cheek. Then, she held me by the shoulders, looked directly into my eyes and told me what a pleasure it was to meet me, that I'm really a good guy, and that they look forward to seeing more of me."

"She said all that? Wow, indeed." And Maggie chuckled softly. "How sweet. I'd say you measured up just fine."

"Well, it's great to feel so embraced—literally and figuratively."

When they pulled up to the curb in front of Maggie's apartment, they both got out and locked the doors. As Rick came around the car, Maggie took a couple of quick steps to him and hugged him. "Listen, you were great with my family. Like I told you, nothing to worry about," she added with a smile and, then, an extended kiss.

Their kiss was interrupted by the noise of a car's roaring engine and squealing tires, quickly pulling out of a parking spot across the street and then zooming past. Maggie stared as it roared off down the block.

"Friend of yours?" he asked with a little chuckle.

"Nah. Just some neighborhood jerk," as she continued to glare at the disappearing car.

"Are you okay? You look a little rattled."

"Yeah. Uh, yeah, I'm fine. Let's go upstairs."

Once back in the apartment, Rick poured two glasses of wine. Settling onto the couch, Maggie put her back against the couch's arm, bent her knees, and tucked her bare toes under his thigh.

"Rick, would you mind if we talked a little more about your parents?"

He shook his head. "No."

"As you were meeting my parents, I kept thinking about how I will never be able to meet yours. I'd like to know more about them."

He coughed and started to speak, slowly, quietly. "Well, um—not sure where to start. I guess you could say that we were kind of a typical hard-working middle-class American family. Dad put in long hours to make his business successful. Mom stayed home and took care of us. When we got older, Mom started her interior decorating business. She had a knack for design and a head for business. She later brought in a partner and they rented office space in Wilton center. At the time of the trip, the business was finally making money. Mom and Dad had never had a vacation by themselves since before I was born, so that trip to Aruba was supposed to be the honeymoon they never had. They'd been planning it for a long time and had been looking forward to it."

"That's so sad."

He sighed. "Yeah. It really was." He looked down, paused, knitted his fingers. He'd always found it difficult to talk about his parents.

"Rick, we don't have to talk about this if you'd rather not."

"No. That's okay." He paused and took a deep breath. "Anyway, Mom finally felt comfortable enough to take a long vacation."

"Do you have a photo of them?"

He stood, crossed the room, pulled a photo from his wallet, came back to the couch and handed it to her.

She studied it for a moment. "How old were they?"

"Uh, forty-five. Both were forty-five."

"They were such a handsome couple. But so young, with so much of their lives still ahead of them." She hesitated to clear her throat. "The tragedy is even more heartbreaking when I see their faces here and their warm smiles." Both stayed silent for a minute before she quietly resumed. "Where did they grow up? How did they meet?"

"Dad—Scott—was an only child, raised on a family dairy farm in upstate New York, outside a little town called Norwich. He had a childhood of farm chores. He worked his way through SUNY Oneonta—the first in his family to go to college."

He paused and looked again at the photo. "Mom—her name was Melissa—grew up in a working-class family in Binghamton. Her father belonged to a union. Worked at a local shoe manufacturer. Her mother stayed home and made money on the side as a seamstress in her spare time. Mom also attended SUNY Oneonta, which was where they met. She studied graphic design. They graduated in 1954 and got married the weekend after their graduation ceremony. It was probably because Mom was pregnant with me. I was born in December. Dad took a job in Stamford with an insurance agency, and then went out on his own a few years later. Since both worked their way through college, they always made a big deal about struggling financially, saying it had been an important character-building experience for them and would be for us, too. So, we studied hard, got good grades, worked after school, and got various scholarships—just as they expected us to do."

"Um—" Maggie paused. "Uh, when did you last speak with them?"

It was a long moment before he answered, hesitant and stuttering at first, then speaking slowly and deliberately. "I, uh, I called them to say good-bye the evening before they left for the Caribbean. My father was still at the office, so I only talked to Mom. I don't remember the last time I talked to him. Maybe a couple weeks before that. We never really talked a lot." His gaze had settled across the room.

She reached out and put her hand in his. He shifted his eyes to hers. "What did you talk to your mother about?"

"Oh, nothing important," he said quietly, tears in his eyes. "I told her I hoped they had a good time. Something like that." He looked down. "The shortness of that conversation still bothers me. I wish I'd told Mom that I loved her. But I was being a jerk. The main reason I'd called was to get them to send me some money to cover graduation fees, but she was balking at sending me any, so I got kind of pissy and ended the call abruptly. I wish I could do it all over again." He dabbed quickly at his eyes with his fingertip as he looked away.

She leaned forward and put her arm around his shoulders and pulled him to her and clasped him. She felt his tears falling on her neck. They were quiet for a several minutes.

He pulled away, wiped at his eyes again. "I'm sorry."

"Rick, it's okay. I understand," she whispered. She hugged him again and then waited another minute. "Tell me about Sarah."

Another pause. "She's a biology major at UConn and just finished her junior year. She's living with friends in New London this summer, while working at the Mystic Aquarium." His voice firmed. "She's lots of fun to be with. I adore her. You would, too. I love both my sisters—very much."

"I look forward to meeting them both. You said Julie lives in Boulder? That she went to the University of Colorado?"

"That's right. She graduated two years ago. She's there because she and my parents had a falling out when she was in high school. They argued a lot… mostly about her choice of boyfriends. Believe me, she dated a real loser for a while there. Fortunately, that relationship was over by the time she left for college. But she still wanted to get as far away as possible. Julie hadn't spoken to them for a month or two before their deaths."

"That's awful."

"Yeah. She still feels badly about it. We talk about that sometimes."

"Is she going to stay in Colorado?"

"I don't think she has plans to move back here. But I wish she would. I miss her. We're on the phone a lot. She's really eager to meet you."

Maggie smiled. "And I want to meet her, too."

"I'd do anything for Julie. And Sarah."

"As I'm sure they would for you, too."

"Maggie, now that I've met your family, do you feel more comfortable telling me more about them?"

"Okay." She paused a long minute before beginning. "Look, Rick, I'm sure you were impressed by my parents' house and their material wealth. The house, the art, the cars. Yet, despite the wealth, despite the comfort and security of all that, I think Mom and Dad did a great job of always keeping things in perspective for Charley and me—unlike a lot of the kids we grew up with. We were expected to, quote unquote, give back. It was a family thing with us—as it had been with my father's family. Which is part of the reason I live down here now. I got familiar with the neighborhood when I worked at the Norwalk Men's Shelter. It's kind of our family charity."

"Really?"

"Uh huh. Dad and Mom gave seed money when the shelter was getting started in the mid-sixties because the homeless problem was so bad here back then. But they felt that just giving money was not enough. So, they got personally involved. Dad is one of the original members of the shelter's board of trustees—he still is. When we were old enough, they brought Charley and me along too, to help out in various ways. I give money now, too. And so does Charley. We support the shelter because of its mission, helping people find jobs and get their lives back on track. We're starting to see a lot more Vietnam veterans nowadays. The shelter has been in operation for nearly fifteen years and the number of former residents with full-time jobs is now close to a hundred. I know that Mom and Dad have had a hand in most of those, giving advice and helping them find jobs. Those guys are all hard-working, tax-paying men now, not dependent on government or charity. Some are married with families. Mom and Dad even went to a few of those weddings. One of them even named his baby son after Dad—Thomas Haines Stanislawski. Cute little boy."

"But he didn't say anything about that when I talked to him today."

"Dad never talks about it, not even to his best friends. It's his thing, and he keeps it within the family. I'm only telling you because this is part of my life and who I am. I don't share it with many people. It's important to me. I'm sharing it with you because, well, you're important to me." She wrapped her arms around him and pulled him close. They snuggled silently.

Maggie's comment struck Rick deeply. No woman had ever said something like that to him. But, at the same time, he was plagued by self-doubt. Who was he to be getting involved with a woman like Maggie who had always had so much more than he? She was the third wealthy woman he had dated. Would it turn out as the other two had?

His life had always been a struggle. From his preteen years, he'd constantly held down jobs, whatever it took to make some money: mowing lawns, delivering newspapers. Anything he could think of. And then, through high school and college, he maintained a variety of menial jobs just to subsist and pay his way through college: bagging groceries, delivering pizzas. Whatever.

Maggie was practically the opposite. With her family's wealth, she had never *had* to work—not if she didn't want to. In fact, she could afford to work for nothing at a charity. What kind of relationship would this become between two people of such utterly different backgrounds?

Maggie pulled away and looked at him. "What are you thinking about?" she asked. "You look like you're like you're worried about something."

"What? Oh. I guess I'm just thinking about how lucky I am to have you." And he kissed her.

25: Confrontation

Saturday, July 5th

Rick needed an early start Saturday. They'd agreed a few days earlier that, on Saturday, he'd work on Maggie's car at "People's Garage" in Stamford, a business that rented out garage bays by the hour. In case he needed any parts for her car that he didn't already have, they had to be mindful that the VW dealer's parts department closed at noon.

His VW was a year older than Maggie's, so the spare engine parts he kept for his car would work on hers, too. Volkswagen made only minor cosmetic changes on the Beetle from one model year to the next. In fact, many times, he had scavenged parts from both older and newer models at Lajoie's junk yard in South Norwalk and found that they worked just fine on his.

Working on cars had become a hobby over the years, and he'd accumulated a full set of tools that enabled him to stay ahead of major maintenance issues. Not once had he taken his car in for service by a professional. He relied on a quirky self-published guide, *How to Keep Your Volkswagen Alive: A Manual of Step by Step Procedures for the Compleat Idiot.* (That intentional misspelling had always puzzled him.)

They planned that, around ten, Maggie would come to People's Garage to see what parts, if any, were needed so that she could drive him to the dealer to get them.

Hopping into Maggie's forest green VW, her unique scent permeated the car and made Rick smile, reminding him of the time he'd smelled her pillow the first time he awoke in her bed.

As he drove to Stamford, he sensed a sluggishness in acceleration and a roughness at idle. Otherwise, it seemed fine. He figured a tune-up and new spark plugs would do the trick. On the way over, he stopped at his apartment to change clothes, get his tools and spare parts, and then to NAPA for three quarts of oil, an oil filter and four new spark plugs.

As he turned onto the short, pot-holed side street where People's Garage was located, Rick noticed in the rear-view mirror that a new bright blue Chevrolet Camaro Z28 had followed him into the turn. As he backed into an open garage bay, the Camaro stopped, the tinted side window rolled down, the driver scowled at him, and then drove on. Looking at him through the VW's windshield, Rick thought he recognized the face, but wasn't sure because the guy was wearing sunglasses.

After checking in with Ralph Bradley, the shop owner, he slid the drain pan under the engine, lay on his back on the creeper to unscrew the oil pan plug and let the old oil out. He could see immediately that it was quite dirty, guessing that it hadn't been changed for far too many miles. He believed you couldn't change the oil in an air-cooled engine too often—he changed his every three thousand miles or less.

As he came out from under the engine, he sat up on the creeper and noticed that the Camaro had pulled into the shop's driveway in front Maggie's car. The driver was walking towards him.

It was Pete Conley.

"Who the hell are you?" Pete asked gruffly as he stopped a few steps into the garage.

"Who's asking?"

"Why are you driving Maggie Haines' car?"

Pete took a couple more steps. "Are you *fuckin'* my girlfriend?" he shouted angrily.

The two other guys working on their cars in the adjacent bays looked up from their work at the sound of the loud, angry voice.

Pete's muscled arms tensed at his sides. Rick stood and wiped his oil-covered hands on a rag. "I, uh, I think it would be best if you just left," he said, his voice quaking a bit.

"I'll leave when I'm *damn well* ready to leave!" Pete shouted. "Hey. Aren't you that little twerp who was talking to Maggie at the Hotchkiss party a few weeks ago?" Rick gave him a silent glare.

"Yeah, that's it. That's who you are. Well, you'd better mind your own *fuckin'* business and leave Maggie alone. She's my girl. I'm dating her and have been for a long time. We just had a little argument. We'll patch things up again. We always do. And you'd better butt out."

Ralph had come out of his office. He and the two other mechanics stood nearby watching the developing confrontation.

"I don't think so. First of all, Maggie is a woman, not a *girl*," Rick said, mocking Pete's tone. "And secondly, her life is her own business, and of no concern to you. She told you she's done with you. I heard her say so myself."

"Hah. That's funny, 'cuz I was by her apartment a couple weeks ago. She didn't say anything like that."

Rick flinched. Sensing his doubt, Pete clinched his jaw, flexed his fists again and took another step forward. He was now close enough to hit Rick if he'd wanted to. Rick braced himself awaiting a punch. Pete glanced sideways at the other men before returning his glare to Rick.

"Get the *fuck* out of our lives." He then turned, strode back to his car, backed out quickly and sped off with squealing tires, throwing gravel in his wake.

After he'd left, Ralph returned to his office and the other two mechanics went back to work on their cars.

Rick was shaken, unsure what to make of Pete's visit. The last thing he'd expected that morning was this meathead showing up and confronting him like that. He thought he'd seen the last of him that night in Salisbury, when he'd heard Maggie tell him that their relationship was over.

He sensed Maggie would not be happy to hear about this. Maybe he shouldn't tell her. She hadn't mentioned Pete at all since the party. But then, why hadn't she mentioned that Pete had gone to her apartment? Or, had he? But if he had, why hadn't Maggie repeated what she'd said at the party, that the relationship was over? Maybe he's lying.

Standing in the shop for a couple minutes after Pete left, worried he might return, Rick didn't know what to believe. As his adrenaline rush subsided, he got back to work, keeping an eye out for the blue Camaro.

Taking the carburetor apart, he discovered it was full of accumulated crud. A couple of component pieces were worn and needed replacing. Fortunately, he had those parts on hand and wouldn't need anything from the VW parts department.

Within a half-hour, the carburetor was clean, and he had put it back together. He'd also replaced the oil and spark plugs. Using his timing light, he was working on getting the timing just right when Maggie pulled up in Rick's car, parked it in front of hers and jumped out.

"How's it going? Anything serious?" and planted a strategic kiss on his cheek, avoiding an oil splotch. "I know it's been running a little rough lately."

At the sound of a woman's voice—a rarity in that garage—the other mechanics looked up from their engines and stared. As usual, she looked gorgeous and sexy. She was dressed in leather sandals, white cotton shorts, a powder blue sleeveless t-shirt and sunglasses. Her hair was tied back under a Red Sox cap.

"Nah. Just the usual maintenance. But I probably don't need to tell you that you should change your oil more frequently. It was pretty dirty. And you should get a tune-up at the same time," he said flatly.

"Well, now that I have a boyfriend who's a mechanic, that shouldn't be an issue," and she gave a little laugh. "Thanks a million."

"This is good to go. You can drive it home and see how it runs. By the way, what's with the Red Sox cap? Trying to get my goat?"

"Don't you remember? They brainwashed me in Boston," and laughed again.

Rick laughed, too, but his bland look didn't square with the laugh, which alarmed her.

"What's the matter? You're not mad about my hat, are you? I can take it off. Or is something else wrong with the car? You seem annoyed."

"No, no. Your hat is okay. And your car's fine. It's just that…"

"What? What's the matter?"

"Let me shut off the engine." He lowered his voice. "Come outside with me for a minute," and led her out of the garage, where he sat back on front fender of his own car.

"Rick, what is it?" a note of alarm in her voice.

"Guess who followed me here?"

"Someone followed you? What do you mean?"

"A blue Camaro."

Maggie's face fell, and she slumped. "Oh shit. *Oh shit. Not Pete.*"

"None other. He had to have followed me all the way from your place. To my apartment. To the NAPA store. And then here. I didn't notice him until he turned the corner behind me onto this side street."

"What'd he do?" Her face betrayed fear.

"Fortunately, not much. But he threatened me and was pretty loud. He wanted to know why I was driving your car. To tell you the truth, he was kinda scary. I'm sure he outweighs me by at least thirty pounds. He was flexing his muscles and rubbing his fists. I thought he was going to take a swing at me. He was certainly close enough."

"What'd he say?"

"Well, for one, he asked me if I was—his words—*fucking* you. Actually, what he said was, quote, are you fuckin' my girl, unquote. He said that you were still his, quote, *girl*. He said you'd just had a little argument. That you'd patch things up again as you always do. Told me to get lost and to, quote unquote, get out of our lives."

"That *bastard*. What'd you say?"

"I told him that your life is none of his business. I also said that you'd told him it was over. That I'd heard you say so myself. After that, he left, probably because these other guys here were watching. Maybe he thought they might jump in if he hit me. But I wonder how far he would've gone if I'd been here alone."

"Oh crap. I was afraid this would happen."

"What do you mean, you were afraid this would happen? Why? I thought you broke up with him. I heard you say so at the party."

"Yes, of course I did. But apparently, he doesn't think so. He's been calling me at the office. I've asked Molly not to put his calls through."

"He's been *calling* you?" Rick folded his arms across his chest, staring at her open-mouthed.

"He even started giving phony names to try to get around Molly, but she knows his voice and wouldn't put his calls through. Then he came by my apartment building late one night a couple weeks ago and made a scene."

"Came by your apartment? When? You didn't mention any of this to me. Pete did say that he'd been by your apartment a couple weeks ago. But I didn't believe him. He claimed you didn't say anything about breaking up."

"He's *lying*."

Now Rick began to wonder who was telling the truth.

"So, what exactly *did* you say to him?"

"I certainly *did* tell him for the umpteenth time that we were through—"

"—*Why didn't you tell me any of this?*"

"Um, well, I didn't tell you because, honestly, I, uh, I didn't want you to be worried—"

"—*Didn't want me to be worried?*" raising his arms over his head. "You should have told me, Maggie. I thought we trusted each other." He refolded his arms and scowled.

"I'm sorry. I thought I could handle this myself. I thought he'd finally get the message and leave me alone."

"Apparently you were wrong." Rick continued frowning. "So, what *really* happened when he came over to your apartment?"

Maggie resumed tentatively, looking away and absent-mindedly fiddling with the zipper tab on her purse. "It was... It was a weeknight, last week. Uh, last Tuesday. Um, late. About eleven. The night you were out of town on business. I'd fallen asleep on the couch reading the paper. He woke me buzzing at the front door. He was pretty drunk. Over the intercom, I said we were through and told him to go away. He wanted me to buzz him into the building so we could talk. I told him there wasn't anything to talk about and to go away. Then he stood on the sidewalk yelling at me until my downstairs neighbor called the police. As the police car came around the corner, he walked away casually."

As she talked, Rick remained skeptically silent.

"At first, I did take two of his calls at work with the intention of telling him again that the relationship was over—which is what I did. *Emphatically.* He couldn't possibly have misunderstood me."

"When was that? You didn't mention that either."

"Back in early June. His first call was the week after the party. He pleaded with me to get back together again. He apologized and said he'd been out of line, that he'd said things he shouldn't have, that he still loved me—his standard speech. But I cut him off and told him it was over and to stop calling me. And I hung up on him."

"And he called again?"

"Yes, he called again. A week later, after having sent a dozen roses to my office—an old tactic he'd used before... Remember at the party when I told him not to waste his money on flowers for me." Rick nodded. "He always does that, and it really irritates me. I left the flowers in the lobby and had Molly throw away the card that came with them. I didn't even look at it. After that, I asked Molly to screen his calls. He's called three more times since then—that I know of." She scanned Rick's face, looking for a hint of sympathy.

"You said he had to have followed you to here?" He nodded. She looked down briefly before returning her gaze to his eyes. "Rick, remember that car that tore out of that parking space last night across from my apartment?"

"How could I forget it? That was pretty obnoxious."

"That was Pete."

"Oh my God, you're right. That *was* a blue Camaro. I didn't make the connection. *He's stalking us!*"

"I'm afraid so Rick. I'm sorry." She was starting to tear up.

Looking at him, lips quivering, she reached out, put her hand lightly on his wrist and gave it a gentle squeeze. It instantly reminded him of the first time she'd touched him the night they'd met. He unfolded his arms, took off her Red Sox cap and wrapped his arms around her, pulling her to him in a tight hug. He could feel her soft sobs begin on his shoulder.

Still holding her, he whispered, "Maggie, I love you. Without reservation. You know that, don't you?" She nodded, her face still buried in his shoulder. But she said nothing, shuddering, continuing to cry quietly.

He held her silently in the hug for several minutes until she stopped crying. "Why can't this guy take a hint? Now I *am* worried, especially considering that he's stalking us. He's obsessive. You gotta wonder how many times he's been hanging around outside your apartment—and when, and for how long. This is one fucked-up dude and he's making me very nervous."

Maggie pulled away, sighed and wiped at her tears. "What do you think we should do?"

"This is not good. I do not like where this is going… Here's what I think we need to do. We should—"

"—Wait. Maybe we should go somewhere else and talk about this."

"Okay, sure. Let me pay the tab for the bay rental and put my tools in my car so we can leave."

She started taking out her wallet. "Rick, let me pay. And how much for the oil and spark plugs?"

"I got it. Not a big deal. You'll recall that I haven't had breakfast yet, and I'm starved. How about you buy me breakfast at Ernie's and we'll call it even?"

"Okay."

"Take your car, and I'll drive mine. I gotta run home, get the grime off me and change clothes. Let me know how you think your car runs. I'll meet you at Ernie's around ten-thirty. I just hope Pete's not lurking around, waiting to follow me again. At least I know what car to watch out for."

"I'm so sorry Rick. Really, I am" and she started tearing up again.

He sighed, hugged her again and then looked into her eyes. "Maggie, this isn't your fault. This guy is a total asshole."

26: Envy

After Rick left for the garage a little before eight, Maggie stripped the bed and added the sheets to her wash load for her weekly run to the laundromat around the corner.

By nine-thirty, she'd finished that day's *New York Times* she'd brought along, folded the laundry and remade the bed. She grabbed her Red Sox cap, intending to tease Rick, before leaving in his car for the garage in Stamford where he'd be working on her VW.

She greeted him and learned about the status of her car. But he didn't rise to her teasing with the hat. She sensed something was bothering him, and soon found out. Pete had followed him there and confronted him. Clearly Rick was upset. For good reason.

In addition to enduring Pete's belligerence and threats, Rick had not been aware of his on-going contacts with Maggie. So, of course the confrontation had surprised and rattled him. She'd not been completely honest with Rick. With each successive incident, each time she told him to leave her alone, she'd hoped that Pete would finally get the message. There was no reason to bother Rick about it. Or so she thought.

In hindsight, that was the wrong choice. Now she regretted it. Maggie feared she'd lost Rick's trust—which was more upsetting than Pete's annoying intrusions.

Dammit, this was getting out of hand. It stunned her to learn that Pete had followed and then confronted Rick like that. Had he lost his mind? She knew he could get carried away with himself sometimes, but this was too much. What would he do next? And what could she do to get him to stop, to leave them alone? Should she confront him herself? Should she call him? Or go to his office and talk to him?

The mounting frustration of trying to be rid of an abusive ex-boyfriend, combined with her fear of losing Rick's trust and love overwhelmed her. She found herself breaking down in tears. Rick gave her the sympathy she craved.

As she drove back to South Norwalk, she was soothed by how

smoothly her car was running. They met outside Ernie's. She hugged him.

"My car runs like new. I guess I'd gotten used to it like that. Thanks."

"Anytime. Tell you what. I'll put your car on the same maintenance schedule as mine. We'll keep 'em both in tip-top shape. If you like, I'll even teach how to do it yourself so we can do our cars together."

"I'd like that."

They walked into the diner holding hands and settled into a semi-circular booth in the rear so that they were seated next to one another. After ordering breakfast and coffee, Rick picked up where they'd left off.

"Do you think Pete is capable of violence?"

"I'm not sure. But probably."

"Did he ever hit you or threaten to?"

"Uh, no. Not really." Her eyes briefly skipped to the side. She had just told him another lie before she was even aware she'd meant to do so.

"What do you mean, *not really*? Either he did, or he didn't."

"No... But he does have quite a temper. There were a few occasions when he was drunk, angry about something, and so amped up that I worried he might get violent. He would pace around, rubbing his fist while shouting. I've seen him punch a hole in a closet door. He's a control freak with little self-control."

"Well, like I said earlier, I'm glad there were other guys at the garage this morning. I think he came close to taking a swing at me."

She sighed aloud and looked down.

"A few days after we met, I asked Bill about him. He told me he was a very aggressive hockey player, got into fights every game and drew a lot of penalties as the team enforcer. In one match, Bill said, Pete missed a check, took a header into the boards and was knocked out cold. He was carted off the rink unconscious, held overnight at a local hospital for observation and missed several games after that."

"Pete once mentioned he'd been injured and missed a couple of games because of it, but not in such detail. He didn't say anything about going to the hospital. That sounds far worse than what he told me."

"Bill didn't spend a lot time with him off the rink, so he didn't know him well. What do you know about his background?"

"He was poor kid from Hamden, raised by a single mother. He got a scholarship to Hotchkiss."

"I guess that makes him a preppie." He chuckled. "Kind of an unusual preppie as far as I'm concerned. Not like the ones I knew at Dartmouth."

"No. You're right. And, honestly, that's kind of what attracted me to him in the first place. He was a preppie, knew that world and could navigate it. But he didn't have the usual attitude that goes with it. You know, like the cynicism, fake suaveness and name-dropping and all that crap. Anyway, after Hotchkiss, he got an athletic scholarship to play hockey at Quinnipiac College and earned a degree there in Business Administration. Then he landed a sales rep job with Stockton Chemical, where he's done quite well. A couple years ago, he was promoted to eastern regional sales manager—one of five regional managers. Their youngest one, in fact. He may be a jerk, but he's smart and he's a hard worker. I mean, he did well enough in school to get scholarships—like you. You know, I admired him for that early on, just as I respect you for getting a full scholarship to Dartmouth. That's really impressive. I doubt I ever could have done that."

Rick continued as though he hadn't heard the compliment. "You said you were together then on and off, from then until late May when we met."

"Mostly off. He could be so sweet and thoughtful, and we did have a lot of spontaneous fun early on. He'd buy me gifts for no reason at all—jewelry, flowers, scarves, a sweater, whatnot. He'd surprise me. Take me a Yankees game or something like that. But he'd have these moods where the smallest irritation would set him off. When he was angry, he'd take it out on me. And that would lead to arguments. Sometimes, when I'd confront him about his behavior, he'd get angrier. I was at the end of my rope so many times and would walk out on him. But then, a few weeks later, he'd be back like a little puppy dog, all apologetic, send flowers to my office, and take me out for a fancy dinner."

Maggie touched Rick's hand and looked into his eyes. "Listen, Rick, I want to make one thing perfectly clear. I was never serious about Pete—I mean, I wasn't looking for a long-term commitment from him. Initially, maybe, as we all do when we first start dating someone. But pretty soon, I realized he wasn't for me. It's just that he could be a fun guy to hang out with. Maybe he was looking for a serious relationship, but I never was. Not with him. We didn't spend a lot of time together. Not the way you and I have been doing this past month. Later on, when he got into a routine and the surprises stopped, when we went out, it was to a movie or dinner, or to friends' places. But he was far more serious about my family's wealth than he was about me."

"How'd you get that impression?"

"Well, he'd ask questions. It felt like an investigation sometimes. How much money was in my trust? Restrictions on it? When did I get control? Who managed it, and how was it managed? Stuff like that."

"Whoa. I'd say that's none of his business."

"Yeah, I know. Anyway, his questions would arise casually. Over time. A stray question here, another one the next time I saw him. It was kind of weird and made me uncomfortable."

"How did you answer him?"

"I never gave him much information. Said I didn't know and didn't want to know. He had money, too, that he'd earned from his job. He makes very good money at Stockton—a lot more than I make. I only learned how much by accident when I saw a paystub on his kitchen table once. I was actually kind of shocked. Jeez, who knew you can make such good money selling chemicals?"

The waitress brought their breakfasts, topped up their coffee mugs, and left.

"Please don't take this the wrong way, but I don't see how you can be attracted to me when you were attracted to my polar opposite. More to the point, why did you keep going back to him?"

She sighed again. "I don't know. *I really don't know.* I've asked myself that question many times. Amanda asked me that a couple weeks ago, too, and it frustrates me that I don't have a good answer. I can only guess. Maybe I was weak, unsure of myself, afraid to confront him. But I've learned a lot about myself in the past year—and even more in the past several weeks that I've been with you. I guess I've grown up a lot, too, and gotten stronger. Experience does that to you, you know—and so does love." She smiled and looked at him as she said it. "I've had similar conversations with Amanda about Pete, when she asked what I saw in him and why I kept going back to him."

"If he was making good money, why do you think he was so focused on your family's wealth?"

"Pete never had much growing up. His mother was a widow and worked a couple jobs to support him and his sister. They lived life from one paycheck to the next. I guess my family's wealth was the closest he'd ever gotten to something like that, the sense of security and comfort that it may have represented to him. Maybe that's why he's reluctant to let go now, refusing to accept that I've broken up with him. Maybe he had his life all planned out—with my money. And he doesn't want to lose that." She looked down and sipped her coffee. Rick let her have the silence.

"After she met him and saw him in action, my mother tried to convince me to break up with him."

"Why? What'd he do?"

"A couple months after we started dating, he started bugging me about wanting to meet my family. So, I brought him to a party my parents threw at the end of last summer. There were a couple dozen guests—mostly Mom and Dad's friends, but also a few of Charley's. As usual, Pete drank too much. At one point, someone politely asked him what he did for a living. He went into great detail, far too much. And then he got obnoxious when he realized people were drifting away and weren't really interested in the finer points of the chemical industry. He got kind of loud."

"Whoa. And he thought he was going to make a good impression on your parents?"

"Yeah. No kidding. And Helen. Oh my God. You should have seen her. She kept looking at him rolling her eyes. She finally pulled me aside and quietly told me to get him out of there. So, we left the party early. I've regretted few things in my life, but that was one of them. I never should have brought him to that party. You know, Pete was the last boyfriend of mine Helen met before yesterday. That's why she hugged you. Mom had obviously told her all about you. And she could see that, unlike Pete, you are a real gentleman."

He laughed. "I'm very curious what else you told your mom and dad about me. They sure seemed to know a lot about me before I'd even met them." He continued grinning, and then kissed her forehead.

Then he paused a moment and his seriousness returned. "I understand what you're saying. Yes, we do grow, and we do learn from our experiences. But, look, I don't think you've answered my question. God knows I've had my loser girlfriends, too. But I didn't keep dating them for almost a year."

"I don't know what to say. You know, Pete could really turn on the charm. He was romantic and sent me flowers many times early in our relationship. He was always telling me how wonderful and how beautiful I am—which, later on, often preceded his blow-ups."

"Doesn't seem like a very charming fellow to me."

Maggie scowled. "Yeah. I guess he was like gum stuck on my shoe. I couldn't get rid of him. But that's my fault. Maybe I just didn't want to deal with what a final break-up would likely lead to. Now, we're seeing it. And it's not pretty."

"Yeah. No kidding."

"But I think, at that party—that scene you witnessed—I finally snapped. Or maybe I just finally admitted it to myself that I had to put an end to it, or I'd be doomed to a life of blow-ups and stupid arguments. Maybe your presence and the way you made me feel gave me the confidence I needed to finally tell him off." Her voice trailed off and she paused a moment.

"Rick, I didn't tell you the truth about why I threw my wine in his face. It wasn't because he called me a lying bitch. It was because… because he called me a lying cunt."

Rick winced, looked down and shook his head. "Oh my God! I don't blame you. What an asshole. I think throwing your wine at him was being too kind."

"And remember what I said to him when I refused to go home with him, about not bothering to call me and apologize, and my reference to his vile behavior?" Rick nodded again. "I'd never talked to him like that before. I'll bet it shocked him. That's what I mean about getting strength from you. I said that in front of you, as you literally stood by me."

She paused a few moments and averted her eyes before resuming. He continued looking at her as he took a bite of his omelet. "I've learned a lot the past few weeks that I've known you. You've helped me rediscover my self-confidence—myself, really." And she smiled, looking into his eyes again. "Rick, I love you" She paused, put her hand on his. Her eyes were bright with tears. She blinked them back.

"I really do. Very much… I've been thinking a lot about this the past couple weeks. It's really been on my mind. It's because I feel so comfortable being with you, so much myself, so natural. You make me feel. Safe to be who I am or what I feel like being or doing at that moment. With Pete, I never felt like that. I had to be on guard. I had to be what Pete thought I was. I was always afraid of doing or saying the wrong thing and setting him off. When I first met you, I think I took a leap of faith. I trusted that. I trusted you. I have even more confidence in myself now because I know that you trust me. And I trust you—totally. I've *never* felt that way before about any man. Certainly not Pete. I've never looked for it or even expected it. And I feel like we are only at the beginning of something entirely new—and beautiful."

As he listened, a smile grew on Rick's face. "Maggie, what you say is true for me, too. You make me feel the same way. I love you for all the same reasons." He paused, still smiling at her. "And isn't it funny that we've gone along this far without saying so out loud. I told myself that it would scare you off if I did, that the words couldn't possibly express my true feelings for you and our relationship."

Now Maggie smiled, too, and laughed quietly. "Me too. I've been wanting to tell you that since a couple weeks ago. But it seemed hasty then. Now, it seems so right, and so true. The words come naturally and so easily." She squeezed his hand and smiled.

Her face shifted. "I'm sure you realize that we're probably not done with Pete yet. I wish it weren't so, but I think we should expect it and be prepared for it. I just wish he'd accept it. I'm so sorry to inflict him on you."

"Well, he'll get the idea and leave us alone."

She smiled, but Maggie wasn't so sure.

27: Beach Serenade

Despite their avowals of love for each other after the confrontation with Pete, Rick was still troubled by Maggie's confession as he learned details about her relationship with Pete that she'd concealed or glossed over in previous discussions. But what troubled Rick most was the nagging feeling for which he was now scolding himself.

Was she still withholding information about Pete? If so, what else would he learn? And if she isn't, why was he so suspicious? He didn't like feeling that way about the woman he'd come to love so much.

The Haines family had long been members of Burnside Country Club, which had both a championship golf course and clubhouse in Darien, and a beach club in Rowayton on Long Island Sound. She suggested they spend the afternoon at the beach, and then have dinner in the dining room there.

After they set up lounge chairs in the sand and grabbed beach towels, they plunged into the water together. The Sound was early-summer chilly. They swam briskly to the club's float, about fifty yards off the beach, to sun themselves there, stretching out and closing their eyes.

Rick had been tormented the past several days, thinking about Maggie's relationship with Pete. Rick would visualize her making love to him, and it would give him an empty feeling in the pit of his stomach. Now that he'd found that she'd been holding back information about the relationship, his torment increased.

His imaginings of their intimacies sickened him. But why? He rebuked himself. What did he expect from Maggie? That she'd be a virgin? For God's sake, she's an attractive woman. And she's twenty-six years old. Was she supposed to sit around and wait until he showed up? He hadn't exactly been Mr. Chastity these past several years. It was time to lay his cards on the table. If he expected honesty from her, then she should get the same from him. Rick interrupted the silence.

"Maggie, can I tell you something?"

"What's that?"

"I want to tell you about my own baggage from the past."

94

"Is that really necessary?"

Leaning on his elbow, he turned to face her. "Well, yes, I think it is. You've been so open about Pete. It's been on my mind, and I think I should be just as open with you."

"But I've only told you as much about Pete as I have because he has intruded so rudely in our lives."

"That's true. But I still want you to know this about my past."

Maggie nodded.

"One night in January of my senior year, I went to a frat party, like we often did. Several girls from Clifford College were there and that's where I met Karen McKenna. Clifford is a small all-girls school not far from Hanover. They often came to Dartmouth for the parties. We kinda latched on to each other amid the party chaos. After that, I started seeing her regularly. Her family has a place at Killington, so we went skiing there a few weekends in February and March" He stopped and averted his eyes.

"And, as you know, that April, my parents were killed—three months after we'd met. So, I was dealing with that. Karen never showed me much sympathy. It seemed like she purposely avoided the subject—like it made her uncomfortable. But, in an odd way, I think I appreciated that. I guess I was looking for reasons to, uh I, uh, I suppose I just wanted to move on. Put it behind me. Karen was unthreatening and put her energies all the time into partying and having fun. I spent most of my free time that summer with her and her friends here in Fairfield County, going to bars and parties. Though I'd just graduated, I wasn't looking for a full-time job, instead taking part-time work as I'd done through high school and college summers. I was feeling pretty disconnected from the world and unmotivated."

"Understandably. I mean, losing your parents all of a sudden."

"Uh huh," he nodded. "Karen's family lives in Tokeneke. Her parents are loaded. Karen never let me forget that she was wealthy. She used to go to Ox Ridge Hunt Club pretty regularly to ride her horse, which she stabled there. I went a couple times and watched but didn't ride with her. We'd go to polo matches there, but it was a weird scene. Real hoity-toity. I'm not too comfortable around the horsy set. Anyway, I was living that summer in my parents' house in Wilton with my sisters while we tried to figure out what to do with the house, trying to sort out my parents' stuff—it's tough not knowing what to do with your mother's dresses and stuff, what to get rid of and how…"

His voice trailed off. Maggie reached out and touched his arm.

"Sorry. Karen and I had a lot of fun and I let her pay for almost all of it. She even bought first-class airline tickets when we went to stay at her parents' place on Sanibel Island in Florida for winter break in February. She always paid for drinks, expensive restaurant meals. But my point is, I became accustomed to a comfortable existence sponging off her. I guess I shouldn't have been surprised to discover how self-centered she was. The world was all about Karen and her needs. I don't know why she kept me around. Maybe I filled some kind of role for her, like a gigolo. She always seemed to have cocaine on hand, though I never indulged, despite her many offers to share."

"Whoa. She's a cokehead? *Jeez.*"

"Yeah, I know. She used to make fun of me because I wouldn't try it. And she once sold some of her inherited General Motors stock and bought herself a brand-new BMW—which I always found a little ironic. I mean, why not sell GM shares and buy a 'Vette?" Rick chuckled.

"Wow. Mom and Dad would never let us to do that."

"No, your parents are special, that's obvious. Remember what you told me last night about their roles in your lives?" Maggie nodded. "I think Karen's parents were the opposite. They were never around. I only met them once, and that was only briefly. They barely acknowledged me. Her father gave me a limp handshake and a *nice to meet you* without making eye contact. Her mother just nodded at me from across the room. I never even heard her voice. They hardly seemed involved in Karen's life. Once during a party at their house, I went to the freezer to get some ice. It was packed to the gills with Stouffer's frozen dinners. The fridge itself was devoid of fresh food—just beer, mixers and snacks. That struck me as weird. But I'm digressing."

"No, no. That's interesting. And very revealing. Go on."

"Aside from the partying, there wasn't a lot of purpose to her life. She led a life of leisure. She never talked about life goals, what she wanted to do with herself, and seemed in a constant search for stimulation. She didn't even read books. The only things she read were magazines like *Cosmopolitan* and *People.* Her idea of an adventure was a new batch of coke, a shopping spree at the mall or on Fifth Avenue in Manhattan, getting extremely drunk or going to the opening night of the latest big-name bar or club. I broke up with her at the end of the summer as she was getting ready to go back to Clifford for her senior year. I was just tired of her nonchalant attitude toward life, toward everything and everybody—including me. She wasn't the least bit upset when I broke the news to her. It was kinda like, *Okay, then. Bye.*"

"Where is she now? In rehab?"

"I don't know. But for her sake, I hope she did go into rehab. But I have no idea. Never saw her or heard from her again. Nor do I want to."

Maggie sat up, turned to face him squarely. "You know, I'm glad you shared that. You've given me a fresh perspective," and she smiled. "I can see why a woman like Karen would alienate you."

He nodded.

"People like her have a compulsive need to control situations, to use people for their own needs. I can see that in your description of her. I would guess she's that way because of the absence of parental involvement in her life. I'll bet she always got what she wanted growing up. It also sounds like she wanted to impose on you her idea of what you should be to fulfill her own needs. Listen, Rick, I care deeply about you. You know that."

He nodded.

"I love you and respect you because of who you are, and because of the strength you've given me, and the confidence you show in our relationship. I will *never* impose my expectations on you. Never. And I know you'll never impose your expectations on me."

"Of course not."

She reached out, put her hand behind his neck, pulled him to her, and they kissed. "Enough talk. Let's swim back to the beach," she said.

After the swim, they lounged on the beach, talking on a range of topics. They both dozed off. When Rick awoke some twenty minutes later, Maggie was still asleep. He sat up and turned again to look directly at her, and then sat still for a minute just admiring her with an expanding grin on his face. Then he thought what his life would be like without her and he shivered.

She stirred, opened her eyes, and looked at him. "Why are you looking at me like that?"

"Maggie, you are *too beautiful.*" She smiled. He paused, still grinning at her. "Do you remember that song we heard Johnny Hartman sing a couple weeks ago at the Village Gate?"

"Which one?"

He cleared his throat and quietly sang the first two verses of "You Are Too Beautiful," in a soft baritone, trying his best to emulate Johnny Hartman.

The two women behind him on adjacent beach chairs had stopped talking to listen to him sing, which he hadn't noticed. When he stopped, they both applauded softly. Rick blushed.

"Very nice," one of them said.

"Very romantic," the other added. Rick turned, smiled and nodded.

"That was lovely," Maggie said. "Rick, you have such a nice singing voice. Where did you learn to sing so well?"

"In the high school choir, and then I sang for a couple years with an *a cappella* group at Dartmouth."

"I do remember that song when Johnny Hartman sang it, and I remember liking it very much. You did a lovely job," she said, smiling. "Say, what time is it? I'm starving."

Rick dug his watch from his bag. "It's just now five-thirty."

"Let's go have an early dinner in the Ocean View dining room. That's the fancy one. You brought your sports coat and slacks, didn't you?"

"As you suggested. They're hanging in my car."

After showering and changing, they met at the dining room door. Fewer than half the tables were occupied. The hostess seated them by the window with a view of the sound. There was still plenty of light in the sky.

"This is my treat, by the way, to thank you for fixing my car. Let's get a nice bottle of wine. We deserve it. I'll pick. Do you prefer red or white?"

"Nice idea. Either is fine with me."

She studied the wine list. "I think we should share a bottle of Champagne."

"Are we celebrating something?"

"Us. Being together. Being in love. Good enough reason for me."

"I agree," and he returned her smile.

She got the waiter's attention and ordered the Champagne. He recited the evening's specials, departed and returned with the wine.

"Cheers," as she clinked her glass to his. "To us."

"To us. And to your beauty."

She smiled. "Rick, I have an idea. How about you move in with me?"

He grinned. "Really? Are you sure? You want to go there this soon in our relationship?

She gave him a toothy smile and nodded vigorously. "Absolutely. I've been thinking about it a lot. You're already spending most nights at my place, and you have a lot of clothes hanging in my closet. And most of your jazz records are there."

He laughed. "Well, I'm game. But is there enough room for both of us and all our stuff?"

"Yes. But, uh… Actually, I have a better idea. Remember how I told you that I needed my parents' approval to tap my trust?" He nodded. "I've been thinking about this since before we met. I want to buy a house. Dad is always saying that real estate is the best investment. Much as I like my apartment, SoNo is getting old. I'm tired of hunting for a parking space, climbing two flights of stairs, the noise of the city, litter in the streets. Anyway, now that now that we're talking about you moving, how about if I buy a house and you move in with me into my house."

"I'd insist on paying rent. My days of mooching off rich women are over. But speaking of that, when I talked to Julie a few weeks ago, she mentioned that she had spoken to my uncle about my parents' estate. She wants to buy a house in Denver. He told her she could withdraw as much as three hundred thousand. I'll talk to my uncle and make sure I could take out that much, too. I think we could share the cost of the house and get a pretty decent house in a good town with that kind of money—five-hundred to six-hundred thousand."

"Definitely. Tell you what. Let's go look at houses next weekend to get a sense of what we both might like in that price range. Probably not in New Canaan or Darien. But maybe Wilton or Ridgefield."

Rick grinned. "Um, getting a house together? Isn't that sort of like getting married?" She just grinned at him. "What are you thinking?"

"Nothing," and she kept grinning. "I told you. I just want to buy a house. And I want us to live together."

"Well, okay. Good idea. Works for me." He smiled and leaned across the table to kiss her on the lips. They clinked their Champagne flutes. Moments later, the waiter interrupted them with their dinners.

28: P.J. Clark's

Sunday, July 6th

They had no plans for Sunday, so, over dinner the night before, Maggie had suggested a hike in Pound Ridge Reservation, just across the line in Westchester County. It took about forty minutes to drive north from Norwalk to the Bergfield parking lot on the reservation's northern side. The Sunday morning skies were hazy, the temperatures in the eighties, the humidity rising.

They headed up the Fox Hill trail, hiking briskly, for a couple miles—too quickly to hold hands as we had at the outset. At Deer Hollow, they turned onto the Brown Trail and continued for another mile or so. They had the trail mostly to themselves, except briefly for an older couple walking the opposite direction with a friendly, sniffing yellow lab off his leash.

Forty-five minutes of vigorous hiking left them winded and sweaty. Maggie suggested a break, smiling to herself and thinking that now would be a good time to tell Rick her story. She suggested a large flat rock just off the trail. She sat. Rick handed her the water bottle as he sat down next to her.

After taking a long swig, she gave it back to him. "Have I ever told you how my parents met?" Rick shook his head as he took his own drink from the bottle.

"I've been thinking about it lately. It's a cute story."

"Okay. But why have you been thinking about that?" tilting his head and grinning.

She ignored the question. "Mom grew up outside Philadelphia on the Main Line and graduated from Bryn Mawr College in 1952. Dad grew up in Yarmouth, Maine, and, like his father and grandfather before him, went to Yale, as did Uncle Henry, who was a year ahead of him. Charley and Hank went there, too."

Rick nodded. "Oh, yeah. They all laid that Yale stuff on pretty thick at the party. Charley and Hank teased me about Dartmouth. Go Bulldogs, Boola Boola, Skull and Bones, and all that. Whoop-de-doo," spinning his index finger in the air.

"Yeah, they're all like that. Gets kind of boring. Anyway, Dad went to work for the family company in 1950 after graduating. They'd relocated the headquarters from Portland to New York City in 1948, and my dad's parents moved to Old Greenwich. In 'fifty-two, after she'd graduated, Mom moved there to look for a job. She rented an apartment on the Upper East Side with a couple of college friends who were also looking for jobs. One Friday evening in late June, after one of her roommates had gotten hired at *Look* magazine as a proofreader, the three of them went out to celebrate. They wound up at P.J. Clark's. The three were seated in the dining room at a table for four. And at the next table was my father with three of his buddies from work, just out for dinner and a night on the town. Clark's was the after-hours hang-out for Haines' young unmarried managers. As soon as Mom sat down, Dad started staring at her, which made her feel uncomfortable."

"I can see why your father would do that. She's a very attractive woman—just like her daughter."

"Stop it," and she smiled. "So, anyway, Dad got up and took the empty fourth seat at her table. Ignoring her friends, he started talking just to her. And you saw how chatty Dad can be. She says she didn't know whether to be offended by this fresh young man—her description—or attracted. Well, she was attracted. After a few minutes of talking, he asked her out for dinner the next evening. And they were married less than two months later."

"*Two months?* Wow. That's amazing. And they've been married for how long? Uh, let's see, 1980 minus 1952. Twenty-eight years. That's impressive that they'd get married so quickly and stay married for so long."

"Your arithmetic is about right. It'll be twenty-eight years on August thirtieth. Charley came along the next year, and me a year-and-a-half later. And they lived happily ever after."

"I should say so. So, you're telling me this story because?"

"Um, I don't know," she said in a teasing sing-song. "I just thought it was a nice story."

Rick laughed. "Well, it's a *very* nice story. But actually, I think that's a fabulous idea. Let's do it, too Let's get married. You and me."

She gasped. "*What?* Are you serious, Rick? Really?"

"*Of course I'm serious.* That's an amazing story and, to me, it makes perfect sense to get married that quickly when you know you've found your life partner, which I have—I mean, which we have. Why not? After all, we will be getting a house together, right? We may as well, eh? So, yes, really. I *really* mean it. Would you be my wife?"

Her face flushed. "Oh my God. Yes. *Yes!* That's wonderful. I can't believe it." And she reached out and hugged him tightly. They sat there for a long minute holding one another. Releasing him, she said, "My parents will be so thrilled to hear the news."

"I want to ask your father first."

Maggie guffawed. "You mean, like ask him for my hand in marriage?" He nodded, grinning. "That's kind of old-fashioned, don't you think?"

"Exactly. That's the point."

"Well, that's probably not necessary." She thought for a moment. "But you know what? Both he and Mom would be tickled by that. Yes, let's do that. How soon?"

"The sooner the better. How about next weekend? Will they be home?"

"I can check tomorrow." And, with a big smile, she paused again to look at Rick closely. "Oh Rick, I can't believe this. Are you *really* sure you want to do this?"

"*Oh my God, yes.* Absolutely. I've never been more certain about anything in my life. Actually, yesterday, when we were both confessing that we loved one another, I almost did it then. You know I'm crazy about you."

"Oh, I'm so excited," clasping his hands in hers. And then she threw her arms around him again.

"I think we may have to have an argument, though, about who's more excited and happiest here," he said, laughing.

"Let's call it a tie," and she kissed him.

They hit the trail after that, with wide grins on their faces, holding hands this time, and walking more slowly, talking and taking in the reservation's quiet beauty.

29: Reading Between the Lines

Monday, August 7th

Around mid-day Monday, Maggie called her mother from her office.
"Hi Mom."

"Oh, hi sweetie. I was so glad to meet Rick. I have to admit, you were right about him. He's such a special young man. Dad and I were both impressed. He's smart, well-rounded and very personable. And so handsome. I think you've found yourself a real gem."

"I know, Mom, I know. He's the greatest... Say, Mom, what're you and Dad doing next weekend? We'd like to invite ourselves over for dinner. Rick says that he didn't get enough of a chance to talk to just you two alone and really get to know you, what with all the others around."

"Well, that's very sweet. Yes, I think that's a fine idea. Let's do that. Let me look at the calendar" And she paused. "Hmm. Oh. Dad has his annual member golf tournament at the club on Saturday, which ends with the awards cocktail party and dinner that night. I'm expected to be there to see him collect his first-place trophy, says Himself with a capital-H."

Maggie laughed. She'd long known that as a term of endearment between her parents when one felt the other was a bit too full of themselves. Unsure how it got started, it always amused her to hear one of them say it.

"How about Sunday night? Would that work?"

"Yes, I think so. Let's pencil it in and I'll double-check with Dad. But I'm pretty sure that'll be fine. Listen, I meant what I said about Rick. And I'm sorry I was so skeptical at first. I can see why you're attracted to him. He's quite a guy."

"I know, Mom, he really is. We've been spending almost all our free time together. He worked on my car Saturday morning and now it runs like a top. Then we went to the beach club that afternoon and stayed for dinner. Yesterday, we went for a long hike in Pound Ridge."

"My, my. This sounds serious."

"We'll talk on Sunday." Maggie was practically bursting to tell her mother her news, but she and Rick had agreed to stick with the plan and save their big news until they could tell them in person.

"Now you're being mysterious."

"We'll talk on Sunday, Mom. Okay? Gotta go. Gotta get back to work."

"Okay. Bye then. Love you."

"I love you too, Mom."

30: Best Man

Friday, July 11th

Maggie went to a baby shower Friday evening for an old friend from Miss Porter's, so Rick went out for dinner with Bill when his roommate got back to Stamford from his job in the city.

"Guess who I ran into last weekend," Bill blurted out, as they took their seats. "Karen McKenna."

"No kidding. Where?"

"New Haven. Janet and I had been at a party the night before. We stayed overnight with Jesse and Betsy. Remember them."

Rick nodded.

"Anyway, we all went out for brunch the next morning and she was there with some guy, apparently her fiancée. She and he live in New Haven, she told me. She's working for a small investment advisory firm there."

"What else did she say? Did she mention me?"

"Only insofar as she recognized me as your old roommate and said so. She looks great, by the way." He looked at Rick's grim face. "Oh, that's right. You're not a big fan."

"No kidding. Was she sober? Did she have white powder around her nostrils?"

"It was Sunday morning, for Christ's sake."

"Well, next time you see her, tell her *hi* for me. Listen, Bill, I have a favor to ask."

"Sure. What is it?"

"I need you to be my best man."

"*What?* Best man? What do you mean? You're getting married? When? You mean to Maggie? Really?"

He was grinning and nodding yes to each of question. "Well, we haven't set a date yet, but I'm hoping it's before the summer is out."

"Who else knows?"

"Just you, me and Maggie. We're going to tell her parents on Sunday."

He reached across the table and shook Rick's hand. "Well, that's just fantastic! By the way, when do I get to meet this Maggie?"

"Well, if you hadn't been spending all your time with Janet at the Hotchkiss party, you might have met her that night. We were together the entire party—outside on the deck."

Though they were roommates, they hadn't seen a lot of each other in recent weeks. Rick had been spending most nights at Maggie's apartment, and Bill frequently overnighted with Janet Pescara, his girlfriend, at her place in the city every weekend and most weeknights as well.

Bill sipped his wine, scratched his chin and grinned. "So, this Maggie, she's *it*, huh? You found the right woman for yourself, did you?"

"No doubt about it, Bill. She's really amazing. She's brilliant, funny, loving and talented. I'd say she's beautiful, but that's inadequate. She has a graceful, elegant beauty about her. When I spotted her, I fell in love instantly. Did you even see her at the party?"

"I don't think so. In fact, I don't think I saw you after you bolted. Shit, I'd just introduced you to a couple of friends and the next thing I knew, you were walking across the room and gone. What the hell happened?"

"Your memory is short, my friend. Have some more wine," and he retold a truncated version of that evening's events.

"Oh, yeah. That's right. And you asked me about Pete Conley the week after the party. Yeah, the dude is a bit intense."

"No kidding. Let me tell you the latest," and Rick related the events of the previous Saturday.

"Holy shit. The guy still operates like he's on a hockey rink, trying to intimidate his opponents." Bill thought for a moment. "Rick, do you think it would be helpful if I talked to him? We're not exactly good friends. The only time we see each other is at Hotchkiss reunions. And we didn't do much more than say hi to each other at the party last month. But we do have that common history, you know, playing hockey at Hotchkiss. Maybe I could tell him that you and Maggie are engaged and that he should just move on with his life."

"Uh, I don't know. Maybe it would work. But, on the other hand, maybe that knowledge would just piss him off even more. Maggie says he's after her family money and may not give up easily."

"Well, think about it. Ask Maggie what she thinks. Let me know what you guys would like me to do. I'm happy to have a word with him."

"Cool. Thanks. I appreciate that."

31: Mom's Plans

As he opened his second beer of the evening while fixing dinner, Pete continued to stew over the turndown he'd gotten from Stacey Russell when he'd asked her out for a date earlier in the week. She was nice about it, but said she had a rule about not dating men from the office, especially someone as senior in the company as Pete.

It's obvious she has the hots for him, always flaunting her tits at him. So, what's with the stupid rule? Fuck that shit. Dumb bitch—

The phone rang.

"Hi, Pete. It's your mother."

"Oh, hi Mom. How are you? What's up?"

"I thought I might catch you before you went out tonight, it being Friday and all."

"No plans tonight. Just staying home to watch the Yankees play the White Sox. What's new with you?"

"Well, I hadn't heard from you in a while and been wondering how things are going. How's work?"

"Great. Been really busy lately, putting in long days. I'm running the eastern sales team, but I guess you knew that already. We hired two new sales reps so I now have eight reporting to me, covering a lot of the territory. We've been landing a lot of new accounts lately, so my share of the commissions has gone up, too."

"That's wonderful, Pete. I'm so proud of you. I'm so glad to hear that you're doing well in your work."

"And how are you and Sam doing? All settled in now in Charlotte?"

"Well, we're getting there, slowly but surely. Jeez, I'm still unpacking boxes three weeks after the move. Since he doesn't have to travel so much in his new job, he's home for dinner most nights, and he's helping unpack, too. We go out for dinner a lot."

"And how do you like Charlotte? Different than Hamden?"

"I'll say. It's a lot different. I like it a lot. But, actually, the real reason I called was to tell you that Sam and I are getting married."

"No kidding. That's great, Mom. Congratulations. When?"

"Well, seeing as how it'll be second marriages for both of us, we're not going to make a big deal out of it. Just a small ceremony here next month, on August sixteenth. That's a Saturday. We're just inviting immediate family and a few friends. Of course, we want you there. Sam wants you to be his best man."

"That's really nice. I wouldn't miss it for the world. I'll make it a long weekend and take that Friday off. I'll get my ticket right away. Should be able to get to your place by early afternoon."

"That would be wonderful. Your sister will be coming, too."

"Terrific. I haven't seen Mary in at least a year. How's she doing?"

"Great. She seems to be settling into her new job in Los Angeles as secretary at a local TV station there. And, apparently, she has a pretty serious boyfriend, too. So that's nice. He's coming to the wedding with her. How about you? Are you still dating Maggie Haines? Maybe she could come, too?"

Pete sighed. "Well, we had a little argument a couple weeks ago. She's still mad and not talking to me. But I'm sure she'll come around. She always does. We'll see. I'll talk to her about it."

"I hope so Pete. Send her flowers. Apologize, even if it's not your fault. You deserve a good woman after all you've been through. Speaking of which, what's happened to Tracy and—"

"—I'd rather not talk about that, Mom."

"Um, okay. Uh, is everything else okay? How are your headaches?"

"About the same."

"Have you had any more black-outs?"

"Not recently," he sighed.

"You remember what your doctor told you, don't you?"

"Yes, Mom. I remember. But I don't have time to do meditation. I'm really busy."

"Are you taking your medications? Have you cut back on the drinking? You know, the doctor said that alcohol aggravates the headaches. And you can't mix alcohol with those medications."

"Yeah, Mom, I know."

"And I hope you're not still buying those little nip bottles. You know what they always say, Pete. The smaller the bottle, the bigger the problem."

"Yes, Mom. I'm only drinking beer. And I'm trying to cut back."

"Good. Work on it, Pete. It's important. And try the meditation, too.

Really. They say the effects of that kind of head injury can linger for years and that meditation helps reduce anxiety and depression, which are common with concussions."

"Like I said, I'm pretty busy and under a lot of pressure. But I'll try."

"Please do. Listen, I have to ring off. I've got to get back to fixing dinner. But I wanted to share our news with you."

"Well, congratulations again. And congratulate Sam for me, too."

"I will do that. Take care. I love you."

"I love you, too, Mom. Good bye."

Though he was glad to hear from his mother and to learn her big news, he found her constant nagging about meditation, his drinking and his old head injury annoying. He didn't see what the big deal was. Everyone drinks. And everyone gets headaches now and then. So what? He felt fine. And meditation is fucking tedious.

Turning his attention to the TV, he began flipping through the channels and found the Yankees pre-game show. They were in Chicago. The game wouldn't start for another forty-five minutes because of the time difference.

Pre-game shows bored him. He muted the TV, put the Rolling Stones' latest album, "Emotional Rescue," on the stereo, and cranked up the volume. Living alone in a house rather than his old apartment meant he could play music as loud as he wanted.

It also meant he could burp and fart as loudly and as often as he wished—which is exactly what he did just then, unloosing a thunderous beer fart.

"Oh, ho, ho! Impressive. Score that one a solid ten."

But then the stench hit. He grabbed a magazine off the coffee table and vigorously fanned the air of the pungent stink.

Sitting down on the couch to wait for his dinner to finish cooking, he looked at the magazine he'd just used to clear the air of his flatulence. It was the latest issue of Playboy, which had come in the mail two days earlier. Popping his third beer, he opened the magazine to the middle and unfolded the centerfold, holding it up in good light so he could see it clearly. He was duly impressed.

"Oh, wow. Nice jugs. Those would be a lot of fun to play with," he said aloud. After checking on his dinner in the oven, he went to the closet to mine his extensive collection of Playboys, particularly his favorite, which was on top of the pile and a bit dog-eared: August 1979, Dorothy Stratten, Playmate of the Month, now also featured in the June 1980 issue as Playmate of the Year, which was the next issue in his pile.

Dorothy is perfect in every way—with the most stunningly beautiful body, Pete thought. He studied her photos closely. Then he selected about a half-dozen more of his favorite past issues and stacked them on the coffee table for closer perusal.

Dorothy should be Playmate of All Time, not just Playmate of the Year, he thought, as he looked at her nude photos for the umpteenth time. He'd been obsessed with her from the first time he'd laid eyes on her photo spread the summer before. Pete spent a lot of time having fantasy sex with her. He'd even seen the films she'd been in, including "Skatetown USA." The movies were pretty dumb, he admitted to himself, and she'd only played bit parts. Pete didn't care. The films gave him a chance to see her move and to hear her voice, albeit briefly with few lines.

But with her latest film, "Galaxina," which had been released in June, she finally got the lead role, playing the title character, a voluptuous blonde android servant in the year 3008. He'd seen the movie three times. For the third viewing, however, Pete had had to drive all the way to Portchester the previous weekend because its one-weekend run in Stamford had ended.

After about ten minutes of scrutinizing Playboys and downing another beer, he was interrupted by the kitchen timer. Dinner was ready.

32: The Great Indoors

Saturday, July 12th

The classified ads in the local papers that Rick and Maggie had scanned the night before made it obvious that Wilton offered the best selection of houses in their price range.

They parked in Wilton town center, dominated by the Village Market where Rick had bagged groceries and stocked shelves part-time through most of high school. Next door was his mother's former shop, "The Great Indoors." He peered in the window and could see her former partner, Nancy Costello, at her desk. They popped in to say hello. Nancy jumped up and briskly crossed the office to greet Rick like a long-lost son, with a hug and a noisy kiss on the cheek, leaving bright red lipstick evidence.

"Rick Hewson! I haven't seen you since well, at least a year."

"Wonderful to see you, Nancy. Uh, Nancy, this is Maggie Haines, my fiancée," realizing as it came out of his mouth that it was the first time he'd ever said it. Maggie grinned, and nodded toward Nancy.

"Fiancée? Maggie, it's a real pleasure to meet you." And they shook hands. "So, when's the big day?"

"Actually, we just decided to get married last weekend. My parents don't even know yet. You're the first to know."

"Well, I'm honored to be first. Rick is a like a son to me and Ted— my husband. We've known Rick since he was a toddler."

"You guys will be at the top of our guest list," Rick added. "But for the time being, please don't mention this to anyone. No one else knows."

"My lips are sealed. So, what are you doing in Wilton?"

"Can you keep another secret? We're looking at houses."

"Terrific. What agent are you working with?"

"No one, yet. We're just sort of window shopping. Actually, today is our first day at it. We're trying to get a sense of what's out there."

"Well, good thing for you, it's a buyer's market. With the mortgage rates as high as they are, there's a lot of inventory out there."

They spent a bit more time catching up, updating her on Rick's job and some background on Maggie. After about ten minutes, he said, "Well, we should get going. You probably need to get back to work and we have houses to see. But it's great to see you."

"Thanks for dropping by. Don't be a stranger, Rick. Do let Ted and me take you guys out for dinner sometime soon. We must celebrate." She hugged him good-bye and shook Maggie's hand again.

There were other local shops around the center: deli, wine store, real estate offices, pizza parlor, and the like. And then there was Anderson Insurance, which had changed ownership and name, previously having been Hewson Insurance.

"This was my dad's business. We sold it to his partner."

"Rick, I'd never thought of your parents' estate until you mentioned it last night. Though it's giving you the leeway to share in the cost of the house, I feel sad about it, what that money really represents."

"I know. I said the same thing to Julie a few weeks ago, almost word for word. But what am I gonna do?"

"Yeah. Well, it is your parents' legacy to you and your sisters. I'm sure they would be happy to see that you're going to buy a house with it."

"Julie said the same thing."

"Well, we should get going. We have some territory to cover. Let's start on the north end of town on upper Nod Hill Road and work our way back south toward here."

Their drive-by tour was encouraging. Two houses they saw on Nod Hill Road were both perfect, with lots of acreage and historic charm. Both were selling in the low five-hundred thousand range. In this buyers' market, they might be able to negotiate a lower price, Maggie said.

They checked out more houses closer to town center. Soon, it was past noon, and both were hungry for lunch.

"How about a slice of pizza for lunch at Wilton Pizza? I used to work there in high school."

"There too? How many jobs did you have?"

"In the summers, I worked there on Friday and Saturday nights, and the Village Market during the day all week. Made a lot of money. I had to. I was trying to save enough money to get myself through college."

33: Phone Message

Sunday, July 13th

Maggie suggested they go out for a morning run together, before it got too hot. Though both ran separately on their own time, they had only run together once before. Rick ran three or four miles in good weather nearly every lunch hour at work on the track atop Hamilton's parking garage. Maggie usually ran first thing in the morning on a route to and around Rowayton along the water. The only regular exercise they engaged in together involved prolonged sex. Today, they would take her longer route of about five miles out and back to the Burnside Beach Club.

As they ran, they planned how they would separate her parents that evening so that Rick could speak with Tom alone. After returning to the apartment, Rick went into the bedroom to undress for showering.

Maggie spotted the blinking light on the answering machine. Pressing the playback button, she shuddered at the sound of Pete Conley's voice again. He'd obviously called the night before, while they were out at dinner.

"Maggie, we need to talk," he slurred. "I'm worried that you've lost focus on what's really important, hanging out with that leech—whoever the hell he is. He's after your money, that's for sure. You're smart enough to realize that. Call me. I love you. And I know you love me, too, despite what you say. Bye."

She felt physically ill at the sound of his voice, offended by his presumption that she loved him.

Rick came out of the bedroom with a towel around his waist. "Are you coming?" Seeing her face, "What's the matter?"

"Phone message from Pete." And she replayed it.

"What an asshole."

"There isn't much we can do about it," and shrugged.

"This guy needs to get a life. Maggie, when I was talking to Bill Friday night, I told him what Pete has been doing. He offered to talk to Pete. Tell him that we're engaged and suggest he just get on with his life—"

"—You told Bill we're engaged?"

"Well, yeah. I wanted to let him know early. I asked him to be my best man. I also asked him to keep it to himself."

"Okay. So, uh, so he's offering to talk to Pete? Are you sure that's a good idea? It might get rid of him. But then again, it could backfire."

"Exactly my thinking."

"It's risky. Pete can be so volatile and unpredictable."

"Here's another idea. Suppose you called Pete. Not really to talk to him but to leave a message on his answering machine when you know he's not going to be home. That way, you could tell him yourself but not have to have a conversation with him about it."

"Hmm. Yeah, that's a possibility. Let's think about it."

They showered, ate breakfast, and then left for more house-hunting. A couple of neighborhoods in Westport, where they went first, looked promising. Then they popped over to Darien, which was mostly out of their price range for the houses they liked, as they'd initially suspected.

Expected by five-thirty for dinner, it was well past four when they headed back to Norwalk to get ready for the evening.

34: Breaking the News

Walking into the house, Maggie carried the dessert pastries they'd picked up earlier that afternoon in Darien. Rick had the wine and a bag of fresh ears of corn they'd bought at Fairty's farm stand in New Canaan on the way over.

"*Mom? Dad?*"

"In here, kids," Louise called from the kitchen.

They found her at the sink washing lettuce in the salad spinner. She turned to them with a big smile.

Maggie handed her the bag of corn while giving her a kiss on the cheek. "From Fairty's," she said. "It's their first harvest of the season, Mrs. Fairty told me."

"Oh, excellent. Thanks. I love Mrs. Fairty. She's is such a nice lady. You know, I still use her pumpkin pie recipe, which she gave me when we first moved here, and I was a new mother. Her secret is using butternut squash rather than pumpkin. Anyway, they have the best corn. It's a treat to have corn grown right here in New Canaan, isn't it?" as she took the bag. "So, to what do we owe the visit?" looking at them with an inquisitive grin and slight tilt to her head.

"We just want to spend the evening with you guys."

"Of course, dear," sounding unconvinced.

"Mom, where's Dad?"

"Out on the patio, getting the barbecue ready. We're having flank steak. I hope that wine you brought is red."

"It is," Rick said, as he put it on the kitchen counter.

Maggie nudged him. "Rick, why don't you go say hi to Dad while I stay here and help Mom get dinner ready."

"I'm fine Maggie. I don't need any help."

"Yes, you do. Someone needs to shuck the corn."

"Oh, and Rick, please ask Tom to light the charcoal. I was holding off until you guys got here." Rick nodded as he left the room.

Maggie turned back to her mother who was grinning at her like the

Cheshire Cat.

"What? Why are you looking at me like that, Mom?"

"What you are two up to?"

"Like I said. We just wanted to have dinner with you guys."

"Sure. Well, you go ahead and start shucking the corn then."

Maggie was so eager to share their news, it felt like she was about to pop. But she had to give Rick time to tell her father. Maybe another couple minutes. She stalled as she shucked the corn. Louise continued preparing the salad, stealing occasional grins at her. As she'd finished with four ears, Maggie figured enough time had elapsed.

"Mom, can I ask you a question?"

"Sure, honey."

"When you and Dad decided to get married, how did you break the news to your parents?"

"*I knew it! I knew it! You two are engaged!*"

"Actually, yes, we are. Rick asked me to marry him last Sunday when we were hiking in Pound Ridge." Louise squealed loudly and ran to hug her.

"*That's wonderful!* Oh, my God, I'm so excited. Let's go tell your father," and she grabbed Maggie's hand to lead her out to the patio."

"Well, I suspect Rick has already done that."

35: Man-To-Man

Rick found Tom on the patio loading charcoal into the barbecue.

"Hi Rick. How're you doing?" shaking his hand.

"Great, Tom. How'd the tournament go? Did you win?"

"Nope. But I still had a good time. I shot an eighty-one, one stroke under my handicap, which is excellent for me."

"I've never played Burnside. I hear that the course is pretty tough."

"It is. Even though I play it at least once a week, I still struggle. The rough is pretty deep, so you're always in trouble if your tee shot gets off the fairway. I'll have to take you out for a round. Are you up for it?"

"I'd really like that, but I don't have any clubs. Maybe I could rent a set at the pro shop. But, yeah. Sure."

"I have a back-up set you could use."

"Oh, that'd be great. Thanks." Rick worried that he was spending too much time on small talk or he'd get out of synch with Maggie. It was time to cut to the chase. He paused to steel his courage. As he did so, his face took on a serious demeanor reflecting his determination. "Tom, I need to ask you something."

"Sure. What's on your mind?" Tom's face shifted to reflect Rick's.

"This may seem old-fashioned, but I'd like to ask if you would—"

—Louise exclaimed loudly in the kitchen.

"What's that all about?" Tom asked, alarmed.

Rick chuckled. "Well, I'd guess that Maggie just told Louise that I'd asked her to marry me, which is what I was about to talk to you about." Tom's jaw dropped. Rick looked him in the eye. "So, Tom, would you grant me your daughter's hand in marriage?"

Before Tom could respond, Louise had rushed out to the patio, holding Maggie's hand.

"Tom! Did you hear?"

"Yes. Rick was just asking me for Maggie's hand in marriage."

"*He was?*"

"So, Tom, what's your answer?"

He laughed loudly, grinning widely. "Well I'll be. I never expected to be asked that question. But yes. Yes. Of course. *Yes!* This is great!" And he shook Rick's hand enthusiastically, as Louise hugged Maggie for the third time. "Louise and I would be honored to have you as our son-in-law."

Then he stepped over to give Maggie a hug. Louise embraced Rick.

"This is all so sudden," Louise said.

"Well, Maggie told me that wonderful story about you two getting married so soon, too. Frankly, it was rather inspirational. By the way, I was just curious and looked up the date. Do you realize that August thirtieth this year is a Saturday, just as it was in 1952 on your wedding day?"

Tom and Louise exchanged glances. "What are you suggesting Rick?" Louise asked, a grin starting to form on her lips.

"Well, I was thinking, how about if we celebrate your twenty-eighth anniversary by holding our wedding on August thirtieth?"

Maggie put both hands to her mouth and gasped. "Oh, Rick, what a fantastic idea!"

"But we won't have enough time to plan," Louise said.

"Yeah. What's the rush?" Tom asked.

"Well, we have some other news," Maggie added.

"You're pregnant?" Louise exclaimed. Both Maggie and Rick reddened.

"Mom! *Really*. No. I am *not* pregnant. Rick and I are house-hunting and we thought it would be better if we're moving in together, that we be married."

"My, my, aren't we old-fashioned," Tom said with a grin. "First Rick asks me for your hand in marriage and now you're saying you don't want to live in sin?"

"Very funny, Dad. But really. We're serious. Sure, we could postpone the wedding. But why wait? Think about it."

The four of them were quiet for a few moments.

"I've long thought of your wedding," Louise finally said. "Probably since you were four and were the flower girl in my cousin Teresa's wedding. Had all sorts of plans"

"We could have the ceremony at the First Congregational," Maggie said, "and then hold the reception here, around the patio. Have it catered. Minimize the hassle."

Louise was quiet for a few more moments. "You know, I really love your idea, Rick. It's so sweet. It shoots the rest of my summer to hell, but this has got to take priority. Yes, I think we can do it. Any reason why not, Tom?" He shrugged. "Then let's do it," she said, beaming.

"I'm going to get that bottle of Champagne." Tom said. "It's been sitting in the fridge for a long time. Maybe just for this occasion."

Louise turned to Maggie and Rick, who were holding hands, both smiling broadly. She grabbed them both for another hug. As she pulled away, she held them each by the shoulder and regarded them in turn with a big smile. All three were tearing up. "This is so wonderful. I'm so thrilled for you both."

Later, as they finished dinner, Maggie said, "Dad, as I mentioned, we want to buy a house." He nodded.

"We've spent most of the weekend sort of window shopping for houses," Rick said. "We think Wilton offers the best choice of houses for what we're looking for, in our price range."

"Whoa. Hold on kids." Tom exclaimed. "Price range? What are you thinking your range is, and how did you come up with a number?"

"Dad, here's our thinking. We know Grandpa's trust is only for special purposes, like college tuition and such. But isn't buying a house that kind of purpose?"

"Yes, I'd say so. Like I've always told you and Charley, real estate is the best investment."

"But Rick is determined to share the cost of home ownership, fifty-fifty, that I not just buy a house outright, which I could probably do by myself"

"And I have some money, too," Rick added. "I'm entitled to a one-third share of my parents' estate. I'm going to talk to my Uncle Frank. He's the executor. He told my sister a few weeks ago that she could withdraw as much as three-hundred thousand. She wants to buy a house in the Denver area. So I assume I could withdraw that much, too. Double that and we could spend as much as six-hundred thousand. Anyway, I'll verify that with him. Maybe we won't even need a mortgage at all."

"Great," Tom said. "That all sounds good to me. And you're right. You can get a lot of house for that kind of money. Let's talk about this again after you've spoken to your uncle. We'll make it work."

36: Emergency Call

Thursday, July 17th

Walking out of her office front door at six o'clock, lost in her thoughts with her head down, Maggie didn't notice Pete Conley leaning on the hood of his Camaro, parked up front, near the door. He was the furthest thing from her mind, until she heard that familiar, dreaded voice.

"Hi Maggie. How ya' doin'?" he said, as he stepped in front of her.

She froze in her tracks a couple steps from him.

"What are *you* doing here?"

"Just came by to talk. You've been avoiding my calls and hanging up when I do get through. I left you another phone message Saturday night and you haven't called me back. Maggie, we *really* do need to talk. So, I thought I'd just drop by and catch you after work."

He reached into the pocket of his sports coat, pulled out a small square light blue box. "I have a little gift for you," and thrust it toward her.

"I want you to have this. Please accept it as my apology for my bad behavior at the party."

She batted it away and it fell to the sidewalk.

"There is nothing to talk about. *Stop buying me things! Leave me alone!*"

"You aren't being very lady-like, Maggie." He took a couple of quick steps toward her and grabbed her wrist. "We need to talk. I mean it," bending down to look into her eyes, continuing to hold her wrist firmly. "I'm worried about you. You're being taken for a fool by a fraud."

"*Let go of me!*" she shouted, wrenching her arm free. "This is private property. Leave right now, or I'll call the police."

She glanced around the area for anyone else who might help her. But she was alone there with Pete.

"*No.* Not until you talk to me. Please. I think you've forgotten how much we mean to each other, how much I care for you and you care for me. We've gotten through these rough patches in the past and—"

She didn't stay to let him finish. Turning and dashing back into the building, she ran up the stairs two steps at a time back into her office, slamming and locking the door behind her. Molly was at her usual station at the reception desk, alarmed to see Maggie rush back in noisily and lock the door, out of breath, her face flushed.

"*What's the matter?*"

"Molly! Quick! Dial nine-one-one and hand me the phone."

"Westport Police. This call is being recorded. What is your emergency?"

"Would you please send an officer to eight-ninety-two Post Road? *Right away?* There's a man harassing me, preventing me from leaving."

"Has he threatened you?"

"He grabbed me, but I got away, ran inside and locked the door before calling you."

"We'll send an officer right over. Please hold." He was off the line briefly.

"Okay, an officer is on his way. He should be there in less than a minute. May I have your name, please?"

"Margaret Haines. I work here at Williams Advertising and I was trying to go home for the day when he accosted me and prevented me from leaving. Please tell the officer to go to the main entrance, on the Post Road side of the building. The man you're looking for is leaning on his car in the parking lot near the front door. It's a blue Camaro Z28. His name is Pete Conley."

There was a pause on the line. She could hear him relaying the information on the radio.

"Okay, ma'am. I've passed along your information along to the officer. Ma'am, please stay on the line until he arrives."

Molly had gone to the window. Maggie stretched the phone cord to stand next to her and looked out onto the parking lot, just in time to see the Camaro pulling out quickly onto Post Road, tires squealing loudly.

"He just left. What should I do?"

"Speak to the officer when he arrives and tell him what happened."

"Okay. Thank you," and hung up.

Molly's mouth was agape. "What did Pete do?"

"He grabbed me roughly by the wrist. Said he wanted to talk to me. I shook free and didn't give him the chance. He claims I still love him—*as if I ever did.*"

When they saw the officer roar into the parking lot with lights and siren, Maggie ran down and told him what Pete had done and said just minutes before in the lot. She also told him about the harassing phone calls, as well as how he had followed Rick to the shop two weeks before.

After taking down her information, the officer shook his head. "Miss Haines, it's none of my business, but if I were you, I'd take out a restraining order against this gentleman."

Maggie drove home, rattled by the cruel irony, mere days after she and Rick had set their wedding date. How much worse would this get? Had Pete lost his mind? This didn't make any sense. He'd never acted like this before. Why wouldn't he just leave them alone and move on with his life?

When she got home, she could hear Rick in the bedroom. Dropping her briefcase and purse on the couch, she ran to him, wrapped her arms around him. She held him tightly and started sobbing into his shirt.

"*What's the matter, Maggie?*"

She told him haltingly through sobs and tears.

"*Damn it.* That cop is right. This stalking has got to end. He's out of control. He sure seemed ready for a fight when he confronted me. I think a restraining order is a good idea. Better to be safe than sorry. Uh, have you given any further thought about having Bill talk to Pete? Do you think it might make a difference?"

She pulled away from him, wiping at her tears.

"No, I don't think so. You should have seen him. I honestly think he's lost his mind. I'm pretty sure he was sober, yet he seemed crazy. He just isn't making sense. I've never seen him like this. I don't think talking reason to him is going to make one bit of difference. In fact, I think it would only make him a worse, more desperate."

37: Do Me a Favor

Wednesday, July 23th

Pete worked late again Wednesday night, but opted for dinner at home—along with a few cans of beers and TV. The Yankees were hosting the Milwaukee Brewers, and the game would start shortly. He muted the pre-game show and turned his attention to dinner and beer.

Starting on a six-pack of sixteen-ounce Schaefer talls as his dinner of leftovers heated in the oven, he thumbed through his Playboy collection. As he settled onto his couch, he noticed the light blinking on his answering machine across the room and got up to check. He was surprised to hear Maggie's voice.

"Hello… Uh, hi Pete. It's me, Maggie. It's Wednesday morning. I'm leaving you a message because I don't want to have a conservation with you. But I do want you to understand me clearly. I do *not* appreciate your behavior lately, the way you talked to me and treated me at the party. The confrontations at the garage and outside my office. The repeated phone calls to my office, and all the nasty, drunken messages on my home answering machine. Our relationship has become a string of unpleasant experiences for me, pretty much since last fall. I should never have gotten back together with you in January and definitely not again in April. It's my fault, it's my mistake and I regret it. It's time for us both to move on with our lives… This morning I mailed you a package. It contains the pearl necklace and diamond earrings you gave me. Those gifts were merely ways for you to ease your conscience after you hit me those two times. I don't want them. They remind me of you and your abuse. I don't want to be friends with you anymore. I don't want you in my life anymore… You should know that I'm engaged to be married. So, um, good bye." And the machine beeped the message's end.

"*What? What did she say?*" he said aloud.

He replayed the message to be sure he'd heard it right.

"Maggie is getting married?" he said aloud. "To that little turd? *No!* She can't do that."

The more he thought about it, the less he believed it and the angrier he got. He listened to the message a third and then a fourth time, trying to catch the tone of her voice, to figure out whether she was serious. She sounded cold and distant, like she was talking to a stranger, as though reading from a prepared script. She didn't sound like the Maggie he knew.

He didn't believe her. She was trying to throw him off with a lie. She'd never marry that guy. They just met a few weeks ago. Or maybe he told her to call him and say that, just to get rid of him. That asshole was probably coaching her, and they rehearsed this together. How could she make such a hasty decision? She hardly knows him. She doesn't see what he's up to.

"Dammit! What the hell is going on? *Fuck!*" he shouted. "That shithead is messing with her head. I've got to get him away from her."

He crushed his empty beer can with one hand, and went to the refrigerator for a second one, tossing the flattened empty in the trash as he thought through Maggie's phone message.

He resolved to get that little prick out of the picture. He's got her confused, and she doesn't realize what he's up to. All he wants is her money. Why can't she see that? And now she wants to marry him? It's time to get rid of that asshole. Got to scare him off. But how?

After several swigs of beer and a couple minutes considering options, Pete hit on it.

A gun. That's it. He'd catch up with that scrawny little butt wipe and scare him off with a gun. First, he'd kick his ass. Then make him think he's going to use the gun on him. Give him an ultimatum. Get the fuck out, or else. "That'll scare the piss out of him," he said aloud, chuckling to himself.

Pete's old friend from Hamden, Dan Wilson, knew his way around guns. Yeah, Dan could get him a gun.

Dan answered on the first ring. "Hey Danny boy. It's me. Pete. Pete Conley. How ya doin'?"

"Pete. You old son of a bitch. How the hell are you? Long time no see. What's up?"

They'd met in Hamden as fifth graders playing youth hockey, shortly after Pete's father was killed in a truck accident in Indiana. They'd hung out during their high school summers when they'd go looking for fun together, when Pete lived with his mother during summer breaks from Hotchkiss. He hadn't seen much of Dan lately. Figuring Maggie wouldn't care for him, he'd never bothered to introduce them.

"Say, buddy, wondering if you could do me a favor."

"Happy to try. What is it?"

"I need a hand gun. Nothing fancy. Something simple. And small."

"Can do, but not tonight. I'm going out in a while. I have some business to take care of."

"That's fine. Not a huge rush, but if I could get it this weekend, that'd be great."

"Saturday night okay?"

"Yeah. Perfect."

"How much you willing to spend?"

"A couple hundred. Three bills, maybe."

"No problem. I have a reliable source. Can you meet me Saturday night at the Downtowner in Bridgeport? Say, seven-thirty? Remember the place?"

"Absolutely. We used to hang out there quite a lot. I haven't been there since last time I saw you. When was that, a year ago?"

"Yeah. It was June last year. We went there after my mom's funeral. You know, I really appreciated you coming for that. And she would have, too. Mom always liked you. You were a hard-working student and she admired you for that. She thought maybe you'd rub off on me," and he chuckled. "That's a laugh. More like it was the other way around."

"Yeah, well, your mom was a nice lady. Easy to talk to. I liked her a lot. I miss her."

"How's your mom doing? I haven't seen her since the funeral either."

"She's doing well. Got herself a boyfriend. They moved to North Carolina a month ago. The guy makes pretty good money, so Mom doesn't have to work anymore. And she told me a couple weeks ago that they're getting married next month."

"Really? That's great news. Tell her congratulations for me. She's a good lady. I know she had a tough go of it after your dad was killed. It's nice to know that she's got herself a good man."

"Will do. Anyway, I really appreciate this, Dan. Thanks a million. I'll see you Saturday."

38: Cold Beer, Hot Waitresses

Saturday, July 26th

The sun was still out when Pete walked into the darkened Downtowner bar about five minutes early. He had to give his eyes a moment to adjust. Before he could spot him, Dan called his name from the far corner booth.

They shook hands and Pete sat down across from him. From the get-go in their youth hockey days, Dan had developed a reputation on the rink as an enforcer, and taught Pete the subtleties of playing dirty, practiced in the fine art of a deftly executed butt end to the ribs or a sharp elbow to the jaw when the ref wasn't looking.

In middle school, Pete had distinguished himself on the ice, nimble and fast on his skates, in addition to his nefarious moves. When Hotchkiss was handing out scholarships to promising disadvantaged urban kids, he filled their need for a strong forward, which assured the scholarship—since his grades were pretty good and he had strong letters of recommendation from his middle school principal and guidance counselor.

Midway through his sophomore year, Pete became one of the varsity's starting forwards. They called him "The Sniper" for his knack for blasting out of the corners with the puck. He was also Hotchkiss' leading scorer his two final years there, setting several school records that still stood.

Meanwhile, while neglecting his studies, Dan was excelling as a starter on Hamden High School's hockey team, the state's perennial public-school powerhouse. Like Pete, Dan played aggressively at forward on the varsity squad beginning his sophomore year.

He was a member of Hamden's state championship teams in 1970 when they pounded New Canaan, seven to zero in the final, and in 1971 when they beat Amity, four to one. His senior year in 1972, however, New Canaan edged them, two to one, for the state title.

After high school, while Pete headed across town to Quinnipiac College to play hockey on an athletic scholarship, Dan's hockey days were over. Instead, he knocked around between short-term menial jobs. He also hooked up with some questionable characters in New Haven and Bridgeport, eventually landing himself in a state minimum security prison where he served eighteen months of a three-year sentence for larceny and receiving stolen property.

Pete noticed that Dan had gained some weight since he'd last seen him. But then, so had Pete, he admitted silently to himself. Both had a fondness for beer, whiskey, and bar food.

The smiling waitress arrived before they could even look for her.

"Hi, guys. My name is Angela. I'll be your waitress tonight."

"I'm Pete and I'll be your customer tonight," he said smiling widely.

She laughed. "Okay, Pete, what can I get for you?"

"I'll have a Michelob draught, Angela," Pete said, still grinning.

She nodded and continued smiling.

"A Michelob sounds good to me, too," Dan added.

"Do you guys want something to eat? Pizza? Burgers? Would you like a menu?"

"Yeah, that sounds good. I haven't had dinner yet. Wanna split a pizza, Dan? My treat."

"Sure. A pizza works for me. Thanks."

"A large pepperoni?" Dan nodded.

As though to read her name badge, Pete checked out Angela's low-cut t-shirt and all that was revealed. "Got it, Angela?" he asked, looking at her name badge.

"Got it," she grinned, as she scribbled the order on her pad. "About fifteen minutes?" Pete nodded and gave her a sideways smile, but she was looking at Dan.

As she walked away, they both checked out her rear end. "*Nice ass,*" Pete said. "Plus, she's got a sweet pair of tits. I like that low-cut tee-shirt. Leaves very little to the imagination. I'd do her. I haven't been to the Downtowner since I was here with you last year. The waitresses are a lot hotter than I remember."

"Yeah. New owner as of last fall. He's decided to improve the image of this dump, starting with the waitresses, recruiting some real babes. I think he's done a pretty good job so far. They ought to hang a sign out front that says, *Cold beer, hot waitresses,*" and laughed.

"I met Angela last time I was here," Dan added. "She was pretty flirty. I almost asked her out, but I was pretty shit-faced, so I didn't. Figured she'd take it as a beer goggles invitation and turn me down," and he laughed at the recollection.

"Maybe you should ask her tonight. I noticed her making eyes at you. She probably remembered you."

"Yeah, maybe I will. Anyway, sounds like you've done all right for yourself. Making good money peddling chemicals?"

"Yeah. I draw a straight salary as eastern regional sales manager that's nothing to sneeze at, plus I get a cut of my sales team's commissions. Last year, I netted nearly a hundred-fifty thou. I go to Boca every year for our national sales conference. Bought myself a new Z28 last December. Fully loaded."

"Nice."

Angela returned with their beers. Dan winked at her. She grinned at him again and left. "What're you doing with all that money?" Dan asked. "Gettin' any pussy?"

"Nah. A hot chick started as a secretary in my office a few weeks ago. Incredible rack. She comes to the office every day showing some delicious cleavage. I'd love to bury my face in those tits. So, I asked her out. But she said she has a rule against dating guys in the office. I mean, *what the fuck*. She flaunts it but doesn't use it? What the hell is that all about?"

Dan shrugged. "Some chicks are cock teasers. They like to give guys blue balls," and he laughed again. "I guess it gives them a cheap thrill."

"Yeah, well, you're probably right. But on top of that, my girl broke up with me."

"Really? Didn't know you had a girlfriend. When was that? How long you been seein' her?"

"Uh, we met last summer. Actually, it was the weekend after your mom's funeral. She's a sweet thing. Terrific body—a real looker. Pretty good in bed, too—that is, when she's in the mood."

"What do you mean?"

"Well, she doesn't exactly fuck like a rabbit. It's like I have to talk her into it."

"She's frigid?"

"Well, yeah, I guess you could say that. But, get this. She's loaded. Or at least, her family is. New Canaan kind of dough. Big bucks. And don't think that doesn't figure into my thinking," he said, grinning.

"*New Canaan?* I hate New Canaan. Those cocksuckers ruined my last year of hockey, squeaking out that state championship with a cheap late goal, a hot freshman goalie, and a lotta help from the refs. Those fuckin' refs were lucky we didn't kick their asses in the parking lot after the game."

"Oh yeah, I remember that. I was at that game. But Maggie—that's her name—she didn't go to New Canaan High School. She went to an all-girls prep school."

"So, what's the problem?"

"Well, shit. We argue a lot. She's a real perfectionist. Always trying to fix me, and it gets on my nerves."

"Fix *you*? That's funny," Dan said, guffawing. "That'll be the day," and took a gulp of beer. Dan pulled out a pack of Camels, shook one loose, and offered it across the table to Pete.

"No. Thanks. I'm trying to quit. Maggie's been on my case. She hates it that I smoke. Doesn't even want to smell it on me."

"Man, you are pussy-whipped," as he lit the Camel for himself.

"Yeah, well, whatever. Anyway, whenever we had an argument in the past, we always got back together. And we had a big one a few weeks ago. But she's not accepting my apologies this time around. Won't even take my calls. Not even the dozen roses I sent to her office last month did the trick. I went to her apartment and then to her office. She just won't talk to me. I think it's because she's got herself a new boyfriend. The guy's a pansy ass. I came close to kicking his butt three weeks ago, but there were too many witnesses. I gotta get him out of the picture."

Dan scanned the room quickly and lowered his voice. "So, that's why you want this gun? You're gonna knock the guy off, are ya'?"

"Yeah, no, probably not. But I can't say the idea didn't cross my mind. Mostly I just want to scare the piss out of him. First, I'll kick his ass and then aim the gun at him or fire a shot in his general direction to get his attention. Tell him to get lost—or else."

"Gotcha. Well, I have the perfect gun for you. In fact, I can give you a choice of two."

"Great. What are they?"

"One is a Beretta 92FS. Made in Italy. It'll take ten rounds." Dan blew a smoke ring across the table over Pete's shoulder. "The other one is a Swiss-made SIG P239. She's a beauty. Carries eight rounds."

Dan rattled on about the guns' features and merits. Pete faked understanding the finer details Dan was citing, as he knew next to nothing about guns.

"And are they small enough I can easily conceal them?"

"Damn straight. Both are pretty compact. You just tuck it under your waist band in the back. That's what I do with mine. In fact, I'm carrying my trusty Smith & Wesson right now."

"You got the guns with you now?"

"Yeah. They're outside in my car. We can go out into the parking lot when we're done here. Which one do you want?"

Pete shrugged. "I dunno. Which do one do you think is best?"

"They're both great guns. Maybe you should take 'em both."

"Hmmm. Not a bad idea. How much?"

"I was going to sell you either one for one-sixty. But since you said you're willing to go as high as three, I can let you have them both for that."

"Do you have ammo for them?"

"Yeah, a couple of boxes of bullets for each, enough to get you started. I'd suggest you go somewhere remote to test fire them a few times. Get a feel for them. They're each gonna handle a little differently."

"Cool. You got yourself a deal." Pete took out his wallet and peeled off two fifties and ten twenties and handed them to Dan. As they were swallowing the last of their beers, Angela brought the pizza, and they ordered another round of Michelobs.

After nearly an hour of catching up, retelling old stories, needling each other, and eating and drinking, they'd polished off the pizza and three pints of beer apiece. Pete pinned three twenties under his empty beer glass and they exited to the parking lot to finish their business.

39: Sunday Evening Call

Sunday, July 27th

As Maggie fixed dinner, Rick poured two glasses of wine. They were talking about the upcoming week when Maggie noticed the blinking light on the answering machine.

She groaned. "Probably Pete again," she said aloud. "He probably called this morning while we were out running errands."

"Hi Maggie, it's Pete." He was speaking quietly and calmly. He sounded the way Maggie remembered him in their better days.

"Listen, Maggie. I'm very sorry for all the rough language lately. I know I haven't been very pleasant. In fact, I've kinda been a jerk. I realize that. But I hope you can see that it's only because I'm so frustrated. You're not giving me a chance to explain myself and apologize properly. I love you, and I *know* you love me. You don't have to lie to me. I know you're not really getting married. That guy you're seeing doesn't really care about you. He's a phony. It's obvious to me. He's messing with your head. You've *got* to realize that. Please call me as soon as you get this message. We really need to talk. I love you, babe. Bye."

"Did you hear that?" as she turned to look at him.

"So, you called him?"

She nodded shallowly and looked down and spoke quietly. "Yeah. I called his home phone Wednesday morning from my office to make sure I wouldn't have to talk to him. Like you and I talked about."

Rick nodded. "Well, now we're seeing the result. I think we need that restraining order, right away—and an unlisted phone number."

40: Aspiring Marine Biologist

Sunday, August 3rd

They'd arranged to meet Sarah, Rick's younger sister, for dinner in New London on Sunday night on their way back from Boston, where they'd visited Amanda and her boyfriend, Jeff, for a weekend of music and museums.

Rick and Maggie left Boston in the late afternoon, arriving in New London in time to meet Sarah at the Chowder House Restaurant at six. Rick embraced her and kissed her forehead before introducing Maggie.

"Rick has told me so much about you." Maggie said, giving her a hug.

"You too. I'm so glad to meet you finally. Rick has been raving about you and—"

"—Miss Hewson? Your table is ready. We've put you outside on the deck. Is that all right?" Sarah smiled and nodded. The hostess walked them to the deck outside overlooking the Thames River and a wide view of the lighthouse and the mouth of the river where it flowed into Long Island Sound.

It was a pleasant evening, with comfortable temperatures and a few scattered clouds in the east that were picking up the light from the low sun in the west, turning them a soft red-orange. The waiter arrived as they sat, read the evening's specials and took their drink orders.

As they studied the menu and made small talk, the waiter arrived with drinks. When he left, Maggie turned again to Sarah. "In addition to us spending every free moment together, I've been immersed in wedding planning the past few weekends. I'm thrilled that you and Julie are going to be my bridesmaids. I hope you got the information about your dress."

"Yeah. I'm all set. Thanks."

"So, Rick has told me you're doing really well at UConn. You'll be a senior? A biology major, right? Tell me about your studies, and what you hope to do after graduation."

"Whoa. A lot of parental type questions. I'm sure you know that Rick is now my surrogate father, at least he thinks so. Always nagging me about my grades. That sort of thing." She gave him a fake scowl. He grinned back.

"The truth is, she has a near-perfect GPA. Doesn't need a big brother to nag her to study hard," he said.

"Yeah, I'm majoring in biology. I really enjoy it and seem to have a knack for it. What will I do with it after graduation next spring? No idea. But I do like working this summer at the Mystic Aquarium. So maybe I'll get a master's in marine biology at Woods Hole. But I don't know for sure yet."

The waiter returned to take their dinner orders. After he left, Sarah raised her glass to toast her brother and Maggie. "Cheers. Here's to the two love birds, Mr. and Mrs. Rick Hewson."

After the toast and further small talk, Maggie paused before speaking to Sarah. "I was really sorry to learn from Rick about the sudden loss of your parents. I know it was devastating for Rick. But it must have been especially hard for you, being the youngest and still in high school."

Sarah sipped her drink and glanced at Rick before answering. "Well, yeah," she said quietly, turning back toward Maggie. "It really was. I was finishing my junior year at Wilton High. I'd been into a lot of school stuff, sports and clubs. That sort of stuff. I gave it all up my senior year and withdrew. Just buried myself in my books and got ready to go to college."

"That was a tough time for all three of us," Rick added. "But especially for you. Aunt Sally and Uncle Frank were super. They really helped us deal with it and did so much for us."

"I hope you don't mind me bringing this up," Maggie added.

"No... No, that's okay," She said quietly. "I know it was more than four years ago, but the pain and reality of losing Mom and Dad is still a big part of who I am, who we are. And you're going to be a member of our family, so it's going to be part of your life, too. You know, there were many nights that summer where I'd keep Julie or Rick up talking far too late. I just needed to talk about everything—and nothing at all. Or I needed them to make me laugh, or someone to cry with."

She paused and looked down at her hands. "Thank God for Sally and Frank. Sally is a lot like Mom in so many ways. I've heard her repeat stories that Mom used to tell. Even their voices are similar. It's kind of spooky, actually. Sometimes, if she talked to me from another room, I'd think I was hearing Mom. But nice as that is, Sally isn't Mom. And Frank is not Dad."

"I cannot imagine what that must have been like. I wouldn't know what to do if I lost my parents so suddenly like that. You've gotten yourself through UConn and worked so hard to support yourself through your grieving.

You have a lot to be proud of—even as you continue to grieve."

Sarah arched her eyebrows and looked at Maggie again. "I don't think I'm still grieving. I mean, it's been more than four years."

Maggie hesitated. "Well, we all grieve in our own way and at our own pace, but I believe we will always mourn the loved ones we've lost, for as long we ourselves live."

Sarah looked down at the table again, thinking, and then returned her gaze to Maggie. She spoke slowly, hesitantly, with a small quaver in her voice. "I know what you say is a generalization about grief and you're probably right. I've just never thought of it that way. I've been focused on moving on—sort of like getting over it, I guess."

She paused again. "But yes, you're right, I do think of Mom and Dad a lot. I, uh, um—" She lost her voice momentarily. Clearing her throat, she resumed, speaking deliberately, looking off into the distance at Long Island Sound over Maggie's right shoulder. "I wonder what they would say about this or that, how they would react to something I said or did. I've never thought of that as grieving. Maybe it is grief when I can't shake that urge to share things with them."

She glanced at Rick and then looked back at Maggie again. "There have been so many times that I've wished they were here to give me advice when I'm having a hard time. Or to be here so I could share my little victories with them. Those are the toughest times, when I feel so alone. It's an ache, an emptiness in the pit of my stomach, and sometimes I find myself almost gasping for breath, like a panic attack. But I've gotten a lot of love and support from Rick and Julie. And Aunt Sally and Uncle Frank, too. And that's helped me get through those painful moments, just knowing they are there for me." She gave Rick a little smile, reached out, and touched his hand.

They were all silent for a few moments before Maggie spoke softly. "You've lost your parents, but your love for them lives on. You live now for both you and them. My Grandma Margaret died two years ago. I was given her name and was very close to her as I grew up. I visited her often in Philadelphia and at their summer place on Cape May. She talked with me about things I couldn't easily talk with my parents about. I treasure her memory and feel like a part of me is living her life every day. What she would do or what she would say, what advice she would give me, and how she would react to something I told her."

Maggie smiled. "I know what made her laugh out loud. And I can still hear her laughter. I think often of her wisdom. She knew when it was best to listen and stay silent. And she knew when it was time to offer advice that I'd listen to—when I was a know-it-all teenager. I've asked myself several times recently, what would Grandma Margaret think of Rick?" and she turned to Rick, smiled, and held his hand.

"I'm sure she would approve enthusiastically. Thinking that way helps me keep her spirit alive—alive in me. It keeps me honest with myself. Sometimes, I talk quietly to her about Rick, about the love and trust we share, and the future we have ahead of us together. I feel like she knows Rick. I often sense her spirit and love surrounding Rick and me."

Maggie smiled again at Rick and paused before resuming. "I owe her that much. But I owe it to myself as well, always to cherish what my grandmother gave me in emotional strength. To remember her and the love she gave so freely. Her memory brings me strength and enriches the love I share with Rick."

Sarah looked at her for a few moments. "I've never really thought about it that way. But I think you're right. And I... And I really appreciate you sharing that." She paused again and looked into Maggie's eyes, her own eyes misty, blinking. "I really mean it."

"Sarah, I know we've only just met, but we're going to be family. You, me, Rick, Julie, my brother Charley, and my parents. You're not alone. You have us, a much larger family in addition to Sally and Frank. You can reach out to us anytime for support and encouragement."

She paused a moment. "My biggest regret will always be that I never had the chance to meet your mom and dad. That's going to be a real hole in my life with Rick. But I will come to know them through you, Rick and Julie. We will keep their memory alive, together, in ourselves and among ourselves, and in the love we all share."

Sarah put her hand lightly on Maggie's and smiled. Maggie gently put her hand atop Sarah's, smiling back at her.

Sensing the subject at its conclusion, Rick craned his neck, looking for the waiter, who noticed Rick looking for him and raised a single index finger. Dinner arrived a minute later.

They lingered over it for a while, savoring their fresh seafood entrées while continuing their talk about Rick and Sarah's parents, sharing stories about them with Maggie so that she might better appreciate who they were, laughing at retold family tales and foibles.

After dropping Sarah off at her place, they got on the Connecticut Turnpike to head home. It would be a long drive back to Norwalk—nearly two hours.

As they hit cruising speed, Rick put his hand on Maggie's thigh and squeezed gently. "Thank you for talking to Sarah about my parents. You bring a different perspective, an outsider's view, that I think is good. And very loving. She has a hard time admitting it, but I know it has been difficult for her. Even Julie and I have a hard time talking about them. I know Sarah misses them terribly. We all do, for different reasons. But she's the baby of the family, and they weren't there to see her graduate from high school or take her to college. Julie and I always have been there for her, but it's not the same thing."

"Rick, have you given much thought to your own grief over losing your parents? When you told me about your old girlfriend and how she never showed you any sympathy, I felt badly. You said you were kind of relieved because you just wanted to get past it. But we all have to grieve our losses, especially something so traumatic as losing both parents at the same time, and so unexpectedly."

"I don't know. Listening to you talk about grief with Sarah tonight was kind of eye-opening. Like Sarah said, I hadn't thought of it that way. But, you know, I think you're right. I never really did spend a lot of time thinking about it. To me, it was a… um, something I wanted to get through, get over… Uh, I guess that sounds a bit cold-hearted. But I'm… I'm just trying to be honest."

"Do you ever feel that you have unfinished business with your parents? You know, you told me that the last time you talked to your mother, that you regretted not telling her that you loved her. What else do you regret not telling her?"

He was quiet for a few moments before he began speaking slowly. "I… I don't know," and paused again. "I've never really asked myself that question. But now that you're asking, I can't say I have a good answer. So did I just want to move on, as though to forget them? I don't know."

"Maybe you couldn't deal with the pain. So, you postponed it. But you continue to postpone dealing with it. I don't think it's healthy to put off dealing with the pain associated with such a profound loss."

He nodded slowly. "Hmm, yeah I guess you're right. But, uh, what should I do? I don't want to start obsessing about their deaths four years after the tragedy."

"No, no, of course not. And I'm not suggesting that. You know, I once read about the five stages of grief. If I remember right, we start with denial—like we deny to ourselves that our loss ever happened. And then we go to anger, lashing out at the whole world. Then to, uh… Oh yeah, to bargaining, like we try to negotiate a better deal. Then to, uh… then to depression. And finally, to acceptance: we come to accept the loss. I wonder if maybe you just skipped ahead to acceptance, without bothering with the earlier stages. In hindsight, I realized that I went through those stages when Grandma Margaret passed away—not consciously, but I did. And though I've accepted losing her, that doesn't mean I no longer grieve her or miss her. But I've accepted the reality of her being gone as part of my life from that day forward."

"Uh huh."

"Rick, I realize that losing one's grandparent after a long illness is a lot different than losing both parents out of the blue as you did, but it's the only personal such experience I've had that I can relate to yours." She paused a moment in thought. "But I have an idea. You don't have to do this. It's just an idea. But give it some thought and do it if you feel like it."

"What's that?"

"Remember how Picasso expressed his grief and anger over the obliteration of Guernica in his passionate painting?" Rick nodded. "How do you think you might best express your grief?"

"Don't know. Probably not a painting," and he laughed softly. "What are driving at?"

"Have you thought about writing about it?"

He shrugged.

"A few months after my Grandma Margaret passed away, I was talking to Amanda about her. I was still depressed about losing her, feeling that I hadn't taken the opportunity to tell Grandma how I really felt about her. Amanda suggested I write her a letter. It seemed silly, but, as I thought about it, I liked the idea. So, I did it. And I'm glad I did. It made me think more deeply about her, my relationship with her, and what she meant to me. It gave me the opportunity to rehash my many fond memories of her and gave me fresh insights into my true feelings about her and how much I appreciated her.

Maybe you should do that. Write your mother a letter. Tell her what you wished you had told her in that phone call. Pretend that, instead of losing her so suddenly, that you had one last chance to tell her how you felt about her. What you're grateful to her for, what she might have done that bothered you... Whatever crosses your mind and is still lingering, still bothering you."

"That's an interesting idea."

"Think about it. Take your time. And do with it as you like. Write it down. Share it with me. Or don't. Whatever. What's important is doing it, of going through the process, of thinking it through. They are your thoughts and no one else's. You're the most important person here. This is your chance to get it off your chest, to talk to your mother one last time."

"I think I like that idea."

41: Beretta 92FS

Closely following owner's guides he'd bought earlier that week at a Stamford gun shop, Pete carefully took apart, cleaned and polished both the Beretta and the SIG on his kitchen table, before putting them back together.

Earlier that day, he'd followed Dan's advice and taken both guns to a remote sand quarry up north outside Oxford where he spent the morning firing off a dozen shots each at old beer cans. He'd gotten comfortable with them and impressed himself with his gun control.

By the time he stopped, the pistols felt natural, like extensions of his hand. Dan was right. Practicing with them helped him feel more comfortable with them. Plus, as Dan said, he could sense the difference between the two. He kind of liked the Beretta better.

As he finished cleaning the Beretta, he thought to himself that it is a thing of beauty, like a beautiful girl with a perfectly proportioned body. The Italians really are good designers.

Wiping it down with a clean rag, he fondled it, turned it over repeatedly, looking at it from different angles, letting the overhead kitchen light reflect off its design details, curves, indentations, and corners. He liked the heavy way it sat in his hand, perfectly balanced.

Holding it firmly, he aimed at the door knob across the room and pulled the trigger. Without a bullet in the chamber, it just clicked.

Nice action on this baby. Real clean.

He slipped both guns, ammo, cleaning kit and guide into a pillow case, took the step ladder to the basement, lifted the ceiling panel in the corner, and stashed it there. Stepping back, he made sure the ceiling looked normal. Not a good idea to keep weapons like that lying around the house out in the open when you don't have a license to carry.

42: Resident Wino

Saturday, August 9th

Rick rolled into the driveway around noon on Saturday and parked between Maggie's VW and Susie James' shiny new Datsun 280ZX, which she'd picked up that week. Susie was the wedding planner that Louise had hired. After spending a couple minutes circling the car admiring it, he let myself into the house, correctly assuming the women were at work in the dining room.

"Hi Rick," Louise called out cheerfully. He walked up behind Maggie, put his hands on her shoulders and kissed the top of her head. She touched his cheek. He left his hands on her shoulders, messaging them absent-mindedly, as he spoke.

"Nice car, Susie. I like it. When did you pick it up?"

"Thanks. Day before yesterday. I only have seventy-eight-point-three miles on it," and she grinned.

"Looks pretty zippy."

"It is. I took it for a drive yesterday up on the quiet roads in Pound Ridge and Bedford. It corners really nicely."

"I'll bet. Maybe you'll take me for a ride?"

"If you're a good groom, I may even let you drive it." She smiled.

"It's a deal. So, how's the planning going? You've been at it all morning."

"Yes, we accomplished quite a bit. I think we're in good shape, considering the wedding is just three weeks from today," Susie answered. She paused and looked at all the paperwork on the table. "I think we're about done for the day. We do need to nail down the dinner menu today before we quit." Turning to Louise, "And I need to get answers to your other questions—which I should be able to do this afternoon when I get back to my office."

The three women shared the menu with him, which he approved of with a nod. "Sounds yummy."

"We're leaving the wine selection to Tom. He wants a role, too, and that's his. He is our resident wino, after all," Louise added with a chuckle.

"After lunch, Rick and I are going to the jewelers to pick up our wedding bands. They're basically identical gold bands. No jewels. We've been so rushed, we didn't bother with an engagement ring. No time."

"And neither did we. More than a year later, after Charley was born, your father gave me this ring," and Louise held out her left hand for Rick to see, a bejeweled golden band. "We've always called it my engagement ring."

"Nice."

"So, we're done here? I'm hungry," Maggie said.

"Susie, you're staying for lunch?"

"Thanks, but I have those calls to make before the end of the day," as she gathered up catalogs and notes. "I'll call you later this afternoon when I get answers to your questions."

After finishing lunch and helping Louise clean up, Maggie and Rick drove into town center to the jewelers on Elm Street. Both rings fit perfectly. They paid the balance due, left and got back in Rick's car, next driving to see the caterer in Greenwich about the wedding cake. After settling on the cake design, they got back in the car. Maggie suggested a detour.

"You know, we're not far from the house where my grandparents lived. Let's go look at it. I haven't been by there since Grandma Abigail passed away six years ago."

Within five minutes, they were in Old Greenwich, stopped at a brick wall and tall, ornate iron gate. They could see the stately red brick home, set back from the road, facing Long Island Sound.

"Grandpa Tom and Grandma Abigail lived here since before I was born. I was only eighteen when Grandpa passed away. Dad was very close to him and I know that Dad was devastated when he died. That was October 1972. It was kind of sudden. He was diagnosed with colon cancer and was gone within two months. He died while I was starting my freshman year at BC. I remember that he got the diagnosis when I was getting ready to leave for Boston. I came home the weekend of the funeral but had to get back to school for my mid-terms. I should have stuck around for a few days to be with Dad. He didn't take it well."

"I'm sorry that your father had to deal with that."

"Oh my God, Rick. Listen to you, after all you've had to deal with. At least Dad got to say good-bye to his father."

"Yeah well, there's that. But that's an insight into Tom I hadn't known. You know how much I admire your father—both your parents. They're really good people. They've been *so* nice to me to me. Tom is becoming my mentor. I'm learning so much about the paper business from him—business in general—and people."

"As if you don't know already, Dad loves you. He talks about you all the time. He's so happy that we're getting married. You're like a second son—to both of them."

As they resumed their drive back to New Canaan, Rick asked, "Maggie, what was your Grandma Margaret's maiden name?"

"Tilden. Why do you ask?"

"And what was her mother's maiden name?"

"Uh. It was Roe, spelled R-O-E. What you are asking for?"

"Oh, just curious," and he grinned.

"What are you up to?"

"Nothing. Just curious." She looked at him with a half grin.

When they got back to the Haines house, Charley and Beth had arrived to spend the night. Beth was in the kitchen talking with Louise. Charley was out on the patio talking to his father, Beth said.

Rick exited for the patio to find Tom and Charley talking, each with a bottle of beer as they sat at the patio table.

"Hi. I'll leave if you're discussing World Paper secrets."

"Nah," Charley said. "Have a seat. We're just talking about Dad's trip this week. Want a beer?" he asked, reaching into the ice chest next to him.

"Sure. Thanks," he said, accepting a bottle of Beck's.

"Yeah, Maggie said you were on the road, Tom. Where to?"

"I was at our mill in Vanceboro, Maine, in the middle of nowhere—actually, north of Vanceboro. Ever heard of it?"

"No, where is it?"

"*Ya cahn't get they-ah frum hey-ah,*" Charley said with a Maine accent and a grin. "That's what the old-time Mainers would tell you," and Charley laughed.

"*Whey-ah* is it and how often do you get *they-ah?*" Rick asked, laughing.

"It's way up north and east, on the border with New Brunswick on the St. Croix River," Tom said. "We have one of our older mills up there. I go about once every three or four months. It's a long drive from the Augusta airport—about three-and-a-half hours."

"Do you go there, too, Charley?"

Charley shook his head. "No. I work in marketing. Haines is one of our four subsidiaries. World has twenty-three paper mills. Most are in North America—the US and Canada. We also have mills in Norway, Sweden and Finland. But I know where Vanceboro is. We've taken a few fishing trips on the St. Croix. Dad was just talking about the situation at the Vanceboro mill."

"The mill's been struggling the past few years," Tom explained. "It's old, and its two paper machines both need upgrades, which the board of directors is not keen to pay for. We last upgraded them when we were still independent, more than twenty-five years ago, in the late fifties. So, we're trying to make do with spit and chewing gum until I can convince the board that it's worth the investment. I go up there to hold their hands and help them squeeze a little more productivity out of those old machines to justify the investments."

"Aren't you worried about sharing your secrets with a competitor?"

"This was all written up in *Paper Age* magazine two months ago," Tom said.

"Oh. I guess I need to catch with my trade publications," Rick said with a laugh.

"It's kind of a Catch-22 situation," Charley continued. "They won't get the investment unless the performance improves, but the performance won't improve without the investment."

"That's what we were talking about when you came out—the irony of it all," Tom added. "That mill employs about five-hundred people, many of whom are third, even fourth generation mill employees. The mill has been the main employer in that area since my grandfather built it in the early 1920s. I'm trying to save the mill. Nearly every job in the area, one way or the other, depends on it. If it ever shuts down, so will the town. I've seen the phenomenon before. Lots of little towns across northern Maine barely exist after the local mill closes."

"We have to build paper and lumber mills near the source—the forests," Charley added. "That's always going to be out in the boonies."

"Yup," Tom added. "So, there are never many other employment opportunities in the area. If you don't work for the mill, you work for one of the businesses supported by the mill workers who live there—the businesses that comprise a community, like diners, bars, hardware stores, grocery stores, mechanics, gas stations, gun and bait shops, dentists, doctors, police, firemen.

Everything and everybody that make up a remote community of a couple thousand people."

"I never thought of it that way," Rick said.

"And neither do most company directors—at my company, nor yours for that matter," Tom said. "One of my jobs is to remind them. The employees are committed to us, and we ought to be returning the loyalty. One hand washes the other. I believe that loyal employees help improve profitability because loyal employees are the best, most productive workers. So, yes, my main job is helping the mills stay productive. And I think we do that by building employee loyalty and commitment. Profitability means those jobs are protected another few years."

"That's a great perspective. I guess I sort of saw that at the Iron Mountain mill, too."

"Absolutely," said Charley.

43: Wedding Parade

"Mom, your wedding was on a tighter schedule than ours. How did you and Grandma pull it off?"

"There were no such things as wedding planners back then. We did it all by ourselves. The wedding was held at the Bryn Mawr Presbyterian Church, and then we held the reception at my parents' house just up the street, close enough that everyone could walk from the church to the house. Your grandfather had the foresight—and the connections—to get the street closed for the occasion. It was really neat, your father, me, my parents, his parents, and the bridal party leading the way up the middle of the street, with the guests following. My sister, Alice, who was my maid of honor, carried my bridal train, and the flower girl threw flower petals in the street ahead of us."

Louise looked into the middle distance. "It was our own private parade. A lot of the people in the neighborhood—people we didn't even know—came out of their houses and stood at the curb. Everybody was smiling. Many applauded. Others took pictures. One little girl ran out of her house with a box of rice and started throwing it at us. It was really special."

"Charley showed me the photos in the library. It looks like it was a wonderful wedding," Beth said.

"It really was."

"How many guests?" Maggie asked.

"Around a hundred."

"Did everything go as planned?" Beth asked.

"Yeah, I was wondering about that, too. I'm kind of nervous about all the moving parts. Thank God we have Susie. How did you and Grandma manage on your own?"

"Well, a lot of it was flying by the seat of our pants. Fortunately, the weather cooperated. If it had rained, I'm not sure how things would have turned out. But it was well planned. As you know, your grandmother was a smart woman and a natural organizer. Everything came off perfectly."

"I'll bet... I miss Grandma I wish she could be at my wedding."

"Me, too, Maggie. Me too. She would be so thrilled to see you marry

Rick. She would love him, as much as we all do."

"I know, Mom. I think about her often, and that's what I ask her. *Grandma, what do you think of Rick?* And I can see her smiling and nodding."

Louise smiled, blinked her eyes rapidly and put her hand on Maggie's arm. "Yes, I think you're right."

"Mom, not to change the subject, but I'm afraid Charley and Dad are probably talking Rick's ear off. We'd better rescue him."

"You go save Rick. Beth and I will start working on dinner. Bring them all in here. Dad and I have a little announcement to make." Maggie looked at her quizzically.

"Go on. Shoo," she said, with an underhanded flip of her wrist.

Maggie stepped out the door and walked to the table where the three men were seated, talking. "Are Charley and Dad boring you?"

"Quite the contrary. I'm getting some great insights into the industry. And I'm stealing trade secrets," he added with a laugh.

"I was just telling Rick about my travels this week to Vanceboro, honey."

"Oh. So, you gave Rick your standard Vanceboro speech? The one about all the people supported by the mill and employee loyalty?"

"Indeed I did, Maggie. This is important stuff. We're talking about people's lives here. It's not just machines churning out tons of paper."

"Maggie, he's right. And I really appreciate your father's perspective. These are critical considerations in our business. I'm new to this, and Tom is a veteran. He can teach me a lot." Tom smiled.

"Yeah, Maggie," Charley added. "I grew up on these talks with Dad. When I joined World Paper, I was way ahead of my peers in my knowledge of the business."

"Okay, you guys, but please come join the rest of us. Let's move the party indoors."

As they all gathered in the kitchen, Louise nodded to her husband. "Uh, Tom, do you want to share our little surprise?"

Everyone turned their faces to him.

"Maggie and Rick, your mother and I want to give you a special wedding gift. When Louise and I were married, nearly twenty-eight years ago, her parents gave us a honeymoon trip to Hawaii, and we want to do the same for you."

"Oh Dad. Mom. That's wonderful. Thank you."

"Yes, that's great. Thank you so much," Rick added.

"But first, the details," Louise said. "Hawaii consists of six main islands. So, we need to be a bit more specific about which one you're going to visit. We think you would really have a good time on Kauai."

"Isn't that where you guys went a couple years ago?" Charley asked.

"That's right," Tom said. "It's west of Oahu, the furthest west of the main islands. It's called the Garden Isle. It's largely unspoiled. And, honestly, the least touristy. We've rented you a cottage on the beach in Princeville on the north shore near Hanalei Bay. It's the same cottage that your mother and I stayed in a couple years ago. We almost didn't come home."

"We've also bought you first class round-trip tickets," she added. "You'll be leaving Sunday morning after the wedding."

"Oh my God!" Maggie exclaimed, turning to give her father a hug, and then her mother as well. "Thank you. Thank you so much."

"Yes," Rick said, "thank you very much. You're being so generous. This and the wedding"

"Well, Maggie's our only daughter. We couldn't possibly scrimp," Tom added, winking at her.

"Hey, what about my wedding?" Charley asked, with a laugh.

"Well, we'll see about that," Tom replied, now winking at Beth, who blushed.

44: Three Nip Bottles

Leaving the SIG safely hidden in his basement ceiling, Pete returned to the sand quarry with his Beretta that afternoon for a second round of practice to confirm his confidence with the gun. On the way home, he spotted a gun shop in Derby and pulled in to replenish his ammo for the Beretta. A liquor store next door provided him the opportunity to restock his glove compartment stash of nip bottles of whiskey.

As he squirrelled away the dozen bottles of assorted brands, he heard the voice of his mother: "*the smaller the bottle, the bigger the problem.*"

"Fuck it," he said aloud. "It steadies my nerves, and I'm gonna need some nerve steadying tonight."

By the time he got back to the southern end of Fairfield County, it was nearing dinner time and he was famished, having skipped lunch. Since he had nothing at home to eat except a couple of slices of two-day-old take-out pizza, he opted for his old stand-by, Victoria Station, and got off at exit thirteen, four exits before his home off-ramp.

Stan was the weeknight bartender, so he wasn't there that night. Pete didn't know the weekend crew—an attractive young woman was working the bar. A larger, rowdier crowd dominated the bar than he was accustomed to. He didn't recognize anyone.

He shouted his order over the shoulder of some guy who was putting the moves on a girl who looked underage and well beyond a buzz. He had to wait several minutes, until nearly seven, before a stool opened up when the guy convinced the girl to leave with him.

The seat wasn't his usual spot on the corner, but he had a good view behind the bar, and could easily check out the bartender as she briskly moved around serving customers.

She wore a black vest that was part of the restaurant staff uniform. A bit too small—probably intentionally—it pushed up her ample breasts. The button-down shirt she wore underneath was unbuttoned at the top so she was showing plenty of cleavage, which pleased Pete immensely, especially when she bent over frequently to retrieve bottles of beer from the fridge below the bar.

The Yankee pre-game show had just started on the TV above the bar. They were playing the White Sox at home that night, with the game set to start in about an hour. It was so noisy, he couldn't even hear the TV.

Pete ordered a second mug of Michelob and a shot of Jack Daniels on the side while he considered the menu. The baby back ribs sounded good, but he hated the mess they made. And since he would be handling his gun later that night, he didn't want greasy fingers. He went for his favorite stand-by: French dip with fries.

He'd finished his second beer when the bartender put his dinner in front of him. He ordered a third mug and another shot of whiskey. By the time the game was underway, he was on his fourth beer.

Pete couldn't focus on the game as he considered whether this would, in fact, be the best night to get that little prick out of the way. He had it all planned out: He'd park and sit in his car to stake out Maggie's apartment, and wait for them to show up. And when they did, he'd grab the little twerp, beat the livin' shit out of him and then threaten him with the Beretta. Tonight's the night, he told himself as he ordered a fifth mug of Michelob.

With the Yankees ahead, one-to-nothing after four innings, he swallowed the last of his beer, paid his tab and left the bartender a twenty-dollar tip under his wet beer mug, winking at her as he left. He'd have to stop in at Victoria Station more often on the weekends. She was a hot number. Maybe come in early, before the crowd gathered, so they could get acquainted.

From Post Road in Darien to Maggie's street in South Norwalk was a familiar ten-minute drive. He and Maggie had eaten a few times at Victoria Station, so he knew the route well. It was about nine-thirty when he pulled into a spot near her apartment door on the same side of the street. After shutting off the engine, he cracked his window, and left the ignition on so he could listen to music quietly. The lights were off in Maggie's apartment.

He was prepared for a long wait, if need be. Pulling a nip bottle of Jack Daniels out of the glove compartment, he poured it down his throat, tossing the empty out the window. Thirty minutes later, he had had his third one when the beige VW pulled into the empty space two cars ahead of him.

It's now or never, he told himself, as he got out of the car, tucking the Beretta in the back of his pants the way Dan had shown him. Then he quietly clicked his car door shut and ducked in behind the car in front of his, hoping they hadn't seen him.

45: Second Confrontation

Because they'd talked so much about Hawaii, Maggie and Rick stayed at her parents' house later than usual. It was nearly ten when they got back to South Norwalk. After they'd parked, Maggie hopped out and took a few steps toward the front door, and then stopped for a moment so Rick could catch up. As she turned around to wait for him, a large man stepped onto the sidewalk from between two cars so that he was facing Maggie, standing between her and Rick in the dim light of a streetlamp.

It was Pete Conley, unsteady on his feet. "Hey Maggie. How ya doin'?" he slurred, looking at her with a crooked smile.

"Pete. What are you doing here?"

"Just came by to talk. You know, we really gotta talk"

Rick moved in, close enough that he could smell Pete's alcoholic stench. "Pete, you really should move on. There's nothing to be said here. Maggie and I are just going home, and so should you.".

Pete turned quickly. "*Your fucking asshole!*" he shouted, lunging at him with his right fist. He caught Rick's cheekbone with a glancing blow. Rick stumbled backwards. Maggie screamed.

Rick stayed on his feet, stepping out of the arc of Pete's next punch. The momentum of the missed punch threw Pete off-balance. He stumbled to the ground. As he hit the pavement face-first, the pistol slipped from the back of his pants and fell to the sidewalk. He grabbed it.

Rick stomped on his hand. Pete yelped in pain and let go of the gun. Rick kicked it aside, into the gutter and under Pete's car, out of sight and out of reach. Pete lay on the sidewalk cursing.

"Maggie, *call the police!* Tell them he has a gun!"

Rick's cheek throbbed. A big ring Pete was wearing had opened a cut on below his eye. Blood trickled down Rick's cheek. He wiped it with the back of his hand as Pete struggled to get up, looking around the sidewalk in the semi-darkness for his gun while still on his hands and knees. With Pete still hunched over, trying to steady himself to stand upright, Rick ran at him and pushed him down to the sidewalk again.

"You piece of shit! I'm gonna kick your ass," Pete roared from his prone position.

As he struggled to get to his feet again, Rick charged him again, kneeing him in the ribs and then pushing him backwards onto the ground again. "Kick my ass?" Rick yelled. "Are you kidding me? You can barely stand up, *you fucking drunk!*"

The shouting had stirred Paul and Lilly Jenkins in their ground floor apartment. Paul came outside to investigate.

Pete lay on the ground, struggling to catch his breath. He rolled away from Rick and jumped up unsteadily. Standing in a low crouch, he took three quick steps toward Rick, swung wide with his right fist. Rick dodged it. Pete followed with a quick punch from underneath with his left, surprising Rick and catching his right jaw. Rick stumbled backwards this time and Pete stayed on his feet, determined to hit him again.

After Pete's punch connected, Paul angled toward him, intent on breaking up the fight. He grabbed Pete's shoulder and tried to pull him away. Pete shoved him away. "Get out of the way, old man. You're a pain in the ass."

Paul stumbled backwards and fell to the sidewalk.

Maggie was back. She helped Paul to his feet.

Blood was oozing from the cut on Rick's cheekbone. He kept wiping at it, and crouched to shrink Pete's target, bobbing and weaving to reduce the chance that he'd connect again. As Pete took another run at him, Rick side-stepped him. Once again, Pete tripped and crumbled in a heap on the sidewalk. He got up and threw three more rapid punches, none of which hit their mark as Rick dodged each one. Now, he was getting winded.

"*Pete! Stop it! Stop it right now!*" Maggie shouted. Pete glared at her briefly and turned his attention back to Rick, lining up for a fourth punch.

They could hear the approaching sirens. Pete didn't seem to notice as he positioned himself awkwardly, reared back and hastily let loose with another roundhouse punch. Rick easily sidestepped it. Pete stumbled and fell to the ground. The squad car screeched to a stop. The two officers witnessed the thrown punch. Both jumped out.

One easily throttled Pete, who was still face down on the pavement, and put handcuffs on him behind his back. The other grabbed Rick. He was about to put handcuffs on him as well before Maggie intervened and quickly explained what had happened. The officer released him and asked where the gun was. Rick pointed under Pete's car. The officer knelt in the gutter with his flashlight and retrieved it. Holding it on the end of a pencil inserted in the barrel, he examined it in his car's headlamp. Then he deposited it in an evidence bag in his car.

Returning, he began questioning Rick, who recounted the episode. Maggie corroborated. "And Rick, tell the officer about the time Pete followed you to the auto repair shop."

Throughout the questioning, Pete snorted his disagreement periodically, muttering profanities.

"Uh, ma'am, am I correct in assuming you and this gentleman were once, uh, friendly?"

"Yes, we dated on and off for a time. But we broke up in late May."

"Maybe you did, but I didn't!" he shouted.

"Shut up," the other officer commanded and put his foot on Pete's back.

"Oof."

"*You're a real asshole, Pete!*" Maggie shouted at him.

"That's not what you said when we made love. *Oh Pete, your cock is so huge!*" he said in a falsetto, laughing, while still on his stomach on the sidewalk.

Maggie's fury flared. She leapt forward to kick him in the ribs. But before her foot could connect, Rick grabbed her by the arm and pulled her back. Her kick went wide. She lost her balance and fell backwards into Rick, who caught her.

"*I told you to shut up,*" the cop shouted, putting his foot on Pete's neck.

"*Ow!* Police brutality! You're gonna hear from my lawyer."

"Oh, I'm so scared," the cop lisped, before adding, "Hey, and by the way, you have the right to remain silent. And I wish to hell you would. Anything you say can and will be used against you in a court of law. And I'll be there in the cheering section."

The other officer turned back to question Maggie. "That guy's a dirt bag," he said quietly. "Don't give him the satisfaction of letting him get your goat... I have a couple more questions" He paused a moment. "Are you okay?"

Maggie nodded grimly. Rick still held her by the upper arm, steadying her as she quivered with rage.

"Okay then... Were you aware that he possessed a firearm?"

"Certainly not. But, then, nothing about this *pig* would surprise me."
Her arm tensed. Rick had never seen her like this.

"We're gonna run a check on this gun. My bet is that it's stolen. And I doubt he has a license to carry. So, he'll probably be facing multiple charges, including illegal gun possession, receiving stolen property, assault with a deadly weapon, drunk and disorderly, and assault and battery. Short of homicide, you name it, he did it. And if that's his car, well, he's parked next to a fire hydrant." Maggie nodded. "So, we'll charge him with that, too. I assume you'll both be pressing charges as well?"

"Absolutely. What Rick didn't mention is that this piece of garbage has been stalking us the past two months, bothering me at work with numerous unwanted phones calls, despite my asking him to leave me alone. He even came to my office last week and accosted me, putting me in fear of my life."

Pete snorted in disbelief. "Oh my God. *Get real, bitch.*"

"Just a moment, please, ma'am." Turning to his partner, he said, "Let's put this horse's ass in the squad car. I'm tired of his act."

He and the other officer each grabbed an arm and picked up Pete roughly, frog-marching him across the sidewalk, into the street, heaving him into the back seat of their patrol car.

By then, several neighbors had joined Paul on the sidewalk to observe the proceedings. The officer returned to Maggie while his partner stayed with the car, Pete safely locked up in the back. A second police car had arrived moments earlier. Those two officers got busy shooing away the crowd.

"Sorry, ma'am. Go ahead," and the questioning resumed.

Maggie recounted Pete's on-going harassment of the previous several weeks, including his late-night foray there at her apartment building.

"That's right, officer," Paul added. "That was late June. It was a weeknight. He was at least as drunk that night as he is now. He was aggressive, loud and obnoxious. Woke up me and the wife—and probably the rest of the neighborhood, too. He threatened me. I'm the one who called you."

"If you called us, we'll have a record of that."

As he wrapped up his questioning, he asked Rick and Maggie to come to the station the next morning to sign the report and to have Rick's wounds photographed as evidence. After getting their names and phone numbers, the officers departed.

Watching the police car pull away, with Pete scowling at them from the back seat, Maggie exhaled aloud. "I guess it's a good thing he was as drunk as he was so that he never got to use that gun," and shivered.

She eyed the congealing blood on Rick's cheekbone and the blooming flushes where he'd been hit.

"Let's go upstairs and clean that cut and put a bandage on it. We should also put some ice where he hit you to keep them from bruising up badly. Paul, thanks so much for helping out."

"Yeah, thanks, Paul. Sorry not to have met you sooner under more pleasant circumstances," and they shook hands. Paul went ahead of them to unlock and open the front door. Maggie led Rick up to their apartment.

46: Tender Loving Care

Maggie went to the bathroom for a bandage and Neosporin while Rick settled on the couch. Returning shortly to the couch with a wet, warm washcloth, she carefully swabbed the cut clean.

"I wonder if this needs a stitch or two. Let's keep an eye on it and make sure it stops bleeding," she said, examining the cut closely. "Hmm. I'll bet this was caused by Pete's Hotchkiss class ring. He wears it all the time. That's a bit ironic, don't you think?" She applied the antiseptic and bandage.

Maggie got up and went to the refrigerator to prepare ice packs. "He's gone too far this time," she said from across the room. "We're going to file assault and battery charges, and every other charge they come up with. Come to think of it, we need a lawyer. I'm gonna call Dad."

"Uh, do you really want to get them involved in this?"

"Rick don't be ridiculous. They're going to find out. What are you going to tell them when they see your cut and bruises? That you walked into a door? C'mon. Give me a break. As soon as Dad finds out, he'll call his attorney. He won't even ask if we want him to. He'll just do it."

"Well, you know him better than I do." She gently applied one ice pack to his chin and the other to his cheekbone.

It looked worse than she'd expected. "This one below your eye looks bad. I hope it doesn't turn into a black eye. Hard to know now. Let's keep ice on it for as long as you can stand it."

"It could have been worse. He got me there with a glancing blow. If he'd hit me straight on, he might have knocked me out. He has a helluva punch."

"Oh Rick, I'm so sorry. This is all my fault."

"No, it isn't, Maggie. Pete's a jackass. You can't control him. Obviously," Rick said, grinning.

She pursed her lips, sighed and continued pressing at his wounds with the icepacks.

After a few moments of silence, Rick asked, "What should I tell the people in my office tomorrow about these injuries?"

"And what are we going to tell everyone else?"

"The truth, I suppose. That your ex-boyfriend tried to kill me."

She sighed again. "Yeah. The truth is always simpler."

She held the ice pack on his wound.

"Here, hold this. I'm going to call Dad."

"Can't it wait until the morning?"

Ignoring him, she picked up the phone and dialed.

Neither of her parents had known anything about Pete's ongoing stalking and harassment of the past two months, so she had to spend several minutes filling in her father to provide context to that evening's events. Louise had picked up the bedroom phone, so she found herself talking to them both, answering their barrage of questions.

In the end, Maggie was right. No sooner had she told them what had happened than Tom said he would call their attorney, Chet Montgomery, that night—even though it was nearly ten-thirty on a Saturday night.

Hanging up, she turned back to Rick. "I feel better already, now that he knows." Then she thought a second. "The downside of all this is that it means that Mom knows, too. So, she and Helen will remind me what a total loser Pete is."

"Well, you don't need them to tell you that. I can do that," he said, grinning.

She punched his shoulder.

"Ow."

47: Interviews

Sunday, August 10th

Tom called Maggie first thing the next morning. Chet Montgomery wanted to interview them both as soon as possible. They were to meet him at the house at eleven-thirty.

Despite the ice pack treatment the evening before, a bruise and some minor swelling had bloomed on Rick's jaw, and he showed the beginnings of a black eye along with swelling. That, plus the bandaged cut on his cheekbone left little doubt that he'd taken a beating.

After breakfast and a shower, they hopped in his car and drove to the Norwalk Police Station to sign the report and to have Rick's wounds photographed. Then, they headed to New Canaan, arriving at the house a few minutes ahead of the attorney. "I'm sorry to put you through this, Dad," Maggie said, as Tom and Louise greeted them at the front door. "And thanks for getting Mr. Montgomery involved." Her parents, too, were anxious about the interview.

Tom and Louise eyed Rick's wounds. "Ow. That looks painful," she said. "Are you okay, Rick?"

"I'm fine. It's just a little sore."

"You're gonna have quite a shiner there, Rick, which will give the wedding photos an intriguing look," Tom added, grinning.

"Stop it, Tom," Louise scolded as Rick grinned and Maggie scowled.

They heard the crunch of gravel in the driveway. Chet Montgomery's car was approaching. A second car was right behind.

Climbing out of his sleek black Mercedes sedan, Chester "Chet" Montgomery was a lanky six-foot-four, with a receding hairline of snow-white hair and a rigid all-business posture. A bit older than her father, Maggie guessed. As she soon learned, he was both a gentleman and thorough.

The second car brought his assistant, a junior partner by the name of Steve McDonough. Both men were wearing dark business suits, white shirts and rep ties, as though they'd come straight from their offices—or church.

After introductions at the front door, Chet spoke to them all.

157

"Before we get started, we need photographs of Rick's wounds as evidence when this case comes to a trial. Did the Norwalk police photograph them yet?

"Yes," Rick said. "We dropped by the Norwalk Police station this morning on our way here. In addition to signing the officer's report on the incident, they took several photos."

"Good. Also, I want you to see a doctor about those injuries tomorrow to get a diagnosis."

"Diagnosis? We know what they are. It's just a cut and a couple of bruises. They'll heal. I'll be fine."

"I know, Rick. But the point is, I want a doctor's professional opinion and a written report saying that he examined you such-and-such number of hours after the incident. And then, using medical language, describe the wounds. If need be, the prosecutor will call him—or her—to be an expert witness. Try to see a doctor tomorrow, today if possible. Or just go to a local emergency room and ask any doctor to do it while the wounds are still fresh. Have the doctor send the report directly to me at this address," as he handed Rick his business card.

"Okay. I can do that."

"Before we start, I thought we'd better give you a few things we've collected," Maggie said, reaching into her purse. She pulled out the cassette tape from her answering machine and handed it to Chet. "First, there's this."

"What's on the tape?"

"Two weeks ago, Pete called us at home while we were out. This is that message. It's his standard apology. Also, I had left him phone message earlier that week to tell him that I was engaged and to please leave me alone. He responds to that here, saying he doesn't believe me."

"Okay."

"Not only that, but he called a couple more times later when we weren't home and resumed his ranting, threatening both of us, but especially Rick. So, there's plenty of incriminating evidence there."

"Excellent."

"Also, he has been calling me at my office since early June. I took the first two calls and told him to stop calling. But I assumed he would keep calling, so I asked our receptionist, Molly Shepherd, not to put his calls through. I also asked her to log the times he called. In addition to the first two times that I spoke with him, Molly has logged three more calls—with the dates and times that he called, as well as the messages he left, a couple of which were rather unpleasant. I'll mail that log to you tomorrow."

"This is all excellent. Good thinking. Also, please tell Miss Shepherd that she may be called as a witness, should this go to trial. I'm sure her log is thorough. But tell her that it would be helpful if she supplemented it with additional notations to remind herself of what the defendant may have said to her on the phone and his tone of voice, while it's still fresh in her mind. For instance, did he use his own name or a false name? Did he try to disguise his voice? How did he react when she refused to put his call through? Was he verbally abusive to her, too? During the time lag before a trial, she may forget small but important details."

After Tom led the group into the house and then into library, Chet turned. "I'm sorry, but I think it best if Steve and I interviewed Maggie alone. Your presence, as Maggie's parents and fiancé, might inhibit what she says and how she talks to us about her relationship with the perpetrator and the events that led to last night's confrontation. We need her to be completely candid. When we're done interviewing her, we'll want to talk with Rick, also alone. This could take up to an hour."

"Of course," Tom said, as he, Louise and Rick backed out, closing the door behind them.

Settling in, Chet began, "Maggie, it's critical that we learn as much as possible about Mr. Conley and your relationship with him. Our questions may seem personal and intrusive at times, but when this comes to a trial, they are the kinds of questions that a good defense attorney would ask you on the stand. So, let's start at the beginning. How did you meet Mr. Conley?"

Both Steve and Chet took notes as she recounted their first meeting on Cape Cod and the weeks and months that followed.

Chet then asked a series of progressively delving questions about how Pete had treated her, their sexual relations, whether he had ever hit her or threatened to, whether he ever demonstrated violent tendencies in other ways, such as throwing things or punching walls or doors.

In fact, she admitted, he did have a penchant for throwing things, and that he had once thrown her new Olympus SLR camera across the room and destroyed it. Another time, he punched a hole in a closet door. Also, he had slapped her hard on two separate occasions. As she was recounting the episodes,

Maggie realized that she had not been truthful with Rick when he'd asked her the same question. She would have to take care of that later.

Maggie was talking about things she'd never contemplated telling her parents—or Rick, for that matter. She was glad they weren't in the room and now understood why the attorneys had excused them.

"Is Mr. Conley at present employed?"

"As of May, he worked for Stockton Chemical as their eastern regional sales manager, based out of their headquarters office building in Darien on Post Road."

"We'll check on that," Steve said.

"I wonder whether they know he won't be at work tomorrow."

"He will still be sitting in Norwalk City Jail tomorrow prior to the arraignment," Steve said. "So, they'll find out soon enough."

Chet paused as he reviewed his notes. "Last question… Are you aware of any previous run-ins with the law Mr. Conley may have had?"

"Uh, yes. He was arrested on a DUI charge about three years ago. That was before I knew him."

"What do you know about that?"

"Well, all I know is what he told me." And she recounted his version of the arrest. "I've seen him pretty drunk and I'll bet that was his condition that night—and last night, too," she quickly added.

"Do you know the disposition of the case? Did he pay a fine, or get his driver's license suspended?"

"No. He got off with a warning from the judge, he told me."

"Was he ever arrested in the period that you dated him?" She shook her head. "Okay. We'll pass along this information to the District Attorney's office tomorrow and they will look into it, as well as his full arrest record. Before I wrap up, do you have any questions?"

"Yes. The officer I talked with in Westport a few weeks ago suggested we get a restraining order. Can you help us with that?"

"Of course. We can take care of that today while we're here. By tomorrow afternoon, the restraining orders should be in force."

"How will Pete know that there are restraining orders against him?"

"If he makes bail, the police will tell him that he cannot come within one-hundred yards of you or Mr. Hewson. Nor can he make any attempt whatsoever to communicate with either of you, either by telephone or any other means. Any violation of the order would send him right back to jail and he would forfeit his posted bond and could be fined. Plus, it would adversely affect his trial defense, obviously."

"Oh, that's a relief. How long will those be in effect?"

"Initially, for ten days. The District Attorney will file it contending that Mr. Conley presents a clear and immediate physical danger to you and Rick. That will lead to a court hearing within ten days, during which time the defendant can ask to have it lifted. The DA's office will argue for a permanent order, which we'll likely get. I can't imagine how any attorney might argue that it be lifted, not after the judge reviews the charges. In that he was arrested with a handgun in his possession during the assault, the DA shouldn't have any trouble making the case that the defendant has shown wanton disregard for your safety."

"What are the chances that he'll be released? I'm not convinced that a restraining order will stop him if he gets drunk—which he's likely to do."

"It's difficult to say at this point what bail the judge will set. We'll know more once the DA completes his investigation. And if the gun was stolen, as the Norwalk police suspect it was, that too will be taken into consideration. If, for instance, he has an extensive arrest record, that would mean a pretty high bail, which he may not be able to post. Do you have any other questions?" She shook her head.

"Now, we'd like to talk to Rick. Would you please get him for us?"

"Of course." And she left the room.

Maggie found Rick with her parents in the dining room. All three were immersed in different sections of the Sunday *New York Times*. After Rick left, Tom asked her how it went.

She walked to him and gave him a hug. "Dad, I'm so sorry to put you guys through this. But thank you for supporting us." She turned to her mother and hugged her, too. "Honestly, it was a lot tougher than I expected. Who knew that filing charges against such a low-life could be so difficult?"

Soon, Chet, Steve and Rick had finished and stepped into the entry hall. At the sound of the library door opening and their voices, Tom, Louise and Maggie emerged from the dining room. They quickly dealt with the paperwork for the restraining orders.

"Okay, then," Chet said, "we'll be in touch with Maggie to let her know what the DA learns about Mr. Conley, court dates and the like."

Chet and Steve shook hands all around and left.

Sighing aloud, Louise said, "Well, I expect you are both hungry after that ordeal. Care to stay for lunch?"

"Thanks, Mom. That would be nice."

Conversation was minimal while the four ate, everyone lost in their thoughts. After she and Rick helped clean up, Maggie turned to him. "Let's go out by the pool and relax a bit. Okay?"

He nodded.

48: Settled

Rick and Maggie stretched out in the sun on lounge chairs by the pool. Aside from a few passing comments, they were mostly quiet, still immersed in their thoughts, thinking about the morning's interviews, which had left them both emotionally drained.

After a while, Maggie quietly asked, "Do you remember after your confrontation with Pete at the garage, you asked me why I stayed with him for so long?" Rick nodded. "And I said I didn't know?"

"Uh huh."

"I've been thinking a lot about that since then. I haven't been happy that I didn't have a good answer—not an answer that I could live with. I think that walking through the entire story with Chet and Steve this morning helped me put everything in perspective. To over-simplify, I *settled* for Pete."

Rick looked at her quizzically. "Settled?"

She breathed deeply and exhaled slowly before resuming. "In the summer of 1976, after I'd graduated, I was living here with my parents while I looked for a job. In late June one of my friends introduced me to a guy she worked with she was sure I'd like. His name was Ron Marion. We went out on a date and really hit it off. He was magnetic, smart and good looking. We had a lot in common and got along well. He was funny. Well-educated. He'd just graduated from Columbia and was working that summer as an intern in the Greenwich law firm where my friend was also an intern. He would be attending Georgetown Law School in the fall. I thought I was falling in love."

Rick paused and looked away momentarily.

"Actually, I thought *we* were falling in love. Our relationship blossomed quickly. I introduced him to my parents. They liked him, too. But at the end of August, as he was about to leave for Washington, he told me that he had to end our relationship. I was stunned. He said his girlfriend from Columbia had been working that summer in her hometown in Colorado during a, quote unquote, trial separation. He said she'd be attending Georgetown with him, also as a first-year law student. They had patched things up and had rented an apartment in Washington. The next day, he was gone."

"What a *prick*. I hope you slapped him. Or maybe threw your glass of wine in his face like you did to Pete."

"Honestly, I was too shocked to react. I felt betrayed, not only by him but by myself for falling for him and his deceit. He'd used me for his own selfish pleasures in the absence of his girlfriend. I felt like a victim. But then, the more I thought about it, the more I realized it was my own fault. I'd been blinded by my emotions. That September, I got the intern job at Williams Advertising. I liked working there and dove into the work. I didn't date at all for more than a year. Just went to work, came home, drank wine by myself, read, watched TV, exercised and ran, went out with my girlfriends occasionally, went skiing with my family. But mostly, I felt sorry for myself and avoided the whole dating scene. I did my job well and put in a lot of extra hours in the hope of getting promoted—which I did."

Rick stayed silent as she spoke, watching her closely.

"Eventually, I started dating again—a guy here, a guy there. Nothing serious and nothing that lasted more than one or two dates. I was wary about men, about getting into another relationship. It was late June 1979 and, for the unstated purpose of fixing me up with Pete Conley, a friend invited me to spend a weekend at her family's summer house in Chatham. In addition to Pete and me, she invited other people, without telling Pete or me of her plan. She thought we'd be a good match. So, I met Pete there. This is where the self-analysis comes in." She paused for a moment and looked away before returning her eyes to Rick.

"I realize in hindsight that I was probably desperate for a relationship. Pete had gone to prep school, but he wasn't really a preppie, as I told you before. He wasn't the rich kind, full of himself. He knew a lot about that world, but he didn't tie his identity to his school like so many preppies do. You know the type. The guys whose fathers and grandfathers all went to the same school, always talking about St. Paul's or Choate or Exeter or whatever."

"Uh huh," Rick nodded. "I know the type. Sure do."

"Pete had more real-life experiences than they did. He held a serious job and was excelling at it, rather than living off a trust fund or still living with his parents. And that appealed to me. I'd had my fill of the Richie Rich types, blabbing on and on about themselves, their prep school and college years and friends, dropping names all the time, talking about their most recent trip to

Europe. Pete had his flaws. I could see that. But I also believed that no relationship can be perfect. Pete was nice to me, so generous and considerate. I was charmed. At least in the beginning. Initially, we had a lot of fun. He could be spontaneous, quirky and funny. He took me to a couple Yankees games—his company has great box seats above the Yankees' dugout. That was a lot of fun. But over time, his defects became over-bearing. He drank too much. He had a short fuse. I thought I could work with him and make him a better person."

"Yeah, you mentioned that."

"It wasn't long before I began to realize the futility of the effort."

"Why do you think he had such a short fuse?"

"I often wondered about that myself. He used to complain of headaches, which usually coincided with his bad moods. You said something a couple weeks ago, that Bill had told you that Pete had had nasty head injury playing hockey that sidelined him for a while."

"Yeah?"

"Pete once mentioned that episode casually but didn't make a big deal out of it and didn't refer to it as a head injury. He just said he'd gotten banged up and had to miss a few games to recover. But now, knowing that, I can't help but think that an injury like that can have long term effects on a person's state of mind."

"Maybe… But what about his earlier life? What was his family like?"

"Well, we never had an in-depth conversation about his background. All I know is what I learned over time. He came from a working-class background. His father was in the Teamsters union. Drove big trucks cross-country. When Pete was in fifth grade, his father was killed in a bad truck accident somewhere in the Midwest. There was a small life insurance policy pay-out, and the Teamsters union helped a bit with his pension. But his mother had to piece together various jobs to support him and his younger sister. She encouraged them in their studies, and he did well in school—well enough to get selected for one of a handful of scholarships to Hotchkiss. He was a good hockey player and that helped him get the scholarship. Beyond that, I'm not sure."

"So, did your talks make any difference in his behavior towards you?"

"Boy was I naïve—and full of myself. I thought I could fix him. In the end, I guess he decided he couldn't change—or didn't want to. People are what they are. They have to want to change. You're not going to do it for them. That

165

was a hard lesson for me to learn. One time, less than two months into our relationship, my attempt bombed. Instead of his usual apology, he got angrier. Called me *Little Miss Perfect* and accused me of trying to control him, and the fight got worse. I told him I never wanted to see him again and left." Maggie stopped talking and looked away.

When she resumed, she spoke more quietly. "Actually, there's more to it than that... Remember you asked me a few weeks ago whether Pete had ever hit me?" Rick nodded. "My answer wasn't truthful. He did. He hit me. Twice."

"What? *Twice?*"

She nodded. "I'm sorry. But, yeah. On two separate occasions. The first time happened last November at his place. He'd been talking as though he'd be coming to my family's Thanksgiving dinner. But my mother had made it clear after that scene at the fall party that she didn't want him in their house again. I argued with her about it, but she was adamant. I couldn't figure out how to tell him that he wasn't welcome in my parents' home. So, that night, he brought it up again. I finally told him the truth. He lost it, saying some really ugly things about my mother with a lot of foul language thrown in. I was insulted and started to walk out the door. He grabbed me by the shoulder, spun me around and slapped me. Hard. I ran out. It hurt like hell and made my ears ring. I had a red welt on my cheek for a couple days."

Rick stared at her. "Why didn't you tell me this when I asked before?"

"Um, I don't know. I guess I was kind of embarrassed?" She looked away again.

"So, you said he hit you a second time? When was that?"

"It was two months before we got back together again, in January. But we only dated twice because the second time we went out, he got drunk. We got into another argument and he slapped me again. It was like an instant replay."

Rick turned pale. "Maggie, are you telling me that you went back to him after he demonstrated that he could and would hit you? And then he hit you again?"

She looked down and nodded slightly.

"And even after those two incidents of physical assault, you *still* went back to him *again* in April?" She nodded again, still looking down to avoid his eyes. "Why? This doesn't sound like you. You're too smart for that."

She shrugged, still looking down.

He paused a few moments, lost in his thoughts. "Honestly, I don't know what bothers me more, Maggie. That you went back to him twice after he hit you, or the fact that you've lied to me again. I asked you directly about this before and you said he'd never hit you. And now you're saying he hit you twice? *Twice?*" He shook his head and looked down at his feet.

After several moments of saying nothing, still looking down, he resumed quietly. "Maggie, this really upsets me. I trust you. Which means that I assume you will always tell me the truth. But how can I trust you if you keep springing new information on me like this? This isn't trivial stuff we're talking about."

"I'm sorry, Rick. Like I said, I guess I was just embarrassed to admit that I allowed a relationship to deteriorate to that point. I guess I was afraid to admit it to you." And she reached out to hold his hand.

Rick sighed, looked into her teary eyes. "So, what you're telling me now, is that everything? There's nothing else you're holding back?"

"Well, a couple more things," she said quietly, in a near-whisper. He winced again. She sighed and looked at him.

"He called me several times—in February, March and April. But I hung up on him every time. When he called again in late April, I finally let him talk. He apologized profusely for hitting me. Said he'd felt really bad about what he'd done. He honestly seemed sincere. He had sent flowers to my office ahead of the call—just like he did a few weeks ago. I agreed to meet him for dinner that night. He fell all over himself apologizing and promised never to get angry with me again and never to hit me again. He gave me diamond earrings as a peace offering. We made up and dated a couple more times."

Rick snorted. "So, you made up with him because he gave you diamond earrings? Did he always give you gifts after he hit you? What other expensive gifts did he give you?"

"Actually, yes. As long as I'm laying it all on the line here… He did give me a cultured pearl necklace in January when we made up then. And one other thing… That day that he confronted me at my office? He tried to give me a gift then, too. It was something in a small Tiffany's box. But I batted it away when he tried to give it to me."

"Oh my God, Maggie. You told me the day that he confronted me at the garage that he had given you gifts of jewelry. But I assumed they were really gifts. Not just attempts at his own atonement."

She sighed and looked down. "I know. Remember how I called and left a message on his answering machine a couple weeks ago?" Rick nodded. "That same day, I mailed the necklace and earrings back to him."

"Well, that's some consolation. But you do realize that that's the way abusers like him operate, that that's how they ease their conscience, until they get abusive again."

"Yeah. Amanda said the same thing."

"You told *her* all about this, but not me?"

"I'm sorry… You know, Rick, I told the lawyers about these incidents this morning and realized that I had to clear the air with you, too. That's why I brought it up now. I feel awful for keeping it from you. But… But I was afraid you'd think less of me if you'd known I'd have gone back to Pete after all that."

She looked into Rick's face and the tears began to flow. Rick reached out and pulled her to his shoulder. She started to cry into his shirt. Soon, she was sobbing and shaking. After several minutes, she shuddered, and backed away from his embrace. He kissed her on the forehead. Her eyes were puffy and red.

They looked like quite the pair: her red swollen eyes, and his bruised and bandaged face, Maggie thought.

She resumed talking, slowly and quietly this time, wiping tears from her cheeks. "Well… Anyway, um, I went against my better judgment and we made up and got back together in April. But I told him that if he ever hit me again or even threatened to, I would file charges with the police. Things were going okay. But then he started getting kind of obnoxious again after a couple of dates and the same old doubts returned. In fact, I avoided him three straight weekends before the Hotchkiss party, making excuses for not getting together. And then came that night on May thirtieth at the White Hart Inn that you witnessed. And in that argument, he brought up those three weekends to use against me. He claimed I was seeing someone else. Well, you know the rest of the story."

She stopped talking and just looked blankly at Rick. Tears still glistened on her cheeks. He leaned toward her again, hugged her while gently rubbing her back. They held one another in long silence before he finally whispered, "I love you, Maggie. You know that. And I know how lucky I am that I was there that night, that we met."

She sighed. "I'm the lucky one. Lucky to have you. Lucky that you were so forward as to follow me out to the porch, so kind and sensitive to what I was going through. I don't know where I'd be right now if you hadn't. It's kind of scary to think about it."

"On the porch that night, when I first spoke to you, I didn't want to be presumptuous, especially as I could see that you were upset. That's why I started to walk away when you were unresponsive. Why did you ask me to stay?"

"I don't know. Maybe it was the way you spoke, so gentle and quiet. And your hesitancy, maybe, which showed me you weren't aggressive, that you weren't just some jerk just hitting on me. Your voice was soothing, and your friendly face so welcoming. I didn't feel threatened by you at all. In fact, it was the opposite. I felt comforted by your presence."

She laughed softly. "You know what clinched it my mind?" she asked, smiling.

He shrugged. "No. What?"

"When you mentioned Winslow Homer. I thought, any man who knows what he's talking about on the subject of Winslow Homer is okay in my book." She smiled widely. "But, why did you follow me outside?"

"As I told you at the time, I was concerned about your safety" He hesitated and grinned. "Well, now I'm the one who's lying. To be perfectly honest, I was struck by how beautiful you were… are."

Maggie looked down.

"I'm serious. I really was struck, as though by lightning. In fact, I remember the adrenaline rush when I first saw you. I literally gasped. But then, as I stood there admiring you from across the room, I realized you were in trouble. I actually started walking towards you to intervene in the fight. I don't know what I thought I was going to do. It was just an impulse. But then you threw your wine in his face and went outside before I could get there and then I followed. It was really obvious to me that Pete had abusive tendencies. I didn't like what I was seeing, the way he was making those stabbing motions at your chest with his index finger, as though he wanted to stab you. It really bothered me and I felt. I needed to get you away from him."

They looked at one another for a long moment before she spoke again. "Maybe that's what he wanted to do. Maybe if I'd stayed with him longer, he might have hurt me—or murdered me." She shuddered. Rick hugged her tightly.

49: Nursing a Hangover

Through his throbbing headache, Pete found it miserably impossible to nurse his hangover without the aid of his usual remedies: aspirin and sometimes, in dire cases, a shot of whiskey—maybe two or three. Neither was available to him today, not in Norwalk City Jail on Sunday morning, the day after his fight with Rick and arrest. He felt like shit warmed over.

All he had was a meager lunch brought five minutes earlier by a young cop: a bowl of warm chicken noodle soup out of a can with a crinkly plastic bag of oyster crackers, a greasy spoon, a bologna and American cheese sandwich on Wonder bread with margarine, and a pint carton of milk.

What the fuck? *Milk?* He hadn't drunk milk since fifth grade, for Christ's sake. He took a bite of the sandwich and then pushed the lunch tray aside before lying down on the hard cot.

Dammit. He shouldn't have gotten so drunk. His head was hazy, and he was having difficulty recalling the details of what exactly had happened. When the police brought him into the station for booking, he was still pretty loaded from his binge at Victoria Station, followed by two nip bottles of Jack Daniels from his glove compartment—or was it three?

Pete denied that the gun was his, insisting that it was Rick's. He told the police that he'd only wanted to talk with Maggie, but that Rick had gotten in the way and shoved him, which is how the fight got started. "He started it," Pete insisted.

The two arresting officers took the statement, but not without a few smirks and elbow jabs between them. "Sure, Mr. Conley, whatever you say."

Now, some fourteen hours later, Pete sat in a hot, cramped, smelly, seven by ten-foot cell with a rigid metal cot and a stainless-steel toilet-and-sink combination, along with a couple other drunks in adjacent cells who were snoozing fitfully and snoring loudly.

He'd been offered one phone call the night before but had asked to postpone it until the next day. Dan Wilson would be helpful, but it was unlikely he'd be home that late on a Saturday night. Besides, Pete wanted a clear head for the phone call. Dan could probably help find him a lawyer. Since

Dan had seen the inside of a jail before, maybe offer some good advice about that, too.

A half-hour later, when the cop returned to collect the food tray, Pete asked if he could use the phone.

"Yeah, sure. Let me go get the officer in charge."

Ten minutes later, an older policeman with more stripes on his shoulder came with a ring of keys and let Pete out. At the end of the hall, he directed him into a room with a phone on a table, along with a pad of paper, a dull stub of a pencil, and a hard metal chair. "Local calls, only," the cop said gruffly.

"Bridgeport okay?"

"Yeah. Five minutes, max. And I'll be sitting here, so don't try any funny business. And no swearing."

He dialed Dan's number, praying that he'd pick up. On the eighth ring, a woman answered. "Hello?"

"Hi. This is Pete Conley. I'm a friend of Dan's. Is he around?"

"No, not right now. He just went out. Can he call you back?"

"Uh, no. He can't. Uh, what's your name?"

"Angela."

The waitress from the Downtowner. Pete thought he recognized the voice. He had a flashback image of her stunning cleavage and grinned to himself. Man, Dan is fast. Good move, my man. Angela apparently didn't connect his name to their previous meeting at the bar. He figured it wouldn't be a good idea to remind her.

"Angela, can you do me a huge favor, please?"

"I'll try."

"Listen, I'm in jail and this is my only call. When Dan gets back, could you please ask him to come to Norwalk City Jail as soon as he can? Tell him that Pete Conley is in a jam and needs his help. Got that?"

"Okay."

"I'm sorry, but would you mind repeating that back to me—what you'll tell Dan?"

"Pete Conley is in a jam. Go to the Norwalk Jail as soon as you can."

"That's it. Great. Thanks a million, Angela."

"Sure. You're welcome."

"You're an angel, Angela, just like your name."

She giggled. "Thanks. Bye," and she hung up.

The cop walked Pete back to the cell and locked the door. Sitting on the cot, he continued to try to clear his head. Then he remembered: His mother's wedding was in six days, that coming Saturday, and he was supposed to be getting on a plane Friday morning.

"Shit!" he said loudly. "*Fuck!* What the hell am I gonna do?"

"Shut up over there. I'm trying to sleep," the drunk in the next cell slurred.

"Fuck off."

If he couldn't get out of there by Friday, he wouldn't be able to make it to the wedding. What the hell is he going to tell her? She's gonna be pissed.

"Fuck! Fuck! *Fuck!*"

"*Quiet!*"

"Go fuck yourself!"

50: The San Francisco Lie

"You know, it feels awkward to learn so much about your past when you know so little about mine," Rick said, as they prepared dinner together that night. "When you were telling me about it this afternoon, I kept thinking about my own experiences and how similar they are and yet, at the same time, how different."

"You don't mean Karen, do you?"

"No. Not Karen. I'm talking about Linda Nash."

Maggie furrowed her brow.

"We met in June 1977. She had just graduated from Harvard. We spent a lot of time together that summer. She was smart, well-read and had strong, well-informed opinions. She got me thinking about things I'd never given much thought to. She was always asking questions and posing even more. She was positive about life and driven—unlike Karen—and clearly going places."

"Did you ever talk with her about your parents?" Rick nodded. "Did she show sympathy and understanding—as Karen hadn't?"

"Yeah, actually, she did. Of course, the topic of my parents did come up—as did hers. In fact, I met her parents, once. They were rather unfriendly. They live in northern Greenwich on a big estate with a gatehouse and stuff like that. Her father is a senior partner at a big Wall Street law firm. Her mother didn't really have a career. She was involved in a bunch of local charities. But, yeah, Linda wanted to talk about my parents' deaths. And she was very sympathetic. But I was a little—I guess I was a less than forthcoming about it and not eager to get into a discussion about my feelings. Yeah, we talked about it, but not about how it affected me. I kind of side-stepped it when she probed too much. At that point, it had been a little more than a year since their deaths and I guess I was still struggling with it."

"So, she basically tried and gave up?"

"Um, yeah, I guess you could say that. But it didn't get in the way of our relationship. I honestly liked her. We really enjoyed being together that summer. It seemed like we were falling in love."

Maggie shivered a little.

"But I didn't know that, late in the summer, she was also trying to rekindle her relationship with her former Harvard boyfriend who'd moved back home to California. She flew out to San Francisco over Labor Day weekend on the spur of the moment and was mysterious about it. As I discovered later, it was to visit him and try to patch things up. She hadn't said when she would be coming back, but I assumed it was just for the long holiday weekend. Well, I assumed wrong. By mid-week when I hadn't heard from her, I called her one evening—she was living with her parents. Her mother answered. She was very cagey. She gave me no information about where Linda was or when she'd be back. It was as though she didn't even know who I was talking about. It was very weird.

"Then, that following Saturday, I got a letter from Linda, postmarked Sausalito. It was a classic 'Dear John' letter. She wrote that she'd gotten a job with McKinsey in their San Francisco office and had moved there. There was no apology, no 'nice to have known you.' Nothing. Not really much of a 'good-bye.' She just said that, if I'm ever in the Bay Area, to look her up. It was only later that I learned, through mutual friends, about the boyfriend."

"Not quite on par with Ron Marion, but close."

"At least Ron had the guts to tell you truth face-to-face," and he guffawed. "I also learned later that there was no job with McKinsey, that she'd lied about that, too. I was stunned. I thought she was serious about me and that we might have a future together. But I had totally misread her. She didn't give a shit about me."

They put dinner on the table and moved the conversation. Both sat quietly for a few moments, lost in their private thoughts as they began nibbling at their dinners.

Maggie finally broke the silence. "You know, I think, in our own minds, people are what we want them to be—whether it's me with Ron or you with Linda. We look for evidence that fulfills our expectations and ignore or rationalize away everything that doesn't. So, even though we thought we knew Ron and Linda, we didn't. But you know, coming out of lousy relationships, we learn a little more about ourselves, who we are, the kind of people we attract, and the kind of people we're attracted to. We also learn the kind of people that use and abuse us, the ones we can't trust."

"I hope you know that I've been completely upfront with you since we met. You don't need to look for evidence that fulfills your expectations."

She grabbed his hand and looked into his eyes. "I know that. I think I sensed almost immediately on the porch that night that I could trust you. And I feel terrible that I've been less than open and truthful with you about my relationship with Pete. I'm so sorry. I am truly sorry." She looked down as she said it and paused a moment before bringing her eyes back to his.

"You know that I love you, don't you?" He nodded and smiled again. "And the best part for me is that I am confident in my own mind that you feel the same towards me."

"Of course I do."

"But think about what you just told me—because I said something similar when I told you about Ron. You said you *thought* you and Linda were falling in love. Did you ever actually tell her that you loved her?"

"Um, no. Not in so many words. Did you ever tell Ron?"

"Yes, I did."

"Did you really love him?

"At the time, I thought so. But in hindsight, no, not really. I think I was willing myself to love him. I wanted to love him. And I wanted him to love me. I guess I'd convinced myself that if I said it and believed it, then it would become true. But, in the end, I was only kidding myself."

"Me, too. I guess I'd assumed that there was love between Linda and me, or that it would grow. In truth, it was just a relationship of temporary fun—at least for her. Well, probably for me too, though I didn't want to admit it at the time—or couldn't admit it. Fact is, I probably didn't really know what I wanted" He hesitated, looking down a few moments before looking again at Maggie.

"Maggie, you know, you're everything to me. As I've learned from being with you, loving you means letting go and putting my trust in you. Maybe I wasn't ready for that kind of commitment before I met you. Or maybe some part of me knew Linda wasn't someone I could or should trust to that degree. But I just hadn't admitted it to myself or couldn't admit it, or just hadn't realized it. I don't really know. Either way, in the end, she proved that she couldn't be trusted—at least, not by me."

Maggie remained silent.

"Regardless. She made the decision for both of us. Maybe it was the right decision and I wasn't strong enough or insightful enough to make it myself. Maybe the pain and sense of betrayal I felt was more about my inability to let go of my ego and own up to that truth. Though it was the right thing in the end, I'm still angry with her for the way she did it."

Still looking into her eyes, he paused again. "Linda and Ron were not our fate. We just didn't know that at the time. But we know it now, now that we have each other."

"You're right. It's all about trust. And I trust you *completely*," she said quietly, and paused briefly. "We are each other's destiny. We both know it. And that's the best thing that's ever happened to us."

51: Revealed Secrets

Tuesday, August 12th

Maggie had just finished a client call when Molly buzzed her on the intercom. "Steven McDonough from Montgomery Winstead is on line three for you."

"Thanks, Molly."

"Good morning. This is Maggie."

"Good morning, Miss Haines. This is Steve McDonough from Montgomery Winstead. We met on Sunday at your parents' home."

"Yes. But please, call me Maggie. How are you?"

"I'm fine, thank you. I hope you are as well. And you can call me Steve. Uh, Mr. Montgomery has asked that I share with you the findings from the initial investigations into your assailant, Peter Conley. I need about ten minutes of your time. Is this a good time to talk?"

"Yes. Go ahead."

"We, the Norwalk Police Department and the District Attorney's office, have uncovered some relevant facts about Mr. Conley that will serve the DA well when this case goes to trial. I'd like to get your reactions and thoughts. Perhaps they will stimulate additional insights or further recollections about him. Okay?"

"Sure… Of course. Go ahead."

"First of all, Mr. Conley is married, and has been since mid-1976."

Maggie gasped aloud. "Wait. *What?* He's *married?* Are you sure?"

"Yes."

"And, are you saying that he still is?"

"We have a copy of a marriage certificate from Stamford city records, dated July seventeenth, 1976, attesting to the marriage of Mr. Conley and Tracy Finnegan. We could find no documents on record to indicate that a divorce has ever been filed for or consummated—not in any state. Mr. Conley's estranged wife and their three-year-old daughter now live outside Nashville with Mrs. Conley's mother."

Maggie gasped again and put her hand to her mouth. "*Oh my God. He has a daughter?"*

"Charlene Conley was born on December fifteenth, 1976. We have a copy of her birth certificate from Stamford Hospital. I personally interviewed Mrs. Conley on the phone. She told me that she had met Pete at Quinnipiac College when she was a nursing student there and he was studying business administration. She confirmed that they are separated, but not divorced. In response to my questions, she said she and her daughter had left Mr. Conley two-and-a-half years ago because of repeated physical abuse."

Maggie gasped out loud.

Steve continued. "In addition, Mrs. Conley applied for and received a permanent restraining order against him. She has not heard from him since she got the restraining order and moved out of state. Nor has he kept up with his three-hundred dollars per month child support payments to which he'd agreed. He currently owes her nearly six thousand dollars, she said. Mrs. Conley's mother cares for the child while she works as a nurse at a local hospital."

Maggie's hand was still over her mouth, as she stared into the middle distance. Steve paused. She could hear him shuffling papers.

"As for his arrest record, in addition to the waived DUI charge of which you are aware, he also has been arrested on six occasions within the past five years, including charges of reckless endangerment, leaving the scene of an accident, and two separate charges of assault and battery. In each case, he either paid a fine or the charges were dropped. The second assault and battery charge was filed against him by a woman he had dated briefly earlier this year, uh, on February twenty-second. She dropped charges before it went to trial. So, he has never served jail time for any of his offenses."

"February twenty-second? This year?"

"That's right."

He paused. Maggie heard his chair squeak.

"Additionally, we learned that, in January of 1978, Stamford police were called to his residence by his wife for a reported domestic dispute. By the time they arrived, Mr. Conley had departed, so there was no arrest, and no charges were filed. According to Mrs. Conley, it was that incident that prompted her to take out the restraining order against him. Shortly thereafter, she obtained a separation agreement from him and relocated to Tennessee with their infant child to live with her mother. So, that's what we have so far. Clearly, based on this information and what you told us about his behavior toward you, he's a serial abuser of women."

She was silent, too stunned to talk.

"Maggie, are you still there?"

"Uh, yeah. I'm sorry. It's just that I…"

"Yes? Go ahead, please."

"Oh… Nothing. nothing. Please go on."

"He was indicted Monday and faces multiple charges, including harassment, assault and battery, use of a firearm in the commission of a crime, receipt of stolen property, and unlicensed possession of a firearm. It turns out that the gun had been stolen. Cumulatively, if convicted on all charges, he could serve as much as forty years in prison."

"Forty years? No kidding? Wow."

"Well, it's not likely that any judge or jury would go that far, but that's what the DA is going to seek. Frankly, I think the DA is building a solid case against him. It doesn't sound like he's going to be open to a plea bargain, so this is going to go to trial. And I cannot envision any judge giving him just another slap on the wrist. Even if he doesn't get forty years, I think he will serve some serious prison time this time around."

"I don't know what to say." She took a deep breath. "Is there anything else that Rick and I need to do?"

"No, nothing for the time being. The court date will likely be set for later this fall—perhaps as soon as October. You and Mr. Hewson *will* need to testify."

"Of course. I understand. And we are both prepared to do that."

"May I assume that you spoke with Miss Shepherd about her possible role as well?"

"I did speak to Molly, uh, Miss Shepherd. Oh, and I assume that our restraining orders against him are in effect?"

"Yes indeed, as of yesterday morning."

"Wow. That was fast. Thank you. One more thing. I'm just curious. Is he still in jail, or has he made bail?"

"He's still in jail. After bail was denied at his hearing on Monday, he was moved to the holding area of the Bridgeport Correctional Center. I attended that hearing. The DA had enough evidence by then to convince the judge that he was a flight risk. That, combined with his possession of a stolen handgun during the commission of a crime, pretty much sealed his fate."

Nevertheless, his attorney is appealing that ruling."

"So, what are his chances of making bail and being released?"

"He'll be in jail for at least another week. The appeal will be heard Monday or Tuesday. In cases like this, the judge will usually set an appropriate bail. Based on his record, his past arrests, the charges in this particular case, plus the outstanding child support payments, the DA told us he is going to ask for bail of a hundred thousand dollars. Conley would have to post a ten percent bond if he wants to get out." He paused a moment. "Did any of this information I've shared with you trigger any additional insights or recollections?"

"Uh, no. No, not really. But I'll be thinking about this and if anything occurs to me, I'll let you know. Oh. Wait. I do have one other question."

"Sure. What is it?

"Have you figured out how Pete got the gun? That was a total shock to me. I've never known him to have any interest in guns. I doubt he ever even fired a gun. But then, apparently there's a lot about him I didn't know" she added, her voice trailing off.

"All we know is that the gun was stolen. The DA's office has correlated the theft to a domestic break-in in Simsbury in May. Ironically, it was the home of a Simsbury police officer, and the gun was his backup service revolver. The thieves were never identified, so we can't know who sold or gave the gun to Pete, or whether he was involved in the robbery himself."

"Well, okay, thank you. Thank you very much Steve This has been eye-opening. Shocking, really."

"I understand. One other thing. Can we assume that Rick has seen a doctor?"

"Yes, he did that on Monday morning. Fortunately, the doctor said the bruises and cut should clear up in time for the wedding and he will be fine."

"I'm pleased to hear that. And the doctor will submit a report to our offices?"

"Yes. Rick gave him Mr. Montgomery's card."

"Very good."

"Is there anything else?"

"No, that's it for now. Either Mr. Montgomery or I will be back in touch with you again as soon as we learn anything further."

"Okay. Well, thank you. Bye for now, Steve."

"Bye, Maggie."

Maggie was dumbfounded. She rocked back in her chair. Staring at the ceiling, she began to feel nauseated. She closed her eyes and took several slow, deep breaths through her nostrils. After a minute, she opened her eyes, sat forward, and started dialing Rick to tell him what she'd learned.

"This will blow his mind," she muttered to herself. She stopped and hung up, not wanting to upset his workday. They would talk about it that evening.

She briefly considered calling her mother but balked again. She was bursting and had to share this new information with someone. Amanda? No. It had to be Rick. So, it would wait. She paused to think about what it all meant.

What had she been thinking? How could she have been so naïve, so trusting, so blind to this horrible human being, this beast, who likely was incapable of an honest relationship? Who lied so easily, who led a double life, who was physically abusive to his wife? Who had abused women with such ease? And he's a father, too? Oh My God. What other surprises will there be? Just like his wife and that brief girlfriend, Maggie had been on the receiving end of his violent outbursts. How many other women had he treated that way that they don't yet know about?

Another fact that stunned her was that, after their January break-up, he had dated another woman and hit her, too. And during that period, he'd made several phone calls to Maggie, trying to make up with her.

Her head was spinning, full of unfathomable new information about a person she thought she knew.

Molly buzzed her on the intercom again.

"Maggie, Mr. Williams needs to see you right away in his office to talk about the Traynor account. He asked you to bring the files."

She snapped out of the haze. "Okay. Thanks." Picking up her notebook and the client files, she walked briskly down the hall to his office.

52: Penalty Box

Thursday, August 14th

Pete didn't yet feel settled into the Bridgeport Correctional Center. The routines were far more complicated and restrictive, the space much larger than Norwalk City Jail. It held hundreds of prisoners, many of whom were in for serious crimes, including murder.

He'd been moved there late Monday afternoon after being denied bail. Assigned to a wing for those like himself who were awaiting trial, he counted his blessings that he was not among the general prison population.

It was now Thursday morning and his mother's wedding would be in two days. He would not be getting on a plane for Charlotte the next morning, and he had to let her know. But what would he say? She would not be happy. In fact, she'd be very pissed off.

When a guard passed his cell, Pete asked if he could use a phone. "Should be okay. I'll be right back."

A half-hour later, another guard came with keys, let him out, and walked him to a room where a half-dozen payphones lined one wall. "Five minutes," the guard told him. "Local calls only or collect if you're calling long distance," and gave him a dime.

"Thank you."

Pete stood still a few moments, collecting his thoughts. Then he called his mother—collect. He could hear her accepting the reversed charges. Finally, "Pete? What is it? Why are you calling me collect?"

"Mom. I got some bad news. I won't be able to make it to your wedding. Something's come up."

"Oh no. Why not? What could possibly be more important than your own mother's wedding? Not business, I hope."

"No, no. It's not business. Actually, I got into a little bit of trouble. This guy picked a fight with me and I got the short end of the stick. They arrested me and put me in jail. But they let him go."

"Pete, what did you do? Were you drunk?"

"Well, a little."

"Pete, we've talked about that before. You lose your temper too easily when you drink. But when do you think you'll be getting out?"

"I don't know. The bail hearing isn't until Monday, so I have to sit tight here in the Bridgeport Correctional Center at least until then."

"*The Bridgeport Correctional Center?* Pete, that's where they put hardened criminals. What exactly did you do?"

"I told you. I hit this guy a couple of times. That's all. But the cops saw me, and they didn't see it when the other guy hit me. So, I'm the one who got busted."

She sighed out loud. "Pete, that sounds like one of your old hockey stories where you got sent to the penalty box while the real culprit got off because the ref didn't see that he'd hit you first. Except this is prison, not the penalty box... I think there's more to this than you're telling me."

"Honest, Mom... But, listen, I'm really sorry I won't be able to be at your wedding on Saturday. I was really looking forward to it."

She was silent for several moments. "I'm very disappointed in you, Pete. You are doing so well in your work, getting promoted, and making good money. Why this? Why now? It's your old self, the angry Pete I thought you out-grew."

"I'm sorry, Mom. I don't know what happened. My emotions just got the better of me." Ahead of the call, he had decided he wouldn't tell her that he'd been fired from his job earlier in the week when his boss learned of the arrest and the gun charge.

She paused again before asking quietly, "Do you need a lawyer?"

"No. Thanks. I'm all set. Got a great lawyer named Seth Farrow. He comes highly recommended. He'll probably get me out next week, but not in time for your wedding, unfortunately."

"Would bail money help? We can scratch some together if you need it—if it means you could get out in time for our wedding."

"They won't set bail for me until Monday at the earliest."

She sighed again. "Okay, Pete. Well, let me know if you need anything."

"Okay. Thanks, Mom. Uh, the guard is telling me I have to get off the phone. Bye for now."

"Bye Pete. I love you. Take care of yourself."

"And I love you too, Mom. I'm sorry."

As the guard walked him back to his cell, he silently scolded himself. What the fuck was he thinking? He fucking blew it. Such an asshole.

Now what? And the more he thought more about the situation, the angrier he got and the less blame he felt for it.

This wasn't his fault. It was that shithead that Maggie is fucking. He's screwed things up for Pete royally.

"When I get out of here, I'm going after him," he muttered aloud. "I'll even things up."

53: Newfield Trio

Friday, August 15th

On Monday, Rick reserved two tickets at the Jazz Cellar to see the Patrick Newfield Trio Friday night, the trio that had been hired to play at their wedding reception. Though he trusted Susie James' recommendation, he still wanted to see them perform himself before the big day, just to get a sense of their set list and style.

Rick also had an ulterior motive.

They left Norwalk when they got home from work and drove straight to New Haven where they had dinner at a restaurant around the corner from the club.

After being seated and ordering drinks, Rick excused himself to go to the men's room. Then he made a detour back stage to introduce himself to Patrick and his band, and to talk briefly about the wedding reception.

He and Patrick exchanged business cards and agreed to talk on the phone the following week. Rick said he wanted to share some ideas for music with him and the band. Patrick was receptive.

Rejoining Maggie in the audience, they settled in for the show. After a half-dozen songs, Rick relaxed, impressed at the trio's virtuosity, pleased to hear that their set included a lot of the standards with which he was familiar, the kind of songs he'd hoped they would play at the wedding reception. Clearly, Susie had paid attention when he contributed suggestions for live music.

The band was good, much better than Rick had hoped.

Maggie was enjoying the music, too, and they were having a good time, much as they had had when they'd seen Johnny Hartman in June at the Village Gate.

About thirty minutes into the set, a group of two women and two men noisily entered the club, taking a table across the room. One of the women scanned the room and her eyes alit on Rick, just as he looked in that direction to determine the source of the commotion. Their eyes connected.

It was Karen McKenna. Each recognized the other simultaneously. She looked away first.

His seat position enabled him to watch her. He decided not to mention it to Maggie.

Occasionally, he'd steal a glance in that direction. Karen was fully engaged in talking loudly with her group, essentially ignoring the band, which Rick found obnoxious. Typical Karen. It's all about her.

A few minutes later, he noticed that Karen had stood and begun walking in his direction. Would she stop, or would she pass by and ignore him? Again, their eyes connected. Karen smiled, and walked straight to him.

"Hi Rick. What are you doing here?" He stood. She gave him a cursory hug and an air kiss. By now, Maggie was watching.

"Hi Karen. It's been a while." Turning toward Maggie, "I'm here with my fiancée, Maggie Haines." Maggie's face was pleasantly non-committal.

"Fiancée? *Really, now.* How exciting."

"Maggie, this is Karen McKenna. An old friend." They shook hands weakly. Maggie stayed seated and gave her a half-smile, saying nothing.

"We came to watch the band," Rick said, facing Karen again. "We've hired them to play at our wedding."

"Oh, yeah? And when is that?"

"End of the month."

"How nice. Well, I'm engaged, too. To Brad Simpson," she added, pointing to him across the room. Brad noticed. He smiled and waved "We haven't set a date yet… Well, funny to bump into you here. Good to meet you, Maggie." Maggie nodded with another half-smile. "Congratulations… Well, I was just headed to the ladies' room. Enjoy the show."

After she left, Maggie gave him an inquisitive look. "So, that's Cokehead Karen, eh? I don't suppose you noticed the expensive dress she was wearing."

Rick shook his head.

"That's a Diane von Furstenberg label wrap dress. Looks like the one I saw last week at Mitchells in Westport. I liked it, but it was too expensive."

"You don't say"

"And did you notice that string of pearls? Oh my God!"

"Uh, you know, we're missing some good music here. Mind if we talk about this later?"

"Sure." She nodded stiffly.

54: White Hart Inn

Saturday, August 16th

Charley called Thursday to say that Beth's trip to South Africa unexpectedly stretched into the weekend and she wouldn't be back to New York until the following Wednesday. So, they would have to cancel the Saturday night dinner in Manhattan they'd planned with Rick and Maggie.

While at work on Friday, Rick made room reservations at the White Hart Inn for Saturday night. She learned over dinner in New Haven Friday evening and was delighted. They left after lunch and drove to Salisbury, planning to sightsee and stop along the way at antique shops. Rick planned a meandering scenic route he was familiar with, through Woodbury, Roxbury, Washington, Warren and Cornwall.

Maggie had been quiet and detached all morning as they ran errands and got ready to go. As they began their drive, her silence continued. He thought he knew the reason, but hoped she'd snap out of it.

As they passed through North Woodbury on Route 47 and into Roxbury, he turned left onto a narrow old farm road, Painter Hill Road. It was to be another little surprise. Rick wanted to show her where Alexander Calder had lived and worked.

He stopped his car in front of an old New England farmhouse. Calder had converted the adjacent old ice house into his studio, its north-facing wall covered in windows, which they could see in the back. A large black stabile graced the side yard.

"I love that stabile. Actually, I love all his work. So whimsical and fun. Calder died nearly four years ago." He turned toward Maggie. "Did you know he's buried here in Roxbury? The family still owns this place."

"Uh huh." She stared straight ahead.

Rick thought she would be excited to see the place, but all he was getting out of her were grunts and monosyllabic answers. She was still brooding, clearly, and Rick knew why.

"Maggie, are you okay?"

"I'm fine," still staring straight ahead.

"You don't seem fine. You're awfully quiet. Is something wrong?"

"Nothing's wrong."

He shut off the engine.

"It's last night. It's Karen. Isn't it?"

"Hmm." She looked into her lap, one hand on each thigh.

"Listen. I understand. It's a natural reaction. And I'd react the same way if we'd run into Ron instead last night. In fact, I'd probably have been worse. I imagine it feels like being smacked in the face by the reality of my past love life, yes?"

"Um, I guess."

"You know that Karen means nothing to me. I walked away from her because of her blasé attitude toward me and our so-called relationship. I harbor no feelings for her whatsoever—not even negative ones. I wish we hadn't run into her, but there you are. What am I gonna do?"

She was quiet for a moment. Rick let her have the silence.

"You're right," she finally said, quietly. "I'm just obsessing about it. It's true. It *was* like slap in the face. She kind of ruined the evening. But that's just me. It's my fault. It's my problem. I let it get to me... Sorry."

"No. It's no one's fault, and there's no reason to apologize. It is what it is. Your feelings are natural. It's fine." He put his hand on her thigh, squeezed lightly. She put her hand atop his. He detected a small smile. He restarted the engine and returned to the main road.

They were coming into the center of Washington, which featured a brilliant red barn near its center housing an antique shop.

"Let's stop here. It looks promising," he suggested. She nodded.

As they began crossing the small parking lot, Maggie grabbed his arm and pulled him to her. "Rick, I'm sorry for being such a pill. I love you," and embraced him in a deep kiss.

They perused the shop for a half-hour, holding hands most of the time. The shop's collection of early twentieth century toys amused them both. Maggie fiddled with an antique doll house for several minutes. They were both taken with an old cedar chest. It was well preserved and was being offered at a reasonable price. They bought it.

Since it wouldn't fit in Rick's VW, they made arrangements to have it shipped to their Norwalk apartment. And they were back on the road.

The direct route would have gotten them to Salisbury in less than two hours. But, with all the stops and the slower, meandering back-country roads, they pulled into the White Hart Inn parking lot after five-thirty, four hours after they'd left South Norwalk.

"Back to the scene of the crime," Maggie said quietly, grinning as she stood scanning the bright white eighteenth-century inn from the parking lot.

"Let's check in and wander around," Rick said. "I want to visit that porch again."

They took an upstairs suite he'd splurged on, full of antique furniture that gave it an authentic colonial feel. After dropping their overnight bags, he led Maggie down the stairs into the lobby and the ballroom, which was being prepared for a private event. After pausing at the entrance to take it all in, he led her to the left end of the room.

"This is where I was standing, next to the bar, talking to Bill and his friends, when I first saw you over there, throwing wine in Pete's face," he said, laughing quietly and pointing to the opposite end of the room near the French doors that led to the porch.

Maggie let go of his hand and slowly walked the length of the room. He followed. She stopped at the spot and, without saying a word, looked back to where he said he'd been standing. She then turned and walked through the doors to the porch outside to stand at the railing where Rick had found her that night.

She leaned forward with her elbows on the railing, just as she had before, looking at the same distant hills. When she turned, Rick was standing behind her. She put both hands around the back of his neck.

"Thank you for being there for me that night. I love you." And she pulled him to her. They kissed for a long minute, until they heard noises inside and looked up to see that an inn worker had come into the ballroom and was moving chairs and tables around. He released her. "Just a second. Stay here."

Stepping inside, he briefly spoke to the young man, who followed him back out. Taking a compact camera out of his pocket, he handed it to him.

"Right here." They put their arms around each other's waists and took a step backward so that they were standing on the same spot at the railing where they'd stood and talked for more than two hours on May thirtieth. "Right here... Okay, Maggie, say cheese." And the young man snapped a few photos from different angles.

"Thank you very much." The waiter gave him back the camera and

Rick slipped him a couple dollars as he returned to his tasks inside.

"That'll be a nice keepsake to show our children and grand-children, and a way to show them where we met," Maggie said.

"What a wonderful thought."

"And what a terrific idea to come back here. It feels like we've come full circle." She paused, looked away, put her hand to her chin and corrected herself. "No, that's not it. We've come a million miles from that evening. And I am in such a good place right now. I don't want it ever to end."

"Not if I can help it," he said, giving her another kiss.

"I'm sorry I was such a brat today. That was out of line."

"Stop it, Maggie. Forget it happened. We're fine. And I love you."

She smiled and kissed him.

"Is it too early for dinner? I'm starved."

"Not at all. Let's go to the dining room."

They enjoyed a long, leisurely dinner, after which they returned to their room and made love into the night.

55: Bail Hearing

Tuesday, August 19th

Maggie had just walked into her office and put her briefcase and purse down Tuesday morning when Molly buzzed her on the intercom. "Maggie, it's Mr. McDonough of Montgomery Winstead for you. Line one."

"Thanks, Molly."

She took a deep breath and picked up the phone. "Good morning, Steve. Got some news?"

"Good morning, Miss... uh, Maggie. I'm calling to give you the latest. The bail hearing for Mr. Conley was held yesterday afternoon and the judge set it at a seventy-five thousand dollars. The judge felt that the defendant presented a clear and present danger to the community."

"Oh, good."

"And, apparently Mr. Conley does not yet have access to sufficient funds to post the ten percent bond, so he will continue to be held in the Bridgeport Correctional Center until his trial, or until he can raise the funds."

"Well, I'm glad to hear that. Do we have a trial date yet?"

"Not yet, but I would expect that it will probably be late October or early November. Before the initial bail hearing last week when he pleaded not guilty, he had retained an attorney, Seth Farrow. I'm familiar with this gentleman. I've represented clients against him in the past. He's a very capable defense attorney. I expect he will argue for a reduction in Mr. Conley's bail."

"Is that likely to happen?"

"That's difficult to say with any certainty. It depends on the judge. As I say, Mr. Farrow is a talented attorney. Knowing him, he's likely to appeal to a different judge, one he feels might be more open to a lower bail."

"Let's hope that he doesn't find one... Have you learned anything further about the defendant?" She couldn't bring herself to say his name.

"Nothing more than what I told you last week. We've given the DA's office our notes from our interviews with you and Mr. Hewson. Oh, and one other thing. I wanted to thank you for forwarding Miss Shepherd's phone log. It is pertinent and most helpful. We've passed those along to the DA, as well as your answering machine tape. They'll definitely want to prep you both for the trial before that begins. Other than that, just try not to think about this case and, instead, enjoy your wedding and honeymoon. You have Mr. Montgomery's and my best wishes and blessings."

"Thank you. And thank you for all you've done."

After calling Rick to update him, she called her mother, who had been upset to learn that there was a chance that Conley might be released.

"Seventy-five thousand dollars? Well, I guess we can relax knowing we won't see him until the trial."

"Well, maybe, Mom. But maybe not. Mr. McDonough said that Pete's lawyer is pretty good and, depending on the judge, he could successfully argue for a reduction in bail."

"Well, I'm sure Chet's team will stay on top of it."

56: Ancestral Surprise

When Maggie walked into the apartment that evening, Rick was already there. Putting her bag on the couch, as usual, she noticed that he had propped up on a dining room chair his framed print of John Singer Sargent's portrait, "Mrs. Charles Inches."

Rick came out of the bedroom, having changed out of his suit, and walked to her for a hug and kiss.

"That's good news about Pete, don't you think, getting hit with that high bail? Let's hope that holds him," she said.

"Yeah, I agree. But, listen, I want to tell you about something else I've found out," and his gaze shifted to the Sargent portrait.

"What is it? And what's with the print? Where'd that come from?"

He grinned. "From the storage locker. It belongs here, on our walls. Not out of sight in that place."

"I agree. It's a lovely painting. I've always liked it. And I know you do, too. But why the change of heart?"

"Sit here. I have a little surprise for you." She settled on the counter-side stool.

"You agree that you look like your mother?"

"Of course. Everyone says so."

"What about Louise and her mother? Would you say that they also shared similar facial characteristics?"

"Uh, yes. I remember Mom saying that. Why do you ask?"

"You told me that your grandmother's mother's maiden name was Tilden and her mother's maiden name was Roe, right?"

"Yes. Just like I told you. Emma Roe Tilden. She passed away in 1957. I barely remember her."

"What do you know about Emma Roe's parents? What was her mother's maiden name?"

"Um, I think her mother's maiden name was Pomeroy. Uh, Jane Pomeroy. Yes. That's it. Jane Pomeroy."

"Then I'm right. Or, I'm pretty sure I'm right."

"Right about what?"

"Well, I've done a little research and made a couple of calls. Got a lot of help from the Genealogical Society of Pennsylvania in Philadelphia, and the New England Historic Genealogical Society in Boston. I found out that Mrs. Charles Inches, Louise Pomeroy," and he paused to nod at the portrait, "that Louise Pomeroy was the youngest of three daughters of Horace Pomeroy and Emma Pierce Pomeroy from Bradford, Pennsylvania. *Emma.* Your great-grandmother's name was Emma, right?"

Maggie nodded. "That's right."

"Louise Pomeroy's older sisters were Alice, the oldest, and Jane. And Jane had two daughters, Janet and Emma—likely named after her mother, Emma Pomeroy. Janet died when she was only fourteen. Emma, four years younger, went on to marry John Tyler Tilden of Rochester, New York, and moved there from Pennsylvania. And their only child, Margaret—your grandmother—married your grandfather, Charles Ainsley Halloway, and moved to Philadelphia where he worked for his father."

"Grandma Margaret was originally from Rochester." Maggie was starting to grin.

"So, the lovely young woman in this portrait is your ancestor—a great aunt." Maggie stared at him, speechless, her mouth hanging open.

"On our first date, I said that you reminded me of Louise Pomeroy Inches. I don't think you took me seriously. But I couldn't get it out of my head. I had to find out for sure—which is why I asked you about your mother's family's names. I was trying to correlate my research with what I could learn from you. A few weeks ago, on my lunch hour, I got on the phone with both the New England and Pennsylvania genealogical societies. They were very helpful and sent me this research," as he pulled a fat envelope from his briefcase and put it on the counter.

"This is how I put all the pieces together," he said, spreading the documents and photos on the counter. "I recognized your face the first time I laid eyes on you, but I didn't make the connection right away to this portrait. It seemed like a lost memory, or I thought that I might have just been imagining it. The night of our first date, I wasn't just feeding you a line about your similarity to Mrs. Inches. I meant it. And now we know that that distinctive, beautiful face has been passed down through generations of Pomeroy descendants, including you, your mother—and it appears your grandmother,

Margaret, as well."

"This is incredible. I can't believe—"

"—Look at this portrait again."

Rick picked up the framed poster and held it so Maggie could see it more closely.

"You and Louise Pomeroy share the same mouth. Look at hers. Do you see it? The slight downward curve to the lower lip and the flat upper lip." He traced his finger across Mrs. Inches' lips.

"And her eyebrows. Same as yours. That soft arch. The narrow, straight nose. Even shape of your chin is like hers. What do you think?"

"Amazing. You're right. And not just me. It's Mom and Grandma, too. And not only that, Mom is named for her great-grandmother's little sister—this woman. And Aunt Alice is named for her older sister. This can't be a coincidence."

"Not likely."

"Funny how Mom and Grandma never talked about this, never even mentioned that the woman in this Sargent portrait was one of our ancestors."

"Maybe they didn't know."

"Not likely, if she and my aunt are named for Pomeroy sisters. I just don't understand why they never talked about it."

"Maybe your grandmother didn't know about the painting's existence but was just picking up on a couple of old family names. The painting is not well-known. After all, it still is in the private collection of Louise Pomeroy's grandson, and not shown in public often. I couldn't find a copy of it in a single reference book. It was pure luck that I should have taken such a liking to it during that show at the MFA that I bought a copy. Otherwise, this may never have come up."

"We gotta share this with Mom! She will be amazed."

57: Cut Loose

Friday, August 22nd

It was Friday, eight days before the wedding. Maggie was eager to leave the office early. There were still many loose ends. Julie was coming in that evening from Denver. And Sarah was expected from New London in the afternoon. Maggie hoped she wouldn't to get caught up in an eleventh-hour crisis at the agency that would waylay her.

Shortly after she got settled, Molly called her on the intercom. "Maggie, it's Mr. McDonough again for you. On line two."

"Good morning, Steve. Do you have some more news?"

"Yes, I do. I'm afraid that it's not good. Mr. Conley's attorney appealed to a different judge yesterday morning, and that judge reduced the bail to ten thousand. Mr. Conley was able to post the thousand-dollar bond and was released late yesterday afternoon."

"*No!* Oh my God. That's *terrible.* Where is he now?"

"Uh, we don't exactly know, but I suspect he's at his residence in Stamford. I do know that he was fired from his job, so I can be sure he's not at work. He was informed of the restraining orders and told not to contact either you or Mr. Hewson through any means. Doing so would revoke his release. He would also forfeit the thousand-dollar bond and be right back in the Bridgeport Correctional Center."

"Well, that's some consolation, I suppose."

"Also, we're reaching out to the judge to ask him to reconsider. But that's not likely to have much effect, not after he's already ruled, lowered the bail, and released him. Generally, they don't reverse themselves unless we can present compelling new information pertinent to the case."

She turned the new scenario over in her mind. "Actually, this makes me very nervous. Knowing him, I'm sure Pete has revenge on the mind. If he gets drunk again, as he is likely to do—immediately—he'll just ignore the restraining orders and come after us anyway."

"I suppose that is a possibility."

"But *how could this happen?* Couldn't you present a stronger argument than his lawyer? I don't get it."

Steve sighed. "It was just one of those things. We were not aware of the appeal until after the fact. His lawyer found a sympathetic judge and made a convincing case. An assistant district attorney was present, but he was unfamiliar with the case. Believe me, we're not happy about this either and, as I said, we've left messages with the judge, but haven't heard back yet. Again, I'm sorry about this. If I learn more, I'll call you back."

"Okay, then. Uh, bye." She hung up, realizing belatedly that she hadn't waited for Steve to say good-bye. A cascade of panic washed over her at the cold realization that Pete was out. Likely to retaliate against her and Rick. She had to call Rick immediately.

"Rick, I'm afraid I have some bad news for you."

"You've changed your mind about marrying me?" and then chuckled.

"No, Rick, this is not a joke. Pete got out on reduced bail yesterday. And nobody knows where he is now."

"Oh shit. That *is* bad news."

"What should we do?"

"Uh, well, uh mostly, we have to be on the alert at all times and keep our eyes peeled for that damned blue Camaro. *Dammit*, this is not good. I do not like this at all."

"Mom is going to freak out—"

"—*I'm* freaking out. I don't need to tell you this, but you have to be super careful when you leave your office. What time are you going home?"

"As soon as I can. No later than three."

"Okay. Before you go downstairs to leave, look out the windows at all sides of your building and scan the area for his car... You know, actually, he could park his car nearby, walk to your front door and grab you. *Wait*. Molly knows what he looks like, right?"

"I think so."

"Then it might be a good idea to have her go downstairs ahead of you to make sure he's not there. *No. Wait*. Maybe we should call the police."

"Rick, you're scaring me."

"Okay, maybe don't call the police unless you see him there. But I'm very worried. This guy knows no limits and I don't think we should trust the restraining orders to stop him if he makes up his mind to come after us. I have no doubt that he's going to want to take revenge on me. Probably both us.

Seriously, Maggie. Please be super careful."

"Of course. Uh, what time are you leaving to go get Julie?"

"What? Oh, I don't know. Probably two-fifteen. Two-thirty. I want to be sure I'm there before her plane gets in at four-fifteen."

"Okay. You guys are going straight to Mom and Dad's, right?"

"Yeah. Right.

"Good. Okay. I'll see there. Bye for now. I love you. You be careful, too, okay?"

"Yes, I will. Oh, and one more thing. I won't tell Julie. I'm sure your mother will tell your father. But otherwise, let's keep it among just the four of us for now. Okay? No sense getting everyone upset needlessly."

"Right. Good idea. Will do. I'm going to call Mom right now. I love you. Bye."

She thought for a few moments, composed herself and then dialed her mother.

"Hi Maggie. What's up?"

"Listen, I got some bad news a few minutes ago. Steve McDonough called to say that Pete got out on a reduced bail and is back on the street again."

"*Oh no!* That's horrible. We need to hire private security. Right now."

"Really?"

"*Yes!* This guy brought a gun to your apartment. God knows what he had mind. To threaten you and Rick with it, or to actually use it? We have no idea what he's capable of. We can't take chances. I'm going to call your father right now and ask him to call Chet and see what can be done. Can we get him back in jail? Chet would know. I'm sure he'll have some ideas. Oh God, this is awful. I thought we were finished with this dreadful person."

"I'm so sorry, Mom. I'm sorry I ever brought him into our lives."

"Maggie. This isn't your fault. Who could have known this guy would turn out to be such a mad man? Give yourself a break."

"I know, Mom. But it's my fault that he's haunting us."

"*No, it isn't!* Stop that. You can't control him. Stop talking like that. And stop *thinking* like that. You did nothing to deserve this beast."

She sighed. "Okay. Uh, listen, Rick and Julie should be at the house by seven. They're coming straight back from LaGuardia. Can we act like everything's normal? Everybody already knows that Pete gave Rick his injuries and that he's now in jail because of that. But I don't want to upset everyone by telling them that he's back on the street. I want them all to have a good time, to just relax and enjoy themselves. So, let's just keep this among ourselves."

"Of course, dear. I'll tell your father, but otherwise, we'll keep it among the four of us for now. Just you, me, Rick and Dad. And we'll hold dinner until Rick and Julie get here."

"Mom, if you don't mind, I'd like to tell Dad about this myself."

"Uh, sure. Sure. Maggie, dear, we will get through this."

"Thanks, Mom. I should be home by four or so to help with dinner."

"Okay. Good. See you then. And be careful."

After hanging up, Maggie immediately dialed her father's office and told him the news. His first response was to say that he would hire private security, starting immediately.

"And then, I'm going to call Chet and give him a piece of my mind. He should have been on top of this. Why was this thug given a reduced bail? It makes no sense at all. Chet said the case was air-tight. Apparently, he was wrong. Or else this bastard's lawyer found himself some bleeding-heart liberal judge. *The victims be damned!*"

"Do you think that's what happened, Dad?"

"I can't imagine why any sane judge would let this guy go. You know these liberal judges. They care more about the criminals than they do the victims. Chet and his team blew it. This is why we pay Montgomery Winstead a retainer. To stay on top of this kind of crap. I'm going to get the security firm lined up right now and put them in touch with Chet's office to get the lowdown on Conley. I want them to know where he is from now until he gets convicted and locked up for good. I don't want him anywhere near you, Rick, or any of us."

"Good. I feel better already. Thanks. Oh, and one other thing. I think we should keep this among us for now. Just you, me, Rick and Mom. I don't want to upset everyone unnecessarily."

"Uh, yeah. Good idea.

"Okay. I love you, Dad."

"And I love you, too, honey."

58: Dorothy Stratten

"Whoo boy, I deserve this one," Pete said aloud, as he reached for the aspirin bottle in the medicine cabinet, hoping to quell his mammoth hangover.

He'd been released from the Bridgeport Correctional Center late in the afternoon the day before. On the pay phone outside the prison, he called Dan to see if he could get a ride. His car was still in the impound yard in Norwalk, fifteen miles away.

There was no answer, so he called a cab to take him to back to Norwalk City Jail. After checking Pete's license, the guard at the impound yard unlocked the gate and walked Pete to the last aisle, pointed to the blue Camaro mid-way down the left side, and handed him the keys.

"Fuck you very much," Pete muttered under his breath as he turned away.

Getting into his Camaro, he gunned it, peeled out of the lot, and headed straight for Victoria Station. It was five-thirty-five when he walked in. The bar was nearly empty. He still wanted to talk to Dan, so he called him on the bar's pay phone. Again, no answer.

Settling onto a bar stool, he saw that the same bartender he'd seen a couple Saturdays ago was working again that evening. "Where's Stan?" he asked her, discreetly checking her out again. She was wearing the same snug black vest and open white dress shirt that he'd admired the last time he saw her. Love that cleavage, he told himself.

"He's off this week. Taking a little vacation time in Florida, he said. I'm filling in for him."

"You usually work the weekends, right? I think I've seen you before. What's your name?"

"That's right. I work Fridays and Saturdays. I'm Tiffany."

"My name's Pete. Pete Conley. Nice to meet you," he said, reaching out to shake her petite hand, noticing a wedding band on her left ring finger at the same time.

"Likewise. What can I get you?"

Pete ordered a long-neck Rolling Rock with a shot of Jack Daniels on the side, both of which he downed quickly. A half-hour later, as he ordered a third round and a pizza, the six o'clock news came on the TV screen above the bar.

Pete was barely paying attention until, a few minutes into the broadcast, a familiar photo popped up on the screen that caught his eye: a fully-clothed Dorothy Stratten, an attractive publicity shot of her in a figure-flattering, snug fuzzy, powder blue sweater and a big smile, a photo he'd seen before. It accompanied an update on a report from the week before and it nearly knocked him off the barstool.

The previous Thursday night in Los Angeles, while Pete was still in jail, Playboy's Playmate of the Year, Dorothy Stratten, had been murdered with a shotgun by her estranged husband, Paul Snider, who then turned it on himself. The bodies weren't discovered until the next morning—last Friday.

Pete was shattered. He'd carried on a fantasy love affair with Stratten for the past year, ever since he'd first ogled her centerfold in the August 1979 issue of Playboy. She was the ideal of beauty. How could this happen? How could one man, a piece of shit like that, destroy such beauty?

As he downed his beer, Tiffany brought him his pizza. He asked for another round.

He had a few more rounds into the evening, losing count along the way. Leaving the bar at close to eleven, he staggered to his car. Though he struggled to work the keys into the ignition, he did manage to find his way home.

When he woke at nine-thirty Friday morning, he was lying face-down on his bed, fully clothed, his shirt drenched in sweat. He was still wearing his shoes and socks. When he looked out the window, he was amazed to see his car parked perfectly in his driveway—though he had no recollection whatsoever of having driven home, much less parking it.

The full impact of Dorothy Stratten's murder hit him again as he nursed his hangover with a long shower, followed by another couple of aspirins and a shot of Jack Daniels. Perusing the two issues of Playboy in which she was featured brought him little solace. Tossing down another shot of whiskey, he unfurled her centerfold photo on the coffee table and agonized over the loss. Then, he was outraged.

Such beauty, such innocence. Gone. Why? Because of some fucking scumbag and his twisted sense of possession? He thought he could own her?

The world doesn't need people like Paul Snider. He should have been wiped out before he could murder Dorothy.

"Fucking bastard! *Burn in hell!*" he yelled at the blank wall.

He mulled it over for several minutes and had a third shot of whiskey. As he thought about it through his throbbing headache and an increasing buzz, he began to see parallels to his own situation. In fact, he was losing Maggie to her own Paul Snider, he told himself. He needed to do something about it— before it was too late.

He resolved to save Maggie, to get her away from that asshole before he destroys her, too.

Later that evening, Pete returned to the basement to retrieve the SIG P239.

59: Mysterious Blue Car

Rick left his office at two-thirty, intent on being at LaGuardia and Julie's gate when she emerged from her plane. Parking in the short-term lot, he slow-jogged the quarter-mile to the terminal, dodging Checker cabs, abandoned luggage carts and disoriented travelers along the way. Julie's Western Airlines non-stop flight from Denver, scheduled to arrive at 4:15 at gate B6, was on time, according to the arrivals board.

She emerged with the other passengers from the jetway at four-twenty-five. Dropping her handbag, she embraced Rick. Julie was somewhat taller than Maggie, with medium-length dark blonde hair pulled back like her sister. She had the tanned, svelte body of a marathon runner.

They held the hug for several moments.

"I'm so happy for you. And I'm so excited to finally get to meet Maggie. We've talked several times on the phone the past couple weeks. She's terrific. She cracks me up. And she's so easy to talk to."

"I know. I know. She's the best. You're going to love her. You'll have a new best friend, for sure. And a new sister, too, I guess."

Descending the escalator to the baggage claim level, they waited about ten minutes for her luggage to arrive. As they waited, Julie told him about her new job with a Denver actuary firm, which would start when she returned from the wedding. Her suitcase finally came around the carousel and Rick grabbed it. They walked back to his car and headed to Connecticut.

Crossing the Whitestone Bridge, they passed Coop City, and got onto the Hutchinson River Parkway. Traffic was moderate, unusual for a Friday rush hour. Julie eyed Rick's wounded face. Though they'd faded to an ugly shade of dull green, she could see remnants of the bruises, the healing cut now raw pink skin.

"So, my big brother's a prize fighter, eh? Maggie told me all about that night, and all that bullshit with what's-his-name—threatening phone calls, stalking you guys, following you across the county. Nasty business. That guy sounds like a total loser. How do those injuries feel?"

"Ah, no big deal. The pain went away long ago. I'm just hoping the bruises are gone by next Saturday. If not, Maggie is threatening to cover them with makeup, which I'm vehemently opposed to."

Julie laughed. "Anything further on that guy, what's-his-name?"

"Pete Conley. He's a dirt bag. But, no, nothing new. We won't see him again until the trial, probably late October or early November. As far as I'm concerned, it's all water under the bridge. We're totally focused on getting the families together and getting married. And I am so happy that you're here, to share in the celebration. I've really missed you," he said with a smile as he glanced at her and touched her arm.

"Me, too. I've missed you," she smiled. "So, I'm staying at the Haines' house? I understand Sarah's staying there, too. Must be a roomie place."

"Yeah. You and Sarah are sharing Maggie's old room. Maggie's best friend from college and maid of honor, Amanda Olsen, and her boyfriend, Jeff, have the guest room. They're coming down from Boston Thursday. And yes, it is a big house. They have a nice swimming pool, too. Hope you brought your swim suit. But better yet, wait until you meet Maggie's parents, Tom and Louise. They're the best. You're going to love them. They're so generous, welcoming and really down-to-earth. They've practically adopted me as their second son. And they'll probably adopt you and Sarah, too, if you let them."

An hour later, as they came up Oenoke Ridge, just south of the Haines house, Rick saw a blue Camaro streak past in the opposite direction.

Was it Pete, or was he just being paranoid? It was overcast, and nearing dusk. The car was going fast, so he couldn't see the driver or make out the license plate.

As he pulled into the driveway at the Haines home, Julie gasped. "Oh my God. This is incredible."

"I know. Don't let it overwhelm you."

"It's like a movie set. Oh. I love the landscaping."

"Yeah, me too. Maggie's parents had the house built twenty-seven years ago, just after they got married. They have more than two acres. Louise designed and oversaw the landscaping, the placement of the azaleas and rhododendrons around the house and along the front. The sugar maples and elms along the driveway pre-date the house. Actually, the trees are quite old. The driveway follows an old farm road, Louise told me."

As they got out of the car, Maggie came running out of the house, greeting Julie with a hug. "It's so good to finally meet you face-to-face." Taking a step back, she said, "You look just like I pictured you. Come inside and meet everybody," and then turned to Rick for a quick kiss.

While he carried the suitcase, Maggie went ahead with Julie to lead her into the house where they found everyone gathered around the kitchen table, each with a glass of wine.

"Everyone, this is Rick's sister just in from Denver, Julie Hewson." She pointed and said, "This is my brother, Charley, and his girlfriend, Beth Meeks, and my parents, Tom and Louise. And look who showed up a half-hour ago," she said, pointing at Sarah, who was crossing the room to hug her big sister, and then Rick, who she hadn't seen since their dinner in New London.

Louise also gave Julie a hug. "I'm so happy to finally meet you."

"And congratulations on the new job," Tom added, as he shook her hand. "Can we get you anything to drink?"

"Yes, please. I'll have whatever everyone else is having."

One Chardonnay coming right up. Rick? You, too?"

"Yes, please."

Dinner was served outside on the patio table. The din of conversation and laughter among eight people and the clang of silverware on china continued through the long, leisurely meal and dessert. The evening went well past eleven, when the guests started heading upstairs. Tom and Louise were cleaning up the kitchen when Maggie and Rick came to say good-night.

"Maggie, we have a private security team in place starting tonight," Tom told her quietly. "I'm telling you now because there will likely be one of their people outside here who will follow you guys back to Norwalk. They'll be parked outside your apartment all night. I didn't want you to be alarmed."

"Okay. Did you talk to Chet? What'd he say?"

"They're working on it. But I'm not happy at all, and Chet knows it. We pay him a retainer so that he stays on top of these kinds of problems. And he blew it. He knows I'm angry about it."

60: Threatening Phone Call

Saturday, August 23rd

Rick and Maggie spent most of Saturday at the Haines house, dealing with last-minute wedding-related decisions and tasks while hanging out with the newly enlarged family. They headed back to their apartment at four to get ready for the dinner they were hosting for the bridal party.

As he pulled out of the Haines' driveway onto Oenoke Ridge, Rick noticed a black Ford LTD, parked at the end of the driveway across from the Haines' driveway, the driver was wearing sunglasses and slouching in his seat, keeping an eye on things. He assumed it was the security detail. When the sedan slipped in behind them a few car lengths back, his assumption was confirmed.

They were well into dinner preparations when the intercom buzzed. It was Hank and Olivia, who lived in the city and were staying that weekend in Darien with their parents.

Julie, Sarah, Charley and Beth arrived next, followed moments later by Bill Crenshaw and his girlfriend, Janet Pescara. Maggie plied everyone with cheese, crackers and wine while Rick finished the cooking duties. By eight, all ten were seated at the dinner table.

People began leaving around ten-thirty. Hank and Olivia were last out the door. Maggie and Rick began clearing the table and cleaning up.

As he was clearing the table, the phone rang. Rick picked it up and said hello.

It was Pete.

"You son of a bitch, I'm coming for you. It's your fault that I'm in this mess. I'm gonna—"

"—You just violated your restraining order. You're going back to jail, and you're going to forfeit your thousand-dollar bond."

Pete laughed. "The fuck I am. Prove it. It's your word against mine. Fuck you."

He hung up.

"Let me guess. Pete."

"Yup. And he threatened me."

"Then he just violated his restraining over. He's busted. And he's going back to jail," Maggie said, smirking.

"Wish that were true, but I'm afraid not. As he just told me, it's his word against mine."

"Hmm. He's got a point."

"Unless… Maggie, do you know whether the security firm has tapped our phone, monitoring phone calls to our line?" She shrugged. "If so, then he's busted. But if not, it'd be a good idea. Because that definitely was a violation of the restraining orders. Did you see the security guy out front this morning when we left?" She shook her head.

"Did you see the guy parked in the black Ford LTD across the street from your parents' house this afternoon who followed us here."

Again, she shook her head.

"He followed us both ways today. I'm glad to see they're on the ball." He walked over to the window and looked out to the street below. "Come here. I'll show you. See that big dark sedan across the street near the street light?"

"Uh huh."

"That's our guy. We're being watched round-the-clock here. Three different private detectives are doing eight-hour shifts apiece. They're following us in their cars. They know what Pete looks like and his car's make, color and plate number. I feel a lot safer knowing they're there. And so should you."

"Yeah, I guess so."

"It won't last forever. Hopefully, Chet will get the full bail re-imposed and Pete will be back in jail, where he belongs. I'm thinking that maybe I should go down there and tell him about this phone call. I'll be right back."

When he got to the street, Rick walked straight to the car and the detective rolled down the window. "Good evening, Mr. Hewson. What can I do for you?"

"Please call me Rick."

"Hi. I'm Phil Strauss. Call me Phil." They shook hands.

"Phil, I have a couple questions."

"Fire away. Uh, that's a figure of speech, you understand," he said with a lop-sided grin. Rick chuckled.

"Were you outside the Haines house last night around seven?"

"No. We didn't take up this assignment until later last night, so I wasn't there until close to nine. I followed you home from there when you left at eleven-fifteen. Why do you ask?'

"I don't want to sound paranoid, but I was driving back there last night after picking up my sister at the airport. As I came up Oenoke Ridge, a little south of the Haines house, a blue Camaro passed me going fast in the opposite direction. Since Pete Conley got out late Thursday, that well could have been him. But I couldn't verify it with a plate. I couldn't see it."

"Hmm. Good to know. I'll mention it to my partner, Walt. Something else? You said you had a couple of questions."

"Yeah. Pete just called and threatened me. But when I told he'd violated the restraining order, he just laughed and said it was my word against his. Is that true? Or do you have a tap on our phone?"

"That's two questions. But, yes, he's right. It's just say-so and inadmissible in a court of law. And, no, we don't have a tap on your phone."

"Could we do that, in case he calls again?"

"I'll talk to my boss about it tomorrow and let you know. I'll be back with you tomorrow, from about four until midnight. Come on down and I should have an answer for you."

"Thanks. Oh, and one last thing. We're all going for a hike tomorrow at Pound Ridge Reservation—eight of us. We'll be leaving the Haines house about noon in the Haines' GMC Suburban. It's dark green. Are you going to be with us?"

"Yes, we'll be there. Walt will be on duty. But he'll be unobtrusive. If you're asking whether he'll get out of the car and follow you on foot, no. But he will be scoping out the area, looking for opportunities for the perpetrator to tail you. I'm sure he's familiar with that area. So am I. Walt and I both grew up in Bedford. Played high school football together," and he grinned.

"So, are you going to the Bergfield parking lot on the north side?" Rick nodded. "And you'll be coming back there when you're done with the hike?" Rick nodded again. "I'll let Walt know. Unless that clown has supernatural powers to know where you're going to be before you get there, he's not going to be there without Walt knowing about it."

"Good. Good to know. Well, thanks. Glad to meet you, Phil," and they shook hands again.

"Same here."

61: Nightmare

Sunday, August 24th

Dawn was faint in the windows when Rick woke Maggie, though not intentionally. His sweating body twitched in bed next to her and he was mumbling in his sleep. She listened to him with increasing alarm as his mumbling got louder and began to take on an edge of panic. He started thrashing about, his legs and feet twitching. She shook him by the shoulder.

"*Rick, wake up.* You're having a bad dream."

"What? Oh. Yeah. I guess I so. Man, that was scary."

"What was it?"

Rick leaned into her and lay still for a moment before speaking.

"What a nightmare. I dreamt that Pete was chasing me, waving a gun, yelling that he was going to kill me. I was desperately trying to get away from him, but it felt like I was knee-deep in mud. I couldn't run. And he was catching up to me, starting to aim the gun at me."

She wrapped her arms around him. "It's okay. It was just a dream."

"But it seemed so *real*. He was chasing me down a street. I didn't even know where I was. I didn't recognize anything. And I didn't know where to go to get away from him. And he was laughing. This real evil laugh, like he knew he was going to get me."

They locked in the embrace for a few minutes without speaking.

Finally, Rick quietly asked, "Do you think that Pete is capable of murder? I mean, he's certainly shown he's capable of hurting people—his wife, you, that other girlfriend, and now me—and God knows who else. It scares me that he had a gun. Maybe he knows how to get a another one."

Maggie sighed. "I don't know. I doubt it. I mean, he can be violent, sure, but he's is a rational person. I, uh, I just don't know. Well, we have twenty-four-hour security. We're safe. You're safe." And she kissed his cheek.

"Let's get up. We can go out for an early run, beat the heat," she said. "Then we can pick up the Sunday *Times* and come back here to read it over breakfast before we head back to New Canaan to meet everyone for the hike.

"Sounds good."

62: Letter to Mom

After returning from the hike, everyone had Sunday dinner at the Haines house. Maggie and Rick departed afterwards.

Rick pulled his car up to the curb outside the apartment and watched Phil pull in a few spots behind them. "Maggie, let's go talk to Phil to find out about the phone tap."

Phil rolled down his window, and Rick introduced Maggie.

"So, what'd you learn?"

"The phone tap is doable. And since you're consenting, we should be able to get a warrant quickly. We should have it set up by tomorrow morning—afternoon at the latest. An attorney from Montgomery Winstead is working on the warrant. When a call comes in, try to keep them on the line a minute or two so we can trace it. We'll also have a tape recorder going."

"Got it. That's perfect. And if we're not home, our answering machine gets the message. Would it be able to trace the call then, too?"

"Absolutely."

"Great. Thanks," Rick said.

When they got back upstairs, Rick said, "Maggie, remember on our way home after our dinner with Sarah, you suggested that I write a letter to my mother?" She nodded.

"I've been working on it in my spare time at work. I rewrote it a few times. It's a kind of short, but I'm satisfied with what I've got. I don't think a long letter is necessary."

"I'm glad you did that. As I said, it's not so much the letter itself that's important. It's doing it, which forces us to think more deeply about our loss and helps us put it in perspective."

"Definitely. I remember you saying that, and you're right. I'm glad I did it. Would you like to read it?"

"I'd rather you read it to me."

He retrieved the letter from his briefcase by the front door and returned to the kitchen. Maggie sat on a kitchen stool to listen. After unfolding the letter, he cleared his throat and began to read.

Dear Mom,

We take it for granted that there will always be another day to say what we should to the people that matter the most to us. Had I known when we spoke the day before you and Dad left for Aruba that it would be our last conversation, it would have been different.

First of all, I would have told you that I love you. I'm sorry I didn't. And then I would have thanked you for all that you gave me, from birth to adulthood. In particular, you gave me my curiosity, and my love of reading and learning. And, you taught me to be a skeptic. New information about known subjects excites me. But, at the same time, I am suspicious of ideas that fly in the face of common sense and traditional values. Just like you.

I remember how you tolerated my wild opinions when I was younger, but would coax me to think more deeply, posing questions about what I took as facts when they were really assumptions and flimsily reasoned conclusions. You led me to that realization rather than simply correcting me directly or telling me I was wrong. In that way, I came to discover their weaknesses and fallacies for myself. So, I learned to think things through more thoroughly.

In hindsight, I marvel at your patience and ability to listen to some of the positions I held as a teenager. I wish we had talked more in recent years because I think I was beginning to see eye-to-eye with you. So, thank you for pushing me to learn, to question, and to read, habits I cherish and continue to nurture.

What I perceived as stinginess for not giving me money when I asked for it, I now understand to be exactly what you said it was: teaching me the value of work and the importance of earning my own way. But I also learned that it's more than that. It also taught me self-sufficiency and independence, far sooner than my peers learned it, and prepared me for the real world in which I am now living. For that lesson, I am grateful.

But most of all, my biggest regret... Uh. But most of all, my biggest regret is that... Uh.

His voice faltered, and his eyes filled. He took a deep breath, wiped at his eyes, cleared his throat. Maggie reached out and touched his hand. He resumed reading, with a quaver in his voice.

But most of all, my biggest regret is that you never got to meet Maggie Haines, my future wife. Just as do I, I'm sure you would adore her for her quick wit, honesty, the depth and breadth of her knowledge and intelligence, curiosity and, most of all, her generous spirit. She is a stunningly beautiful, graceful, deeply caring and selfless woman. I am a lucky man to have found her and fallen in love with her—even luckier that she also fell in love with me. I know you would love her as much as I do.

Thank you, Mom, for all you have given me. I miss you terribly. I always will.

He refolded the letter and put it on the kitchen counter. Maggie got off the stool. Without a word, they wrapped their arms around each other and stood silently in the kitchen, embracing one another for several minutes.

63: Little White Lie

Tuesday, August 26th

Rick felt no guilt about the little white lie he'd told Maggie Monday evening. It was for her benefit, and the harmless truth would be revealed soon enough. He said he had to spend a little time in the office Tuesday afternoon, despite the fact that he'd previously said he was going to take the whole week off.

A report to which he'd contributed needed some elaboration to satisfy the questions of a higher-up, he explained. He'd have to be in the office from late morning until mid-afternoon and would meet her at her parents' house afterwards.

In fact, he left the apartment late in the morning, right after Maggie, and drove to Westport to meet with Patrick Newfield and his band in Newfield's sound studio behind his house on the north side of Westport. Though the three were part-time musicians, all with unrelated full-time jobs, they were able to get away to spend an hour with him.

Heading there and then to the Haines' house afterwards, Rick wasn't tailed by the black LTD. He'd consulted with Phil the night before, told him of their day's plans. They agreed it would be better if his partner stayed with Maggie.

Rick was nervous that Pete might be following him. Just to be sure, on his way to Westport from South Norwalk, he got off an exit early, and turned off on a side street where he did a U-turn a quarter miles later before returning to the turnpike. But no blue Camaro followed him off the highway or onto the side street.

When Rick got to the Haines' house a little after four, he saw the LTD parked across the street and stifled the urge to wave. Maggie, Louise, Sarah and Julie were out on the patio, chatting, laughing, and drinking iced tea. "Is it okay if a man intrudes on this all-female confab?" he asked jokingly as the four turned simultaneously to look at him.

Maggie jumped up to give him a kiss.

"Rick, Mom has invited us all for dinner downtown. Dad is traveling, and Charley and Beth had to be in the city today for work and won't be back until late. So, it's just you and us. Can you handle four women by yourself?"

"Whoo boy, that sounds like a real challenge, especially four who are so good looking. But, yes, I'm up for it."

""I've made reservations for the five of us at six o'clock at Fat Tuesday in town," Louise said. "I knew you'd be keen to join us."

"Absolutely."

When it was time to go, they all piled into the Suburban and Louise drove them into town to the restaurant. The maître d' walked them to a semi-round booth and Rick sat between Louise and Maggie.

The waiter arrived to take their drink orders. After Louise ordered a bottle of wine for the table, the waiter recited the evening's specials.

As he left, Louise spoke up. "Kids, I am so pleased to see all of you having such a great time together. It does my heart good. You know, we strive and work hard our whole lives for moments like this—for weeks like this. I doubt I've ever enjoyed myself more—unless it was the week of my own wedding. But that was a bit more chaotic."

Looking at Maggie, she added, "We didn't have Susie James back then to save us," and laughed.

"I can't thank you and Tom enough for your hospitality" Julie said. "This has been such a wonderful week. And I can't believe it's only Tuesday. It's been so relaxing, and so much fun."

Sarah nodded in agreement, adding, "I wish it could go on forever."

Louise was about to respond when the waiter arrived with the wine. He poured the five glasses, finishing the bottle. "I should have ordered two bottles," Louise told him. "Please bring another."

Turning to Julie and then to Sarah, she continued. "Julie and Sarah, your presence and the chance to get to know you both have been a real pleasure for both Tom and me. You can stay as long as you like. Heck, I wish you'd both just move in. Since we'll be losing Maggie to the Hewson clan, maybe we should just do a straight-up one-for-one trader—or even a one-for-two trade."

Everyone laughed.

"But I know you have get back to Denver and your new job and your life. And Sarah, you have to start school again in Storrs. Alas, the world goes on, with or without us." She paused, took up her wine glass, and proposed a toast.

"Here's to the Haines-Hewson clan. We're unstoppable now." And they clinked wine glasses around the table.

After the toasts, Louise turned to Rick. "We were talking earlier on the patio about the remarkable work you did researching my mother's family. I wanted to thank you for doing that. I've always known about the Pomeroy connections and the fact that I'm named for my mother's great aunt. But I never knew that she had been painted by John Singer Sargent."

"Sure. I enjoyed it. But mostly I enjoyed it because it confirmed my initial feelings about Maggie," as he grinned at her. "But you know, what I find intriguing is that the Sargent connection hadn't come down through the family lore. I wonder why."

"Yeah, I guess knowledge of that painting went with my Great Aunt Louise's family. Maggie said you told her that Louise's grandson is still in possession of the painting? Is that right?"

"It seems so. He lives in Cambridge, Massachusetts. It's just pure happy luck that he loaned it to the MFA and we got to see it at that Sargent show there five years ago."

"Well, maybe I could talk Tom into buying the portrait from her grandson. I wonder how much he would take for it."

"Mom, that's a nice idea, but I doubt you could afford it. I know that the Stella lithograph was expensive, but a nineteenth century masterpiece like that is museum quality and likely run well into the millions. All we can hope for is that her grandson donates it to a museum, hopefully the MFA."

"Perhaps," Louise said, and then raised her glass again. "Well, here's to the Pomeroys. May they feel generous in their wills." And they all laughed.

64: Spilt Milk in the Dairy Aisle

Friday, August 29th

Friday morning, the day of the rehearsal dinner, dawned bright, with blue skies, temperatures in the lower sixties, and a forecast of the low seventies by mid-afternoon. Louise had offered to make a big, hearty brunch for everyone to tide them over until the rehearsal dinner that evening.

Maggie and Rick pulled into the driveway at nine-thirty. The black LTD had followed from South Norwalk. As Rick turned right into the driveway, it turned around and parked across the street.

They'd neither heard from Pete nor seen anything further of him since Saturday: no phone calls, no phone messages, no sightings of the blue Camaro. The phone tap yielded nothing. Rick was pleased at that, but still nervous. He didn't think it a good idea to relax until Pete was securely behind bars.

When they walked into the kitchen, Louise was staring into the refrigerator with hands on her hips. "What's the matter, Mom?"

"I *know* I asked Doug at Gristede's to bring me an extra dozen eggs yesterday morning. I was going to make a couple of big spinach and bacon soufflés. They brought the spinach and bacon all right. But they must have forgotten the eggs. There are going to be ten of us for breakfast and will you look at this? I only have eight eggs. I should have gotten a fresh dozen in yesterday's delivery."

"Louise, let me run down to the A&P for you and get them," Rick said.

"I'll stay and talk with Amanda, Jeff, Sarah and Julie," Maggie said.

"Need anything else while I'm at the store?"

"Nope. Thanks, Rick. I really appreciate it."

Maggie went out to the patio, bringing along the pot of coffee to freshen everyone's cups.

Rick drove down the driveway and turned left to head into town. The black LTD slipped in behind. As he pulled into the A&P parking lot, Rick looked in the rear-view mirror and saw the LTD still behind him, about three car lengths back. Glancing in the mirror a second time a moment later, he saw a blue Camaro further back, behind the LTD.

Oh shit. Is that Pete? The LTD took a spot on an aisle as Rick pulled into a space nearer the store's right entrance—as did the Camaro, four spots to his right. He eyed the Camaro over the top of his VW as he got out and walked toward the store. But he couldn't see through its tinted windows to see whether it was Pete—though he recalled that Pete's Camaro had tinted windows.

He also couldn't see the license plate unless he walked in the opposite direction from the store. No one emerged from the Camaro. He worried. He hoped that Walt Sendor had seen the car and was watching and following.

As he walked briskly toward the far rear corner of the store to the dairy section, Rick kept looking over his shoulder. No Pete.

Grabbing the eggs, he pivoted to return to the checkout counter—and there he was, about fifteen feet away, aiming a pistol at Rick from hip level.

"Pete, you're in violation of your restraining order. You're going back to jail."

"Fuck you, Snider! I'm going to do to you what you did to Dorothy." Pete yelled, and straightened his arm to take aim, his finger on the trigger.

As Rick ducked, he looked over Pete's right shoulder and shouted, *"He's got a gun, Walt! Get it!"*

Pete flinched, dipped reflexively and looked over his shoulder to see who was behind him. Simultaneously, Rick dropped the egg carton, ran at him, grabbed his wrist and twisted his arm.

In the struggle, Pete's arm went up. He pulled the trigger, firing a shot into the ceiling. The overhead fluorescent light explored, showering them with glass chards.

Nearby shoppers screamed and scattered. A middle-aged woman skittered across the floor on all fours away from them and around the corner of an adjacent aisle.

As Rick would later learn, Walt Sendor, meanwhile, was at the front of the store, striding quickly across the ends of the aisles, trying to figure out where Rick and Pete had gone.

At the sound of the gunshot and screams, he took off at a sprint toward the other side of the store, at the opposite diagonal from where he had been. As he ran past the customer service counter, he shouted at the stunned store manager.

"Call the police!"

As Rick and Pete continued struggling over the gun, Pete squeezed off another shot, this one toward the floor that ricocheted off the linoleum and shattered the adjacent freezer case glass door. They continued wrestling.

Pete fired a third shot, this one missing Rick's neck by inches and blasting into a nearby shopping cart. A carton of milk exploded.

Continuing to struggle, Rick finally pried the gun loose from Pete's grip. At the same time, he shoved him into the adjacent egg display case with his shoulder.

Pete's heft squashed several cartons of eggs. After tossing the gun onto the top of the dairy case, Rick took off at a sprint toward the front of the store.

As he ran, with Pete momentarily impeded, he hoped that Walt was indeed in the area.

Pete got up to take up the chase.

The Topsiders Rick chose to wear that morning were not the best running shoes. He feared Pete would easily catch him. Rick had a momentary memory flash of his nightmare earlier in the week, that sense of being impeded.

Running as fast as he could, Rick looked over his shoulder and saw that Pete was gaining on him, though he lagged by nearly half the length of the aisle.

Waving a knife, he shouted, "*I'm going slice you up, Snider, you piece of shit!*"

As Rick learned later, Walt was at the end of the adjacent aisle. When he heard Pete's shouted curse, he turned and came up the aisle behind Pete.

As Pete slowed at the end to turn the corner, Walt tackled him into a display of glass juice bottles. The stack of bottles came crashing down loudly on them both and Walt wrestled the knife away from him.

Pinning Pete face-down in the spilled juices, Walt reached for the handcuffs on his belt. Though Pete struggled, Walt was bigger and stronger. He held him firmly.

With one knee in his back, he snapped on the handcuffs.

Two New Canaan Police squad cars had just pulled up to the front of the store. Sirens wailing.

A third car was right behind, turning off Elm Street into the parking lot. Tires squealing. Siren screaming.

Pete had cut himself on the broken glass. He whimpered at the pain of acidic fruit juices in his open wounds.

Shoppers and store clerks stood back, gawking at the scene.

Walt held him fast, awaiting the police. When the four police officers found them, Walt handed over his captive, lifting him roughly from the floor. As two officers walked Pete from the scene, one began reciting his Miranda rights: "You have the right to remain silent. Anything you say can and will be used against you—"

"—Yeah yeah. Blah blah blah," Pete interrupted.

"Where's the gun?" one officer asked Rick.

"I got it away from him, and tossed it on top of the dairy case," he said, breathing heavily as he leaned over, hands on his knees.

"Jim, call the forensics team," the officer said. "And then go to the front of the store and wait for them there. Bring them to the dairy department." The other officer nodded and left.

Turning to the store manager, Rick asked, "Could we borrow a ladder, please." He nodded. "Have your guy meet us back at the dairy department, at the egg display." The manager got on the intercom and passed along the request.

As Walt caught his breath, Rick thanked him.

"I'd say this guy just cooked his own goose," Walt said with a wry smile, as he panted and brushed glass shards off himself.

"I can't believe he got his hands on another gun. The Stamford police thoroughly searched his house after his arrest. All they found was a gun cleaning kit and a manual for the Beretta. He had to have gotten this second gun from some other source. I'm eager to find out if they can trace it. No doubt it's stolen like his Beretta."

"Where did he come from? I first saw him a couple cars behind you as we pulled into the parking lot."

"He followed you and Maggie all the way from South Norwalk, further back behind me."

"Really? I didn't see him."

"Yup. He was there. Not sure where he'd been parked in Norwalk. He must have been sitting around the corner from your place. When we got here, he kept going and then turned around further up Oenoke Ridge and parked, partially hidden by the curve in the road and a big tree. And then, when you came out again a few minutes later, I followed you and he fell in right behind me. I honestly don't think he realized who I was. He's either stupid or wasn't

219

paying attention. As soon as you went into the store, he got out and followed you. I ran across the lot trying to catch up, but he was too far ahead, and I lost him in the store. Until I heard the gunshot. And you know the rest."

"When he first confronted me with the gun, he said, *Fuck you, Snider. I'm going to do to you what you did to Dorothy.* Who's Snider? Does he think that's my name? And who's Dorothy?"

"No idea. I heard him yell that name at you as he chased you. But that's good to know. I'll add that to my report. The DA will look into that."

The single policeman was quickly jotting down notes as Walt and Rick talked about the incident.

"Yeah. I realize now that Pete probably doesn't even know my name, or anything about me. Why he called me Snider is weird."

The other officer returned from the store front with two investigators from the forensics unit. "Okay. Show us where that gun is."

A clerk had set up a ladder. Rick told him where to place it. The officer climbed up, spotted the gun, retrieved it, slipped it into an evidence bag, and climbed down. As he alit on the floor, the forensics team began their work, combing the area for bullet holes and other evidence.

"Mind if I take a quick look at that gun?" Walt asked the officer, who held it out in front of him. "Hmm. That's a SIG. Nice piece. I wonder how he got his hands on that," he said.

After thanking the clerk, the officer in charge roped off the area to prevent anyone from touching anything while the forensics team did its work. He then turned to Rick and asked for a complete recounting of what had happened.

When Rick finished telling the story, the officer said, "I'll need to take your fingerprints to match them with any that we might get off the gun. You did handle it, right?"

Rick nodded.

After the forensics unit got his fingerprints, he said, "Okay, we're all set here. Thanks." Turning to Walt, he said, "We'll meet you back at the station." He and his partner left to return to their patrol car.

Rick grabbed another dozen eggs before they left the dairy department. The ones he'd originally grabbed were on the floor next to where they stood, most of the eggs broken. He and Walt then started walking together toward the checkout counter.

"Boy, my ears are really ringing."

"No surprise. That's what happens when a gun is fired near your head and you're not wearing hearing protection."

"Yeah. Guess so… So, what happens now?"

"After we're assured that the perp is back at Bridgeport Correctional, our work on this case will be done. There's no further reason to tail you or Maggie. I'll probably be getting a new assignment. We'll also take off the phone tap."

When they got to the checkout area, the store manager was standing there, grimacing, with his hands on his hips.

"Go ahead and just take the eggs," he said, waving his hand at the eggs. "We've had to close the store. Police orders. I sent my clerks home."

Walt and Rick walked out to his car. Stopping to say good-bye, they both finally broke into smiles and shook hands. "Well, take care. And again, thank you, Walt. And give my best to Phil, too. You guys do terrific work. You're real pros."

Returning to the Haines house some forty-five minutes after he'd left, Rick walked into the kitchen to find Tom and Louise talking quietly, looking concerned. The four young women were still outside talking. He put the eggs on the counter as Louise and Tom looked at him quizzically.

"Here're your eggs, Louise."

"Thanks, Rick. But what took so long? We were worried. We called the police. The place sounded pretty frantic and they wouldn't tell us anything."

"I ran into someone at the A&P."

"Who?" Tom asked.

"Pete Conley." Both their jaws dropped. And he told the story.

Louise rushed across the kitchen and hugged him. "I am so glad you're okay, Rick. And I'm so relieved that this nightmare is over."

"Yeah, I'm okay. That is, other than the ringing in my ears from having that gun fired right next my head three times."

"Well, I guess that settles his hash," Tom said. "We can release the security detail. I'll give Chet a call right now. He needs to know about this. He also needs to get on this *right now* and make sure that that piece of garbage goes back to prison and *stays there*. No bail, this time."

"Tom, would you please ask your daughter to come in. She needs to hear this, but we don't want the others to know."

"Right. Will do."

When Maggie came into the kitchen, she could sense something was up. Looking in turn from her father, to her mother, and then Rick, she grew alarmed. "What's going on?"

"Good news," Rick announced with a smile. "Pete's going back to prison. In fact, he's sitting in New Canaan's jail as we speak," and proceeded to tell her what had happened.

Maggie ran to him, clasping him tightly. "I am so relieved that he didn't hurt you again. Thank you, Daddy, for hiring those detectives." Then she turned to her father and hugged him, too.

"Well," Louise said, with exaggerated irritation in her voice, "Pete just ruined my brunch plans. Not enough time to make soufflés. I guess we'll just have to settle for a big platter of scrambled eggs and bacon, instead." And the four of them laughed, more in relief than humor.

Maggie turned serious again. "You know, I get all the tradition stuff about the bride and groom about not seeing each other before the wedding. And I know I'd planned to spend tonight here. But, in light of all that we've been through today—well, all that Rick has been through—I don't want him to be alone. Don't you think so, too, Rick?"

"Uh, yeah. I think that's a good idea. I guess I am a little rattled. By the way, do you think we should tell everyone else about this episode at the A&P?" he asked, with a nod toward the patio door."

"Sure," Louise said, before Maggie could speak. "I think that's a good idea. And I also agree with you, Maggie. I think we can put tradition aside. Rick shouldn't be alone tonight."

"Great. So, I'll just come back here tomorrow morning in my car so I can get ready. Rick can come later to the church in time for the ceremony at two o'clock."

"That'll be fine," Louise said, smiling. "Well, let's get started on that brunch."

65: Deeper Than Skin

Saturday, August 30th

The guests were seated under the massive tent in the Haines' back yard. The dinner plates had been cleared. It was time for wedding cake and toasts. Once all ninety-six Champagne glasses had finally been poured, Rick rose to speak. Several at the head table tapped their glasses for quiet.

"Thank you, everyone. Maggie and I are so pleased and honored that you're all here with us to share our special day. I have a few things to say," and he took an index card out of his tuxedo pocket on which he'd scrawled some notes.

"I'd like to start by recognizing that this day, August thirtieth, is doubly significant. Not only is it the day Maggie and I got married. You may or may not know that it's also the twenty-eighth anniversary of the marriage of my new in-laws, Louise and Tom." Rick looked at them and smiled broadly. Julie had applied makeup on his faded bruises. They were barely noticeable.

"So, I raise my glass first in a toast of love and respect to Louise and Tom, to the longevity of their bond, and the deep, abiding love and affection they share, not only between themselves but also among their family and all of us. They have set a high bar for Maggie and me, a sterling example of what love is all about and where it can take you. May Maggie and I share the same joy twenty-eight years from now. And may we also spread our love and generosity as widely among as many people as Tom and Louise have."

The whole crowd stood and applauded Tom and Louise. They both beamed. Tom leaned over to kiss his wife. As the applause died down, Rick resumed. "I am indebted to Tom and Louise for giving us this special day. I am grateful to be so welcomed into their joyful and generous family. But, most of all, I am indebted to them that their marriage produced this most remarkable and beautiful woman, Maggie." He turned to her, smiled, and paused a moment.

"The past three months have been the high point of my life, with a promise for so much more. These ninety some summer days have given me comfort in the knowledge that the rest of my life, my many thousands of days still to come, can only get better with Maggie by my side. I am a better man because of her. Meeting Maggie was sheer happenstance—luck, as they say. Quite simply, I was in the right place at the right time. And it all led to this amazing evening, here under this tent in Tom and Louise's back yard, united in eternal bond to Maggie before you all—our families and dearest friends." He looked over at Maggie again.

"I am pretty darned lucky. Yet, I know that I must earn Maggie's love and trust every day going forward, and never take her for granted. And so, I promise you, Maggie, that I will forever strive to make you happy. And, in so doing, I hope that I can measure up and be the good man that you truly deserve." And he leaned over to kiss her before resuming.

"Some say that beauty is only skin deep. But Maggie's beauty goes far, far deeper. Her beauty is her wisdom, her passion for life, and her generous spirit and love of giving. I think Maggie is *too* beautiful. And I've told her that many times. In fact, one day at the beach last month, I spontaneously sang one of my favorite songs to her. The inspiration was my telling her that she's too beautiful, because it's also the title of the song. It truly was a spur-of-the-moment expression of my love and appreciation for her. But I only sang the first two refrains that afternoon. And I sang it unaccompanied, *a cappella*."

After scanning the audience again, he resumed: "So, this evening, as my first gift to my bride, I want to sing the entire song. And since we have musicians, I made sure they had the score so that I wouldn't have to sing unaccompanied again. We even rehearsed earlier this week." He looked at Maggie and winked. Her eyebrows arched, and she smiled. "Mr. Newfield?"

With Patrick's opening chords on the piano, Rick looked at Maggie and began to sing "You Are Too Beautiful."

As he finished singing the first part of the song, the musicians started an extended instrumental interlude. Rick guided Maggie to her feet to dance. As the interlude reached its conclusion, they stopped dancing, Rick held Maggie's hand and, looking into her eyes, sang the last refrain to finish the song.

People began clapping and, one by one, rising until everyone was on their feet, applauding. As she hugged him, Maggie's mascara was beginning to run, but she was smiling broadly. Rick was pleased—and relieved—that he and the band had pulled off the performance exactly as they'd rehearsed in their secret session on Tuesday.

When the applause subsided, Rick resumed. "Thank you. I should also tell you that I'm quitting my job because Patrick wants to add a singer to his band and make it a quartet," he said grinning. The crowd laughed. Maggie gasped. "*I'm kidding. I'm kidding,*" he said laughing, looking at her. She smiled and punched his shoulder.

"So, where was I? Oh yeah. A toast." Lifting his Champagne glass, "I raise my final toast to the most beautiful woman in the world. My Maggie."

She hugged him again and whispered in his ear, "I love you madly," as the crowd resumed its applause. He looked over Maggie's shoulder and winked at Tom and Louise who were smiling broadly, standing and applauding with everyone else. He thought they both looked a little misty-eyed.

Turning to the crowd, Rick announced, "Now, let's cut the cake."

Maggie stepped in front of him. "Hey. Not so fast, buster. The bride has something to say, too," smiling and dabbing at her eyes with the corner of her napkin. Rick grinned and stepped back. Everyone quieted, and she began.

"I know that tradition says that the bride sits by, quietly smiling, while the groom toasts her and sings her praises. Well, Rick literally did sing, which was *really* special. Don't you think?" she asked the crowd, smiling broadly at him, nodding, and applauding. The crowd joined her.

As the applause died down, she continued. "But I have a couple other things I want to say to you all. Especially, I want to say this." And she took a deep breath and looked at Rick before beginning.

"It would be wrong on this glorious day if we failed to acknowledge the two most important people who can't be with us for this joyous occasion: Rick's parents, Melissa and Scott Hewson." Rick's smile flattened.

"We all know of the tragic loss that Rick, Julie and Sarah, suffered four years ago—and I hasten to add Sally as well, who also lost a beloved sister and brother-in-law. While falling in love with their extraordinary son this summer and getting to know Rick's two brilliant, charming and engaging sisters, I've come to realize how truly sorry I am and how much I will miss having never gotten the chance to meet their parents. They must have been truly exceptional people to raise three such outstanding children."

She paused, looked at Rick, their eyes connected. She smiled.

"When I first learned of Rick's loss, I wondered whether I might ever, in my own small way, help ease his pain and perhaps fill that void for him. So, when I see how quickly he and my parents bonded, how much love and respect they have for one another, my heart is full. But, at the same time, I ache for the loss that he must feel in the absence of his mother and father, now and forever more. And so, I would like to offer a toast in honor of Melissa and Scott, whose love and spirit continue to live in all of us and through all of us." And she turned and raised her glass to touch the rim of Rick's, while smiling at him, and then turned toward Sarah and Julie, smiling, and raising her glass toward them as well.

After a moment's pause, she turned to face her parents. "I also would like to say a few words of thanks to my two best friends, my mom and dad. Through tough times and now, today, through the best of times, they've always stood behind me. Their generosity, support, love and patience have known no limits. I am eternally proud and grateful to be able to call myself a Haines, daughter of Tom and Louise Haines." She raised her glass to them, and they responded in kind.

"The past three months with Rick have been both exciting and life-affirming. Our relationship is a piece of art still in its creation—forever in its creation. Like Leonardo DiVinci and his *Mona Lisa*. Did you know that DiVinci felt that he'd never finished it and kept it by his side, always working on it, nearly until his final days? It's a good metaphor for explaining how our love will continue to evolve. That our love and our marriage will be full of joy and pain, celebration and grief, always moving forward toward greater beauty, but never complete, never finished." She paused a beat and looked at Rick who stood a half-step back, grinning slightly. She reached out and took his hand, pulled him next to herself.

"I am undoubtedly the luckiest woman to have met Rick," turning to him. "I'm grateful for the strength he's given me, and the boundless confidence, trust and love he has bestowed on me and our relationship. And as proud as I am to be a Haines," she looked at her parents again before turning back to Rick, "and though I will forever be a Haines, I'm even prouder now to adopt Hewson as my new name, the best tribute I can make to both Rick and his family."

She paused again before resuming, raising her glass toward Rick. "So, here's to my husband, Rick Hewson, my destiny, the love of my life, my life partner. I am so blessed. I have so much joy ahead of me in my life, a life to be shared with this wonderful man." She leaned to him and gave him a kiss.

"*Now*, let's cut the cake."

Acknowledgements

This story has been in gestation for some three decades, coming to fruition within the past three years. That it became a reality at all is due in no small part to the support, encouragement and assistance of friends who volunteered to read early drafts and offer suggestions and criticisms for its improvement. To each, I am utterly grateful.

They include Caroline Greger, Ed Montalvo, Midge Denham, Guy Tichy, John Leonard and Mignon Montalvo. I want to single out for special thanks Alexandra Ballantine, who provided me with highly detailed feedback and a suggestion for a new book title (that I happily kept).

For checking and adjusting my hockey terminology, I thank both Guy Tichy and Don Carey. Thanks, too, to Charles Foster for his ongoing encouragement, for being my reality check, and for kicking around ideas with me.

I especially want to thank my long-time friend and confidante, John Leonard, who provided invaluable input, guidance, and sobering skepticism. He also designed the book's cover.

I am also appreciative for all the lessons, ideas and insights I gleaned in the many classes I took at GrubStreet from its fine instructors, especially Ursula DeYoung who gave me the perspective of a published author, helping me refine my characters, and polish my narrative voice and pacing.

41743903R00139

Made in the USA
Middletown, DE
09 April 2019